Indiscretion

"You must be mad!"

Carlyle sat down on the bed and loosened one of my hands from the bedcovers to hold it in both of his. He looked me over very carefully and I hoped he could not feel how my hand was trembling.

"I did ask you for a dance at the Severn ball, didn't I? I've come merely to claim that dance."

"But this is my bedchamber—I'm in bed," I stammered. "You shouldn't be here. You'll ruin me!"

"There, there," he said as if I were a small distraught child. "We are more than adequately chaperoned." He raised his voice a little and said, "Are you there, Mrs. Collins?"

"I am, sir," came the calm reply from just outside the door.

"There, you see. We have a nonpareil on guard. Mrs. Collins is the widow of a former vicar. Her reputation is impeccable. I assure you she will be on the alert to curb any untrammeled passion I might be tempted to visit on your lovely body."

"You are mad, you must be," I whispered. "No one behaves this way, not even the wildest rake!"

"I am hardly 'no one,'" he said, his voice haughty now. "Kindly remember that, Miss Ames. . . ."

Midnight Waltz

Barbara Hazard

A SIGNET BOOK

SIGNET
Published by New American Library, a division of
Penguin Putnam Inc., 375 Hudson Street,
New York, New York 10014, U.S.A.
Penguin Books Ltd, 27 Wrights Lane,
London W8 5TZ, England
Penguin Books Australia Ltd, Ringwood,
Victoria, Australia
Penguin Books Canada Ltd, 10 Alcorn Avenue,
Toronto, Ontario, Canada M4V 3B2
Penguin Books (N.Z.) Ltd, 182–190 Wairau Road,
Auckland 10, New Zealand

Penguin Books Ltd, Registered Offices:
Harmondsworth, Middlesex, England

First published by Signet, an imprint of New American Library,
a division of Penguin Putnam Inc.

First Printing, July 1999
10 9 8 7 6 5 4 3 2 1

For
Lori Rood Ghidella Hazard
with my love

Chapter One

The first anonymous letter arrived in early May.

I remember the occasion clearly. I was sitting at the breakfast table with my cousin Louisa. It was a bright, blustery morning. The sunlight streamed through the windows, setting the crystal and plate to sparkling and turning a prosaic dish of marmalade into a heap of shimmering amber. Since my aunt always had her breakfast in bed and Lord Moreston had left the house early, Louisa and I were free to amuse ourselves as we wished while we ate, I with some letters that had come in the first post and she with the latest romance from the Minerva Press.

My first reaction to the letter was confusion. I felt no fear. That would come later. Much later. But at the time I only stared at it as if in doing so I could learn the writer's name, or discover it had been misdirected after all. But no, my name was written plain—Miss Constance Ames, Moreston House, Park Lane, London.

I did not recognize the handwriting; it was small and cramped. The paper the note was written on was ordinary, the wafer a garish blue. That wafer bore no crest or initial, only the crude sketch of a daisy.

Frowning, I read it again. There was no salutation. Instead, it began abruptly by telling me I was nothing but a country rube, for all my fancy ways. And that there were things the writer knew about my family that would shame me and send me home in disgrace if they were ever to become known. The note ended there. There was no threat of

exposure, no demand for money, money I would in any case
have been unable to provide.

What could it mean, I wondered as I dropped it on the
table and wiped my fingers on my napkin. I felt almost as if
they had become soiled just by handling the thing. There
was a malevolence in those few words I felt strongly as well.
This was no prank. Whoever had written the note wished me
ill.

Chancing to look up I saw Louisa staring at me. At least
I thought she was staring at me. Sometimes it was hard to
tell, for she had a habit of looking right through you when
she was preoccupied. Just in case, I made myself smile.

"I trust you've not had bad news, coz," she said in her
low, husky drawl. "You look a bit concerned."

"No, no, it's not bad news. Just a tiresome letter from an
acquaintance in Yorkshire. I wonder she wrote. We were
never close."

As I spoke, I poured myself another cup of coffee and
wondered at my powers of invention. My uncle had brought
me up to tell the truth no matter the consequences, yet now
I found myself embroiled in a falsehood and I didn't even
know why.

"You'll reply of course. You're so conventional," Louisa
said, sounding bored. "I suggest you tell her all about your
new gowns, the wonderful parties you are attending, the
handsome, wealthy, and sophisticated men you are meeting
who write passionate notes and beg you to marry them. That
would serve her right, don't you think, Connie?"

For at least the hundredth time I wished Louisa would not
call me Connie. I hated that name. But even though I was
careful to call her Louisa instead of Weeza as her brother
did, she had not taken the hint. I wondered why I hesitated
to ask her straight out not to do so. I'm not generally so dif-
fident.

"But no handsome or wealthy gentlemen do those things,
coz," I said instead.

She shrugged. "Since none of your acquaintance in the north could possibly know that, why do you hesitate?"

I saw she had raised her book again and so did not require an answer. She was soon engrossed and I was free to stare out the window and consider this note I had received, and my situation. I had arrived in London one month ago. How could I have made an enemy in that time, one, moreover, who professed to know something detrimental about my family? When I had arrived in town I had known no one, not even my widowed Aunt Lavinia, the dowager Lady Moreston, and her two stepchildren, the current viscount and his younger sister, Louisa. Of course I had met any number of people this past month at parties, strolling in the park or shopping on Bond Street, as well as attending my aunt when she made her calls. Could one of those people have taken such a dislike to me that he or she had penned that nasty note? I would have said rather that most of them had been so indifferent they would have had a hard time remembering my name.

But no, I thought suddenly, it had not been done by a man. Surely anonymous letters were more a woman's weapon. A woman would be more apt to be devious and cunning, using this way to remain unknown and therefore in no danger of having to face the consequences.

But who could know anything about my family, detrimental or otherwise? I had not met a single soul from Yorkshire. I did not question that I was a country rube. I knew that only too well. But who believed I had "fancy ways"? I thought I had behaved as modestly as any young lady being presented this season, in fact a great deal more circumspectly than my cousin Louisa, who was always in someone's black books for her care-for-nothing ways.

I looked down the table to where she sat enthralled. Absently, she dipped the scone she was holding into her coffee cup, then gasped and dropped it. I had to smile. Obviously the heroine of her book had found herself in yet another dire situation, one I was sure to hear about in minute detail as soon as Louisa could tear herself away from the story. Gathering up my letters I rose, determined to go away before that could happen. I dislike listening to plots, even plots of books I have no intention of reading. At the door to the breakfast room I paused to say, "Don't forget the carriage is called for at noon, Louisa."

She wiggled the fingers that had lately held her scone and I left her to her romance.

In the hall I encountered the Moreston butler. Mr. Hibbert did not like me any more than I liked him, and his bow was perfunctory. Horrid man, I thought as I swept by him up the stairs. Then I wondered if he had been taught to write when a child. Of all the people in London, he was the most likely to have vicious thoughts of me.

Our antipathy had begun the very evening I had arrived in town, sore and tired from the long journey from North Yorkshire. With me as chaperone and companion had come the late governess of some neighbors of ours. Miss Angela Wardell, no longer needed for the post, had been sent forth glowing reference in hand, to seek another position. It had not been a pleasant journey. Miss Wardell was overcome by her misfortune and prone to weep quietly in her corner of the coach. I pitied her but I could not like her. And the bad cold she had which caused her to sniffle almost constantly had sorely tried my patience.

Still, when Hibbert had tried to send her on her way, I had risen to her defense and insisted she spend the night at Moreston House. It was much too late in the evening for her to find lodgings even if my coachman had known where to look. A lifelong Yorkshire man, this was his first visit to the capital, and I could tell he could hardly wait to set off for home where *decent* folk lived.

Hibbert had been forced to bow to my wishes since neither my aunt nor my cousins were at home, but he had hated me from that day. Certainly he had reason to chastise me for my "fancy ways."

Miss Wardell had been long gone when I came down the

next morning; I hoped she had found a good place, poor woman.

I myself had had trouble sleeping that first night. My room was situated on the back of the house, but I could still hear the din that was London, only slightly muted now it was dark. And of course the tradesmen's calls early the following morning and the rumble of heavy traffic on Park Lane woke me early the next day.

Louisa had come herself to escort me to the small parlor the family used for breakfast. I had marveled she was up and about. I had heard distant church bells striking three when she and my aunt came home. As for the viscount, I never did hear him come in.

Louisa had surprised me. First there was that husky, low voice, the knowing look in her eyes, both so at odds with her slight, almost childish figure. She was twenty-one, a year older than I. Since she had always lived in town she was sophisticated in a way I could not even imagine being. She made me feel quite the country cousin and it was not comfortable. Only knowing she was not behaving that way deliberately made it possible for me to accept her and the way she talked and acted.

My Aunt Lavinia had surprised me as well. My father's youngest sister, she had married Moreston a year to the day after the death of his first wife. I suppose it was possible I had seen her at family gatherings in Yorkshire when I was a child, but I did not remember doing so. Certainly I had not seen her since her marriage, making our reunion in London more like a first meeting. She must have been a beautiful woman at one time, my aunt, but now her face was drawn and lined and she appeared distracted, even fearful most of the time. Between her and her stepchildren there was little affection. On occasion she might offer a timid suggestion to which neither Louisa nor the viscount paid any attention at all.

How shall I describe the viscount? His name was Cameron James Langley. He was twenty-six years of age and had come into the title when he was only twelve. I could never make up my mind whether he was a handsome man or not. Tall and slim like his sister, he had the same black hair and gray eyes, the same white complexion. Those complexions had put me off when I first arrived, they seemed so unhealthy. I since learned that not only ladies but gentlemen of the *haut ton* strove to attain the look. Pallor and well-cared-for white hands proclaimed the aristocrat who had no need to engage in any commercial or agricultural endeavors. Both Langleys had been aghast at my own rosy face. I could only be glad I had not come in July when I was generally as brown as a berry.

Cameron, as he had asked me to call him even though we were only stepcousins, was difficult to get to know. For one thing, he seldom bothered to speak. Indeed, he was the most taciturn individual I had ever come across. Then too, he was rarely at home, coming and going as he pleased and only occasionally informing his sister or my aunt of his destination and plans. Just last week he had been absent for three days, and when Louisa questioned him on his return had only murmured that there had been a horse. She had been left to make what she would of that statement for he did not elaborate.

But of course it was not Cameron who had sent me that horrid note. He did not even seem to care I was residing in his house for the season, although I suspected if I were to displease him, he would have arranged for my removal with alacrity. You understand, I had no firm reason to think such a thing. It was only an impression I had formed of him.

Putting aside the viscount, I realized there were others in the household who might have sent the note. For some reason Louisa's maid, Emma Pratt, had taken a dislike to me. Perhaps Hibbert had spoken to her? They were the two most senior members of the staff. Then there was Miss Henrietta Mason. This elderly spinster had no clearly defined role in the household. I assumed she was my aunt's companion for she often sat with her, ran her errands, and served as her intermediary with the staff. She was given to muttering under her breath as she left a room and sniffing when she was displeased with something, although I had noticed she rarely sniffed when the viscount was present.

I heard the maid my aunt had insisted I needed enter the dressing room that adjoined my bedchamber and I went to put the note I had received away in my jewel case. There was a secret drawer in it that was perfect for concealing things. As I tucked it away, I wondered why I did not simply burn it. I had memorized it, there was no need to keep it to hand. Still, something made me save it.

I had chosen to wear a new emerald green carriage dress that afternoon. My aunt had disliked the color, claiming it much too bold for a miss making her come-out. She became quite authoritative, but I had fallen in love with the fabric at first sight. Besides, as I pointed out, since I was twenty I was well past the age where I had to wear only white or pastels. Still, my aunt continued to argue until Louisa spoke up, taking my side. She subsided then and I found myself in possession of a very handsome dress and matching bonnet.

When I was ready at last with my hair dressed and that smashing bonnet set carefully on my curls, I felt the equal of any lady in town. As I went down the stairs, I knew I would be first on the scene. Louisa was never on time, and my aunt could be just as tardy. Sometimes the coachman had to walk the team up and down Park Lane several times before the ladies appeared. I could not admire such behavior. Putting aside the horses' welfare, there was the inconvenience to the servants. I had to smile as I went to the library to wait. When had either of them considered the servants? And why should they, I could almost hear Louisa asking.

Things were not done this way in Yorkshire, but of course I was not in Yorkshire now, and had learned to keep my own counsel. Most of the time, anyway.

Chapter Two

It was half an hour later before the Langley carriage set out for the Bath road. My aunt and cousin sat facing forward while Miss Mason and I took our customary seats facing back. I thought my aunt looked tired and she was very quiet. I wondered if she had passed a bad night. Louisa, however, more than made up for her reticence. Dressed in a gown of deep blue mousseline de soie with an audacious hat that tipped over one eye, she almost bounced on the squabs in her excitement. I wondered at her vivacity. We were only going to visit an old friend of the family, a Lady Beech. Louisa told me gaily that Lady Beech had married several years before and immediately left the country to travel to her husband's estates in Jamaica in the West Indies. This was her first time home since.

"Dearest Rosalind," Louisa sighed, her sparkling eyes robbing her statement of any real sorrow. "Imagine if you please living in exile all this time in that awful place. No new gowns, no balls or parties of any kind. How terribly, terribly dreadful! I am sure she must have been bored to distraction."

"I have heard Jamaica is a beautiful island and the weather delightful," Miss Mason said stiffly, as if daring Louisa to contradict her.

"I have heard that myself," my aunt volunteered.

Louisa rolled her eyes at me as if to win me to her side against such stuffiness. Miss Mason sniffed. She held her tongue, however, for which I for one was grateful. Too often

I suspected she baited my cousin till she became angry. Since Louisa had a truly monumental temper, it was not a pleasant thing to witness.

"I do hope Lord Bryce will be there," Louisa continued. "I shall have something to say to him for deserting us all so far this Season. It is too bad!"

I smiled, not to encourage her but to show I was listening. As I did so, I wondered who this Lord Bryce might be. No one had told me anything of the people we were to visit. I only knew they lived a few miles from London on Kensington Road, and I had looked forward to the outing mainly because it gave me the chance to see the countryside again. You may be sure I had not mentioned this to Louisa for she would have been sure to deplore my insipid taste.

The palatial building I stepped down before a short time later was set behind a high wall that separated it from the busy thoroughfare. Indeed, once behind that wall it was all country charm; green lawns stretching away to gardens and groves with fountains sparkling in the sunlight and, over all, the fresh aroma of newly scythed grass. I took a deep breath.

"I can see you feel right at home here, coz," Louisa said, putting a hand to my aunt's back to urge her up the shallow broad steps. "Do get along, ma'am," she added impatiently. "Are we to dawdle about here indefinitely?"

She ignored Miss Mason's disapproval as we climbed the steps. "No doubt you will be happy to explore the plantings, coz. I, on the other hand, shall not waste a moment on 'em. It's humans I care about.

"Why, Mr. Carlyle, I did not expect to see you here," she said as we entered the hall.

"Miss Langley," the gentleman said, his voice as emotionless as hers had been spirited. "Lady Moreston, and, er, et ceteras."

His bland gaze, the obvious boredom in his voice when he reached the "et ceteras," which were surely Miss Mason and myself, made me smile. I could summon no indignation at one of the *ton*'s most outrageous gentlemen. Rather, I almost pitied him, for surely it must be difficult and time-consuming to have to keep coming up with yet another way to insult one's peers only to retain a firm grasp on that most questionable distinction—being more outrageous than the next man.

Carlyle entered the drawing room with us where we were announced to Lady Beech. I warmed to her at once. She was a very tiny lady .. th blond curls and a child's round blue eyes, and she had a smile that seemed to say she had been waiting all day just for us to come to see her. I thought her charming. I noticed even the supercilious Mr. Carlyle had a smile for her.

"Damn, he is not here," Louisa muttered not quite under her breath as she looked around the crowded drawing room. An elderly dowager nearby turned slightly and raised not only her brows but her pince-nez. Louisa ignored her, but she did allow me to take her arm and lead her somewhat apart.

"Who is not here?" I asked.

"Bryce, of course, goose! Didn't I say I intended to part his hair for deserting us all this Season?"

The drawing room was filled with London's elite, all standing about in various poses that best displayed the expensive clothing they sported. I knew most of them by now and of the mysterious Lord Bryce there was no sign.

"He may come later," I said soothingly, noting Louisa's pout, the dangerous flash of her eyes. "We are bade for the afternoon, remember."

"I want him here *now*," she persisted, and I wanted to shake her. Hard.

"Oh, there is Cameron! What on earth? I did not think he would be here, did you? I wonder he did not drive out with us."

Without another word she left my side to hurry to her brother. I moved from group to group exchanging pleasantries. As I did so, I could not help but wonder if my mysterious letter writer was in the room, perhaps watching me to see if there was any sign I was upset or uneasy. Was it you, ma'am? I asked Mrs. Boothby-Locke silently. Or you, perhaps, m'lady? Or your daughter, making her come-out with me and even now staring at my carriage dress in disapproval?

I moved on and found myself face to face with a young gentleman who had danced with me two evenings ago. Strange he could not seem to remember my name, nor the occasion, and spent the next few minutes chatting with me while staring over my left shoulder in a desperate search of someone—anyone!—more important. I excused myself as soon as I could.

Eventually I found myself before the doors that opened to a broad terrace that faced the gardens behind the villa. The day had continued bright and breezy, so breezy I saw no one had ventured outside as I was longing to do.

To go out alone would no doubt call attention to myself, something I was sure would not be approved. On the other hand, perhaps no one would notice if I were quick and deft enough. I had just reached for the door handle when a voice behind me spoke. I gasped.

"Did I startle you?" Hugh Carlyle asked. I turned, not at all sure he was speaking to me. I found him close beside me, staring down at me from his considerable height. I wondered what he wanted—why he had bothered to seek me out—and I resolved to choose my words carefully.

"But surely it can come as no surprise that I was startled, sir," I said. "After all, you have not done me the honor of conversing with me before this."

He nodded. "Very true. But there is no one else here this afternoon worth talking to, and you may be. Shall we stroll the terrace, Miss Ames?"

"You know my name?" I asked before I thought.

He did not bother to answer as he opened the door wide for me, and I cursed my stupidity. I had no great desire to become friendly with the mighty society leader, but neither did I care to have him refer to me to his friends as an imbecile or an antidote.

Once outside, I took a deep breath and turned my face up to the sun. The breeze set my skirts to dancing, and I held them down with both hands.

"You will become brown, Miss Ames," Carlyle said as he took my arm.

"I don't care," I told him. "The pallor that the *ton* holds in such esteem seems ridiculous to me. But then, I am a countrywoman."

"And proud of it. I hear it in your voice. One wonders why," he said. "I understand you have come to stay at Moreston House for the Season. May I ask how that came to be?"

I explained my relationship to the dowager Lady Moreston and he said, "You are to be congratulated you are not kin to Lady Louisa and the viscount. In fact, I suggest you count your blessings."

"What can you mean?" I dared to ask as we turned to start back across the terrace.

"Louisa Langley is one of society's originals," he said. "She has been since she burst on the scene when she was seventeen."

"Seventeen?" I echoed. "I am surprised. Somehow I thought she had delayed her come-out until a year or so ago."

His smile only twisted a corner of his mouth. "It is known she had a prodigious temper tantrum when she was not allowed to do so at sixteen. By the time her seventeenth birthday came round, there was no denying her. And once presented, she proceeded to scandalize society through one mad-cap adventure after another. Surely you must have wondered why she has not wed. After all, she is of the nobility, handsome, and, I assume, well-dowered. And she is almost witty and charming when she sets her mind to it. Many men have settled for a great deal less. But you see, Miss Ames, there was no man brave enough in the *ton* to dare. Nor has there been anyone in the years since."

"Why do you tell me this?" I asked, stopping and turning to face him and look at him squarely.

He seemed amazed that anyone, never mind insignificant me, would dare to question him. At last he said, "Because you are now an intimate of the family, forced to live in close proximity to the lady. Do correct me if I am wrong. I suspect your reason for coming to London is the same as any other young woman's, but a husband may be difficult to find if Louisa gets up to her usual pranks. Guilt by association, you see."

I did not know what to say. It was true I had been sent here with the idea of finding a husband, for my Uncle Rowley had told me it was past time I did so. "There's no great number of Prince Charmings littering the ground here in Yorkshire, Constance," he had said. "Humor me. Accept Lady Moreston's kind invitation and go and see what's what. You don't have to wed if you've no mind to, and the visit will be a change for you and ease my guilt I've kept you to myself so long."

Remembering this now, I hoped I was not blushing. I refused to tell him how close he had come to the truth. Instead, I said, "It seems to me you have much in common with Louisa yourself, sir," I said as we began to walk again. As we reached the top of the steps that led down to the lawn, Carlyle paused to stare at me.

"I mean you do and say exactly what you wish, just as she does, don't you?"

He nodded. "Of course. That is a major advantage of my status and reputation. It is one of the few things that make this tedious London round bearable. There are only a few of us able to amuse ourselves thus and escape censure. Severn for one, and of course Prinny for another."

"What of Lord Byron? And Brummel?" I asked, intrigued.

"Byron? He has become an actor playing the part of tortured romantic poet. As for the Beau, well, he has his merits. At least he's set men to bathing regularly, even changing their linen on occasion."

I swallowed a bubble of laughter. Glancing around, I saw the roofs and chimneys of another palatial building some distance away beyond the wall. "Who lives there, do you know, sir?" I asked.

"Very well," he said with a sudden grin. "That is my house, Miss Ames. But I am not the most notable of its inhabitants. Many years ago, in 1744 I believe it was, an amazing woman lived there. She privately married the third Earl of Bristol but kept the marriage secret so she could continue her role as maid of honor to the Princess of Wales. While countess, she became the mistress of the Duke of Kingston. She brought a suit of jactitation to get rid of her then unwanted husband."

"What is jactitation?" I asked, for I did not know the word.

"Literally it means a restless tossing of the body in illness, a twitching of all the muscles and limbs. I've often thought it was the earl who must have got the twitches living with such a woman."

"Why? What did she do?"

"Her most memorable antic was going to a ball one night wearing nothing but a pair of shoes and, er, a discreetly placed spray of ivy. She had decided to champion nudity, you see."

"You're making that up, it can't be true," I accused him, sure he was trying to see how gullible I was. That I should have pretended to be shocked never even occurred to me.

"No, I am not. She was naked as the day she was born. Larger though, of course," he said. "How sad it is I missed the occasion by so many years. I have often wondered how everyone behaved when she was announced."

I nodded thoughtfully. "Yes, of course. Did other women guests faint or scream? Men snicker? Or did they pretend nothing was out of the ordinary, do you suppose, and kept their eyes studiously on her face? surely it must have been taxing for the servants. Oh, I wish I had been there, too!"

"How refreshing you are," he said, and I could hear the approval in his voice. Then I remembered he should not have told me such a warm story.

"Did you think I might faint or scream at the tale?" I demanded. "Have I passed some kind of test, sir?"

"I told you because you asked about the house. That is all. What need have I to test you, Miss Ames? Why should I do so? You forget yourself."

"As you did even mentioning such a woman," I replied. "Oh do look at the lilacs. What a shame the blooms are past their prime."

"And the roses have yet to enchant," he agreed smoothly, following my lead.

"Connie! What are you doing out here?" Louisa's voice demanded, and we turned to see her coming toward us on the arms of her brother and another man I had not seen before.

I wondered if I were sorry to have this tête à tête with Carlyle interrupted. I knew I should be. There was no telling what he might not take into his head to say next, and although I knew it was sure to be fascinating, it would not do. I reminded myself I was unmarried and twenty. Hugh Carlyle was well into his thirties. As for our situations, they were separated by far more than a difference in age. We could meet on no common ground. For a stabbing moment I was sorry it was so.

"Constance," my cousin Cameron said wearily.

I curtsied both to him and to the man Louisa still clung to. He smiled at me and I returned that smile. Whoever he was, he had a nice face and a warm manner, and of all the men I had met in London, he looked the most like one of my countrymen in Yorkshire. Well-muscled, pleasant-natured, open—*good.* I told myself I would surely find out he was addicted to drink and dueling, for nothing in this upside-down world of the *haut ton* was at all what it seemed.

"Coz, this is Paul Hamilton, Earl of Bryce," Louisa said as if conveying a piece of information of great importance.

"My lord," I said. "I am Constance Ames," I added, since Louisa had not bothered to introduce me to him.

"Isn't he adorable?" she asked, cuddling closer to him.

The earl removed her hand from his arm and stepped away. When she would have followed, he held out his hands. "No, Louisa, none of that now," he said, sounding as if he wanted badly to laugh. "Just because we have known each other since childhood is no reason for such outrageous familiarity."

"Carlyle, servant."

"Bryce."

Strange how only three words could reveal these two gentlemen did not care for each other and never would.

"Are we to stand about here forever?" Cameron Langley asked. "Let us return to the house. It is too windy out and the day grows colder."

A cloud covered the sun just then and it did seem colder. Darker, too, I thought as I took Mr. Carlyle's arm again and started back. Or was that simply because my cousin Cameron had such a dampening effect on everyone?

Once safely within doors, Carlyle released me, bowed, and begged to be excused. A little bemused, I watched him make his way to his hostess, exchange a few words with her and quit the room.

"I haven't the slightest idea how you managed that, coz, you sly puss, but it has made your fortune," Louisa whispered.

I didn't have to ask her what she meant. I could see only too clearly the envious looks I was receiving and the whispers of those closest as they wondered what on earth the fastidious Mr. Hugh Carlyle, a man known more for his cuts than his kindnesses, had found to approve in little Constance Ames from Yorkshire. I tilted my chin and tried to look as mysterious as possible.

"Now if he will but continue to honor you on other occasions, you will be firmly established in the forefront of society," Louisa went on. "Where Carlyle leads, others follow, you see. Why, you won't even have to pretend to your tiresome correspondent in Yorkshire."

I was suddenly reminded of the note I had received that morning. Indeed, although I had several pleasant conversations with other guests thereafter, I could never quite banish it from my mind. I wished Louisa had not mentioned it.

My cousin Cameron stayed beside me for some time. He even introduced me to two of his acquaintances and seemed pleasanter than ever before. Indeed, he was so much nicer it made me think more charitably of him.

Eventually Lady Beech joined our circle, closely attended by her doting husband. I saw this gentleman, still tanned from his recent stay in Jamaica, never took his eyes from his tiny wife. I wondered how it would feel to be adored in such an encompassing way. Would I care for it? In thinking it over, I came to the conclusion that while it was no doubt flattering, I was afraid I would feel smothered and end up longing, if not for indifference, then for some periods of solitude.

I asked Lady Beech about the island they had so recently quit, but before she could reply, she was summoned to some domestic crisis. "I shall call on you, Miss Ames," she promised before she left. "Indeed, I'm afraid you will hear more of my adventures than perhaps you would care for."

Not long after, feeling I had neglected her, I went to sit beside my aunt.

"I hope you are enjoying yourself, Constance," she began. "Such a gay crowd as Lady Beech has assembled! I find it a bit overwhelming myself."

A burst of loud laughter from a group nearby made her wince. Miss Mason, seated on her other side, patted her hand. "We'll be able to leave soon, Lavinia," she said. Looking past her to me, she added, "Saw you with Carlyle. Mind what you're about there, my girl. Mark my words, Carlyle will only bring you trouble. He earned the nickname 'Rogue,' you know."

I wondered why she had put it quite that way. "Louisa says his patronage will give me distinction," I told her.

Miss Mason sniffed. "Oh, *Louisa* says." Her voice was a sneer.

"Oh please, Henny, don't start," my aunt begged, one thin hand raised in distress. I saw it trembling. Miss Mason must have seen it as well for she said no more of my cousin and did not even sniff when later, as we were taking our leave, Louisa insisted that Bryce come to call the following day. I thought the earl's voice cold when he finally agreed, and wished I could warn Louisa that her possessive behavior was apt to put him off.

It was strange. No matter how women pursued men—and of course they did, everyone knew that—everyone also pretended it was no such thing. Only gentlemen were allowed, nay, *expected*, to engage in the chase.

As our carriage turned into Kensington Road and passed the gates of the mansion next door, I was reminded of Hugh Carlyle and his story of the nude lady and her suit of jactitation. I wondered again if it were true. Looking around, I saw my aunt lying back on the squabs, her eyes closed, Miss Mason reading a book she had brought with her, and Louisa wearing a frown as she brooded out the window. Obviously I couldn't ask any of them, even if I had been so inclined, not without revealing how indelicate he had been to tell such a tale to a young unmarried lady like myself.

How tiresome it was to be that young lady! It almost persuaded me to marry as soon as I could manage it, to escape all this hedging propriety. For the first time I felt a kinship with Louisa, who was as shackled about as I was myself.

Chapter Three

The Earl of Bryce came as requested the following afternoon. I was in the drawing room when he was announced and although I could tell by Louisa's glares that she wished me to leave, I could think of no comfortable way to do so. I saw the earl was aware of my predicament and was amused by it, and I had to smile. Too late I remembered letters I had to write and an errand for my aunt I had promised to undertake.

"There's no use looking daggers at Miss Ames, Louisa," Bryce told her as he took a seat facing us both. "I want her to stay."

"Whatever for?" Louisa demanded. "You've come to see me, haven't you?"

"You are the most direct, alarming person," Bryce said lightly. "I've no idea what you have in mind for me—no, no, please don't tell me!—but I can see it behooves me to be on my guard. Please stay, Miss Ames. I may need you."

I held my breath, but Louisa did not take exception to his remarks. Instead, she smiled and leaned back in her chair. "I haven't the slightest idea what you're talking about, Paul. Of course I was anxious to see you. You have been in the country for some weeks now, have you not? I merely thought to spare Connie boredom, listening to you go on and on about the problems you have been solving on your estate."

"While you, of course, will hang on my every word," he retorted. "It was just so pleasant in Dorset I could not tear myself away. Then, too, the spring planting has begun . . ."

He paused, then laughed as Louisa raised her hand to hide a tiny yawn. "Forgive me, do, Louisa. Boring stuff indeed.

"Tell me all the town gossip, and don't pretend you don't know any for I'll know that for the clanker it is."

Thus encouraged, Louisa proceeded to relate any number of tales, including all the details of a divorce currently before Parliament. I thought the subject much too warm even if they had been close since childhood. The earl must have agreed with me, for he changed the subject as soon as he could.

"You say the Severn ball is in two weeks' time?" he said. "I've yet to wade through the invitations that have arrived. No doubt you'll be attending, Louisa, and your guest as well?

"Tell me, Miss Ames, are you enjoying London?"

I thought him kind to try to include me in the conversation and managed a few sentences before I excused myself.

As I curtsied, I caught sight of the bouquet that had come for me three days before. It was sadly wilted and I reminded myself to ask a maid to remove it. How sad the flowers had faded so rapidly. My first bouquet from a gentleman, too. When it had been delivered at breakfast that morning I had blushed, for it came from a man I had danced with the evening before. I had even gone in to supper on his arm. John Geering was a nice man. I liked him.

I had wanted to have the bouquet placed in my room so I might admire it at leisure, but something warned me it would not do to make too much of it. Louisa had been in a dangerous mood that morning for she had planned to ride with friends and the steady downpour that lashed against the windows put paid to such an outing. I had learned how Louisa hated to have any plans of hers thwarted.

Upstairs, I went to my aunt's room to see if she had any other commissions for me before I summoned my maid and changed for the street. A few minutes later I was on my way to the bookstore my aunt favored, trailed by my maid. As the door of the house closed behind me I heard Louisa's gay laughter coming from the drawing room. Surely the earl had overstayed his time, not that Louisa would care a snap of her fingers for that. I wondered she should be so intent on Bryce. He seemed much too ordinary a man for her. I had met several gentlemen I would have thought more to her liking—the exotic Lord Fells, the dangerous duelist Mr. Havers, the well-traveled Viscount Payton. For her to choose a childhood friend more interested in his country home than the delights of town was incomprehensible. Then I wondered if his reluctance to come to heel was the reason she was so determined to win him. But surely Louisa would not throw her cap over the windmill just for that.

My aunt's book returned, I set out for Bond Street, walking as briskly as possible in my narrow skirts. I got very little exercise in London, and that and the late nights were affecting my sleep. We were bidden to attend not one but two parties this same evening, one of them a soiree. I reminded myself I must reach home in plenty of time to prepare. Fortunately I found the shade of ribbon I wanted without any trouble and the box of pastilles my aunt required.

Halfway back to Moreston House I was hailed by Mr. Geering. He was driving his phaeton and offered to convey me to my destination. I did not like to leave my maid, but Mr. Geering insisted there would be plenty of room for her as well. I thought him optimistic when we were all three crammed into a seat built for two and I was far closer to him than was conventional. I could tell from his self-satisfied expression he was delighted with the turn of events. Fortunately, we reached Moreston House before I was seen by any of the starchier dowagers, and thankfully the viscount himself was there to lift me down.

He gave my escort a very cold greeting and sent him off with heightened color. For myself, he waited only till the maid had scurried inside before he proceeded to tell me it would do my reputation no good at all if I were considered to be *fast*.

I thought he would do better to see to his sister's reputation. As if he had read my mind, he said, "Yes, Louisa is fast, but the *ton* is used to her. You, however, are new this Season. I suggest you heed my warning, coz. Surely you must agree I am a bit more familiar with the world than you are."

I told myself it was kind of him to bother. Certainly this was the first time he had shown any concern for my welfare. I thanked him as kindly as I could. I know I do not take instruction very well. It is one of my greatest faults; my Uncle Rowley has told me so time without number.

Cameron waved carelessly as he went toward the library, leaving me to ponder this strange family I found myself living with. For they were strange, each and every one of them. The viscount with his unexplained absences, his secretiveness and general indifference. Louisa with her tantrums and sulks, her care-for-nobody attitude. Even my Aunt Lavinia, so fragile and nervous and helpless when it came to dealing with her stepchildren. And surely it was odd that she had asked me to stay, a niece she had not seen since babyhood, if then. I had suspected my uncle had begged the favor, but he had denied it vehemently by return post when I wrote and accused him of doing so.

But why had she asked me? It was true that in the beginning of my stay she had fussed over me, given me instruction on how to behave in the *ton,* how to dress, even how to comport myself with gentlemen. But as time went by and she grew accustomed to my independent nature, she had stopped that and left me very much to Louisa's mercies. It was almost as if she had washed her hands of me. I was sorry for it, but still I could not regret being free of all her little orders. I did not think my aunt was as much the authority on social niceties as she thought herself, and I knew I had more sense than she did.

Then there was Henrietta Mason, or Henny as my aunt called her. What a strange bird she was when all was said and done. Her disapproval of the viscount and his sister, her cryptic warnings to me—what could they mean?

Well, I told myself as I ran up the stairs, it is not forever. I'll be gone back to Yorkshire no later than July first. That was the date I had set for my departure. As I rang for the maids to bring the tub and copper cans of hot water so I might have a bath and wash my hair, I told myself I could even leave sooner than that if I wanted to. I was not bound here for any definite period of time.

The reception we attended first that evening was crowded with the same people I was sure we would encounter later at the soiree. Louisa became impatient after she looked around, and declared we should leave. I thought such a thing impossibly rude, for we had barely arrived, but I was unable to make her see that.

I was told I was henhearted. Who cared what our hostess thought? I felt for the poor lady, however, for others were following our lead. It was almost as if Louisa's move had precipitated a flood. My aunt, who was accompanying us without Miss Mason's support, was as helpless as I to make Louisa see the error of her ways.

The three of us sat silently in the carriage as we were driven to Sir Grant Abbott's house in Portman Square. Since the first crush of guests had come before us, we were for once able to drive right up to the front door. I was glad for I disliked having to inch forward to the steps at these events. Sometimes it seemed we spent more time waiting to gain the front door and then waiting again for the carriage to convey us home than we did amusing ourselves inside. But I knew it was all part of the London scene, as were the common folk gathered to watch the wealthy and comment on their clothing, their demeanor, and their reputations. I had heard more than one remark about Louisa and now I was to hear another.

Two gaudily dressed women, demimondes by the look of them, were standing nearby. As I stepped down after my aunt and Louisa, I clearly heard one of them say, "There she is! There's the wild 'un everybody wuz talkin' about last spring. Glad she ain't in our line of work, ain't you, Sal? She'd get all the best gentlemen first, she would."

I ignored the women as did my aunt, but to my horror, Louisa turned to face them and drop them a mock curtsy, for all the world as if to thank them for the compliment. I found it necessary to support my aunt up the steps, she was so distressed by the excited chatter of some of the other newly arrived guests. She knew as I did, Louisa's escapade would be common knowledge among the *ton* in a matter of minutes.

Louisa left us as soon as we had been announced by the majordomo, but it was not until I had seated my aunt next to an old friend of hers and had asked a footman to bring her a glass of negus, that I was free to move about the ballroom. I saw Louisa in a gay circle of young bloods and beauties. Of the Earl of Bryce there was no sign. I hoped he would come. Louisa was in a dangerous mood this evening and her old friend might calm her down.

Mr. Geering bowed to me and asked me for the next dance. Even as I smiled I wondered if he had heard the latest news of the Langley family. Surely not, or he would not have been so anxious to associate with me.

"I am so glad, Miss Ames," he said as we waited for the music to begin. "I was afraid your cousin might have warned you away. He didn't seem at all pleased when I brought you home, did he?"

"I think he objected to the way we were all crowded together," I said. "But that was my fault. I should have sent my maid home on foot. I'm afraid I'm not up to all the rigs and rows in town yet."

"I think you are perfect," Mr. Geering exclaimed, taking my hand and pressing it to his heart. I retrieved it as quickly as I could. Glancing around to see if we had been observed, I saw Hugh Carlyle watching us, an enigmatic expression on his haughty face. Quickly I pretended to be searching for someone in the crowd behind him. I wondered why I bothered. I was sure he had seen my little trick for the sham it was.

Robert Geering's dancing was more eager than polished, but we managed the quadrille without incident. Still, I was glad when a friend of Cameron Langley's asked me for the next set and took me away from Geering. He was nice and I supposed I liked him, but I did not care to linger in his or any man's company. I looked around the room casually. Louisa was flirting gaily with an elderly beau who should have known better, even if she didn't. Of Carlyle there was no sign now. Had he already left the soiree? Gone on to another, more brilliant party? Perhaps retired to his club? I scolded myself. What difference would it make to me it he were here or not? Surely I did not expect a man of Rogue Carlyle's stature and consequence to ask me to dance, did I? Yes, I thought, determined to be honest. That was exactly what I had hoped. What a silly fool I was!

The Earl of Bryce never did come to the party and by the time we all went in to supper, Louisa was smoldering with resentment and frustration. I stayed as far away from her as I could, although I saw my aunt watching her nervously, her handkerchief clutched in trembling hands. But outside of laughing too often and too loudly, and insisting on dancing a waltz at double time so all the others on the floor were forced to retreat to the sidelines and watch, she did nothing truly scandalous. Still, I was glad to leave the party at an early morning hour and I was sure my aunt wouldn't leave her room all day.

As the carriage taking us home rumbled over the cobbles, I caught a glimpse of Louisa's face in the flickering light of the candle in the side holder. She was pouting, her expression disgruntled. I wished I might speak to her honestly, tell her how unbecoming her behavior was, and how unfair to those around her, but I did not dare. Yes, it was cowardly of me, but I told myself it was not my place to reprimand her. I was only a visitor here. I saw my aunt was lying back on the seat looking tired and distracted. It was her place of course, but anyone could see she would never dare to assert her authority. And as I already knew, Louisa wouldn't pay any heed to her if she did.

I was happy there was no sign of a mysterious, threatening note in the early post the next morning. Perhaps whoever had sent the first had come to their senses and realized nothing good could come of such venom. As I tucked into my breakfast I realized how relieved I had been to find only a letter from my uncle, how thankful there was no note sealed with a daisy on an improbably garish blue wafer.

That morning Louisa had some errands in Bond Street and she asked me to accompany her. She was quieter this morning, indeed she had barely spoken at breakfast. Instead, she had stared out the window as if deep in thought, a forgotten piece of toast growing cold in her hand. I wondered what was on her mind, but of course I did not ask, coward that I am.

We took the carriage. Louisa avoided walking and did as little of it as possible. When I had protested early in my visit, she had only laughed at me and told me the famous story of a lady who lived in Berkeley Square who had called for her carriage to convey her to a party being held two doors away. I knew Louisa was strong and athletic. She rode like a centaur, she could run up the stairs faster than I, and I had seen her pick up a pile of heavy books without any straining at all. Would I ever understand ladies of the *ton,* I wondered as I followed her from the carriage at the first shop she intended to patronize. Next to the door there was a ragged little girl with a thin face and big dark eyes. She had a basket of violets and she was holding one of the posies out to us, her eyes pleading. When Louisa ignored her she edged closer, partially blocking the shop door.

"Get out of my way," Louisa snarled, pushing her with one gloved hand.

The child stumbled and fell, dropping the basket and scattering her flowers on the walkway and in the road. A horse trotting by rode over two of them and I heard her cry out in distress as she hastened to gather up the rest. I bent to help her.

"Connie, what are you doing?" Louisa demanded. "Come inside at once."

I gave the last posy to the little girl and smiled at her before I obeyed. I was furious with Louisa, furious, and it must have showed for she said, "Don't look at me that way if you please, coz. Dirty beggar! She, all her kind, should not be allowed to bother the nobility."

"She wasn't doing any harm," I said coldly. "You were very rude to her and your actions cost her money she could probably ill afford to lose."

Louisa shrugged. "She's not important. There are hundreds of children like her begging. Surely you've seen them about, haven't you, all running sores, or crippled or blind? Did you know their families deliberately blind some of them to make them more pathetic? They are of no more account than animals."

I shuddered. I hated to think of such cruelty to children, even though I had seen things in the country I would rather forget. Still, it was Louisa's attitude toward them that distressed me. I was determined to buy all the little girl's violets when we left the shop. But by the time Louisa had bullied the mantua maker into promising her new gown would be ready by week's end and we left, the child was gone.

I was looking around for her when I heard the dressmaker speak to my cousin. I only caught a few words—payment overdue . . . something on account . . . these past three months now . . .

Louisa silenced her with a glare. We rode in silence to our next stop, to purchase sandals. It seemed I always needed a new pair for the silk and satin confections with ribbons to lace about the ankles were not durable. Sometimes a strenuous evening of dancing or a clumsy partner could ruin a pair never even worn before.

At another shop I saw a handsome silk shawl in soft

shades of green and gold that I knew would compliment my eyes. It was very dear and for that reason I hesitated.

"You are going to take that, aren't you?" Louisa asked. "It becomes you so. You there, wrap this up for Miss Ames."

"But coz, I'm not at all sure—my word—two guineas!"

"You can't be feeling pinched, coz. Not you," she scolded.

I did not know what to think. Louisa seemed to imply I had all the wealth of the Indies at my disposal. That was not so. My uncle had given me a considerable sum of money to see me through the Season, and banked more with his man of business here. Uncle Rowley had said I was to call on this gentleman whenever I needed more. Still, I knew we were not wealthy. Certainly we lived very modestly at home, for we were, when all was said and done, farmers.

Leaving the shop with the neatly wrapped shawl safe in my arms, Louisa was hailed by her closest friend. Miss Gloria Hefferton had not visited for over a week for her mother had been ill. Now she ran to embrace Louisa and begin a torrent of talk. She ignored me, and I amused myself by looking in a shop window nearby. Miss Hefferton did not care for me. Louisa had said she was jealous, the silly thing, which I thought very unkind. After all, Miss Hefferton was just about her only friend. I suddenly realized the only ladies who came to Moreston House did so to see my Aunt Lavinia or Miss Mason. None of them brought their daughters either. Louisa had only male callers, and not so many of those.

Louisa easily persuaded Miss Hefferton to come home with us for some refreshments. Taking the seat facing back, I examined the girl carefully. She was an ash blonde with a rather long face and a sharp chin and she was even slimmer than my stepcousin. She was not pretty. Even her handsome brown eyes did not help. Besides, she had a peculiar style of dressing. I wondered what had possessed her to wear a puce walking gown with a bright yellow cottage bonnet, a green reticule and navy sandals.

Suddenly I gasped and coughed to hide it. Could it be

Miss Hefferton who had sent me that vile note? Could she be that jealous that she thought to make me go away so she could have Louisa all to herself again? I wondered what her handwriting looked like and how I might obtain a sample of it.

Arrived at Moreston House, I discovered a note had arrived for me while we were out. I saw it was sealed with a pale gold wafer; still, I broke that seal with some trepidation. I was relieved to see it came from Lady Beech, begging my company for a walk that afternoon in Hyde Park.

"Is that an invitation, coz?" I heard Louisa ask, and I looked up to see her and Miss Hefferton regarding me. "From a gentleman?" she persisted.

"It is from Lady Beech," I said. "She has asked me to walk with her this afternoon."

Louisa frowned. "Why, how nice," she said, her voice scornful. "No doubt this comes about because of the way you emptied the butterboat over her the other day when we called on her. I wish you a pleasant afternoon."

She turned and walked quickly into the drawing room, following by her crony, who could not resist giving me a triumphant glance as she did so. The door closed behind them with a decisive snap and I was left alone with Hibbert and a footman.

Angry, I went to my room to immediately pen an acceptance to Lady Beech's kind invitation. It occurred to me that it might be a very good thing if I had some friends of my own. That way I would not have to be so constantly in Louisa's company. Because, I told myself as I sat down at the writing table, I was finding it hard suddenly to like my stepcousin.

Chapter Four

I did not see Louisa before I left to meet Lady Beech at the Stanhope Gate. I had not joined her and Miss Hefferton for nuncheon. Instead, I shared a tray with my aunt in her room, then spent some time on my needlework.

Lady Beech was waiting for me at the Gate, and she dismissed her maid as soon as she had greeted me.

"There, now we can be comfortable," she said with her charming smile as I did the same. "Servants are all very well, indeed I do not know what I would do without my Katie, but they do tend to make one watch one's tongue, don't they?"

I agreed as we set off, reminding myself to shorten my steps. I am only of medium height but I was sure I had a longer stride than that tiny lady.

For a while we chatted of London and the newest fashions before I asked her again about her stay on Jamaica. I was surprised to see her frown.

"I loved it there," she began, tilting her parasol against the sun. "Reggie did too—well, it is his home, of course. But since the slave trade was abolished a few years ago, things have become difficult. Many of the slaves are unhappy—surly, even. Reggie has always treated his slaves well, but there is unrest even among them. And then there are the Maroons . . ."

"What—no, who are they?" I asked.

"Slaves who escaped from their masters during the uprisings many years ago. They fled to the mountains. Reggie fears they've not only joined with the fierce native tribe there, but are beginning to influence our field hands as well. We are back only because he felt it was not safe for me to remain anymore."

She wiped her eyes quickly with her gloved hand. "Forgive me, I am not usually a watering pot. It is just that Reggie is determined to return, leaving me in England. I am afraid for him. You may be sure, Miss Ames, I am doing everything I can to persuade him to sell the plantation and buy an estate here. Or if not here, on some other West Indian island where there is no danger."

"I hope you will succeed, my lady," I said. "I had no idea things were so perilous there."

"The snake in Paradise," she agreed. "It is such a shame, too. Jamaica is so beautiful. I wish you could see the white sand beaches, the strange colorful birds and flowers. I tell Reggie he is too cautious where I am concerned, but he will not listen."

"He loves you very much. I could see that at your party."

She laughed. "Yes, he is overwhelming, isn't he? But I have learned how to circumvent that."

I must have looked a question for she went on, "I send him on long errands, you see. Today, for example, he is gone to Kent to look at a horse for me. Somehow I did not like the one he purchased when we arrived. Perhaps I won't like this one either.

"I do love him, Miss Ames, but not every second of every day. It was easier in Jamaica. He was busy there from morning to night overseeing the place. Here, well, he has little in common with the other gentlemen of the *ton* and so he tends to . . . to . . ."

"To hover?" I supplied.

She nodded, laughing again. "I do like you!" she said, and I felt warm inside. I liked her too.

She asked me then about Yorkshire and my home, and listened with interest as I talked.

"It sounds grand," she said at last. "However, I don't

think Reggie would take to the cold winters, or consider raising sheep a good substitute for sugar. He knows nothing of sheep.

"Oh, do look there. I believe Rogue, er, Mr. Carlyle, is signaling you, Miss Ames. See where he has pulled up his mount on Rotten Row? Perhaps we should go and see what he wants?"

I wasn't a bit reluctant to do so. Carlyle was mounted on a handsome bay and he bowed over the saddle as we approached.

"My lady, Miss Ames," he said politely.

I wondered he did not dismount. If I were uncomfortable looking up at him, surely Lady Beech must feel as if her neck were breaking. She surprised me, and I suspect Carlyle as well, when she said, "We shall be off in a moment if you continue to regard us from on high, sir. We are not your humble servants staring up at an idol they regard with awe. Get down, do!"

What Carlyle thought of her order I had no idea; his face was as expressionless and cold as ever. Still, he did dismount.

"Is that better, m'lady?" he asked in his sardonic drawl.

"If you were as short as I am, sir, you would have more sympathy," Rosalind Beech scolded. "Of course it is better. Not perfect, you understand. I must still look up at you a considerable distance, but there is nothing to be done about that.

"But you signaled us, sir. Why?"

"I only wished to greet you both," he said smoothly. "You are looking very well and it adds to my consequence to be seen with two such lovely ladies."

"Carlyle, you are unbelievable! As if anyone but royalty could add to your already much too considerable eminence. My dear Miss Ames, do not pay any heed to the man. His compliments are false."

"I believe I have taken the gentleman's measure correctly," I said with composure. I thought him very handsome this afternoon in his shining top hat and form-fitting gray coat. His cravat was tied to a nicety, and his long, well-muscled legs were clad in skin-tight paler gray above black riding boots you could see your face in. Yet I knew there were many men more handsome. I wondered what there was about his face that pleased. Taken one by one, his features were unremarkable. Below a high brow and straight dark hair, his eyes were only blue, his nose a trifle long and narrow, the thin mouth too wide and the jaw decidedly too firm. Still, other more conventional-looking men appeared insipid in comparison.

"So you've taken my measure, have you?" he asked, one mobile dark brow raised in astonishment. "And after such a short acquaintance, too. I intend to inquire what you think of me, Miss Ames, but not now while my beauteous neighbor is listening."

Lady Beech laughed. "I've no intention of going away," she warned. "Tell me, Carlyle, are you for Severn's ball? I understand it is to be the event of the Season and I am so looking forward to it. There were no balls in Jamaica. Think of all I have missed."

"I will be there. You must save me a waltz," he ordered. "Perhaps Miss Ames might also honor me."

I was astounded, so astounded I could only nod and mumble how pleased I would be. I am sure I sounded almost incoherent. Carlyle smiled, well aware of my confusion, before he took a graceful leave.

Rosalind Beech and I stood watching him trot away before we resumed our walk.

"My, my," that irrepressible lady said as we did so, "how interesting. The audacious Rogue Carlyle culls you out from all the others. You should be feeling exalted, for I do assure you he never takes any heed of young ladies. I have heard him say they are all of them silly, witless, and inane. It appears he has made an exception in your case. Wait till I tell Reggie!"

"I beg you will not make too much of it," I said, trying

to belittle her expectations. "He asked you to dance, therefore he was forced to ask me as well, out of courtesy."

"Courtesy?" she echoed. "Carlyle is never courteous."

"Well, I daresay he will have forgotten me completely by the time of the ball."

"We'll see, won't we? I intend to wager on the Rogue. How could he forget your charming face and handsome figure?"

"Oh, please," I said, raising one hand in distress.

"You don't like compliments? How strange. I adore them myself. And they were not empty compliments I gave you, no, indeed. You are very good looking. I especially admire your chestnut hair. It is naturally curly, is it not?"

When I nodded, she sighed and went on, "And you have such a little waist, such beautiful breasts."

"I've always hated them," I admitted, stung into speech. "They are much too large."

"Why, no such thing," she protested. "They are perfect. You may take my word for it that they are much admired by the opposite sex. Just watch where the eyes of the next man you meet go first."

She seemed to realize then that I was embarrassed for she changed the subject, to my great relief.

It was a lovely afternoon and many of the *ton* were taking advantage of it in the park. We often stopped to chat with others although Carlyle did not come around again. We did see the Earl of Bryce, however. He was driving a phaeton, alone except for a tiger clinging to the perch behind. Rosalind Beech waved to him.

He stopped obediently, and when the tiger ran to hold the team's bridles, climbed down to greet us and offer us both an arm.

"Shall we stroll?" he asked. "The team can follow us."

I thought how easy and comfortable he was and what a wonderful smile he had, so different from Carlyle's half twist of the lips.

He inquired first for Lord Beech, explaining to me they

had been good friends at Cambridge before my lord left England.

"It is wonderful to see him again. Good old Reggie! I wish I could convince him to remain here."

"I wish you could too," Lady Beech said fervently.

"I intend to ask you both down to Kent to visit in July. Perhaps if he sees the land there, he might consent to be my neighbor. There's a good property of some two hundred acres coming up for sale shortly."

"If you mention it, do it casually," Lady Beech warned. "My darling Reggie gets so stubborn when he thinks he is being maneuvered in any way."

"A failing most men have, don't you agree, Miss Ames?" Bryce asked, turning to include me.

"And women as well," I said. "Have you ever wondered why something recommended to us for our own good is always so unappealing? While something we are warned to avoid immediately becomes tantalizing?"

He laughed and nodded and we continued along the walkway. I was surprised that he went with us such a distance. Behind us I could hear the jingle of harness and the occasional snort of one of the team as they were led along at a discreet distance.

When we reached the gate we took leave of each other. Lady Beech's carriage was waiting to convey her home. On learning I had sent my own maid back to Moreston House, Lord Bryce insisted on driving me the short distance.

Much to Lady Beech's amusement, I could not dissuade him. She pressed my hand in a meaningful way as we parted, saying she hoped we would meet again in a short time. Lord Bryce helped me to the seat. He had a handsome rig, all shiny black except for the wheels which were picked out in gold.

"This reminds me of a tale Louisa told me about a lady who called for her carriage to take her to a party being held two houses from hers," I said as we set off.

"Yes, it is much too brief," my escort said. "However, I hope you will do me the honor of allowing me to drive you sometime in the near future." He glanced down at me and smiled. I felt a wave of warmth inside. It was as if his smile had the same properties as a steaming cup of tea on a frigid day, able to warm one from inside out.

Moreston House was very quiet when one of the footmen admitted me. I wondered where everyone was, and went upstairs to see if my aunt was in her rooms. As her gentle voice bade me enter, I thought how like a sanctuary those rooms were to her, a place where she could retire and not have to deal with whatever difficulties arose, either in the management of the household or, more likely, with one of Louisa's mad starts.

I wondered where Louisa was as I greeted her and Miss Mason. It was strange. I knew somehow my stepcousin was not there, for the house was entirely too quiet to contain her.

"Did you have a nice time, my dear?" my Aunt Lavinia inquired as she measured out another strand of pale blue for her needlepoint.

"Yes, I did, thank you," I said with a smile. "Lady Beech is so nice. I like her."

Miss Mason nodded. "Pleasant young woman. Thinks just as she ought. Good manners. If others I could name were more like her . . ."

"Henny, please," my aunt interrupted. "It does no good to talk about it, and you know how it distresses me."

Miss Mason subsided. I wondered why she so often spoke of Louisa when she knew how the subject upset her friend. In her place I would have tried to give the lady's mind another direction. Certainly I would not have harped on it as Miss Mason so often did.

Quickly I spoke of the people I had seen in the park and those I had spoken to, although I did not mention either Hugh Carlyle or the Earl of Bryce. My aunt smiled, added a bit to the conversation every now and then, and seemed a lot happier.

When she left her sitting room to lie down for a short rest, Miss Mason moved her chair closer to mine and said in a soft voice, "I can tell you don't like me to speak of Louisa, do you, Constance? Can't agree. Should be spoken of, for it's not too late even now to do something about that young lady. Lavinia is far too gentle and retiring. She should have exerted her authority over the girl years ago when she first married Moreston."

"How old was my stepcousin when my aunt became viscountess?" I asked, intrigued in spite of myself.

"Twelve. A very willful twelve, I might add. She was still mourning her mother and her father's new marriage brought nothing but tantrums and hysterics."

"I'm sure it must have been a difficult time for her," I said. My own mother had died giving birth to me, my father six months later, so I knew nothing of such pain. Still, I could sympathize.

"Yes, she adored the late Lady Moreston." Miss Mason shook her head. "Cameron was seventeen and away at school most of the time. Lavinia should have taken a firm rein with Louisa instead of allowing Emma Pratt to cosset and pet her."

"Her father died only two years later, didn't he?" I asked. "She must have been inconsolable, poor thing."

"She wasn't," Miss Mason contradicted me. "I think she stopped loving him when he married Lavinia. No, she was not a bit sorry for his death. Fact is, I always thought she was pleased. She never shed a tear, and it was then she began to defy convention."

"Pleased?" I repeated. It seemed a singular word even for someone who did not mourn. He was her father, after all, and his passing left her an orphan.

"Yes. The viscount had kept her firmly in line, not standing for any of her nonsense. After his death she knew she

could ride roughshod over Lavinia, and so she did. So she
does to this day, as you have seen for yourself.

"I warned Lavinia over and over, but she would not heed
me. And now we see where her diffidence has led us—a
young woman gone wild, one moreover who is looked at
askance by everyone in the *ton*. Mark my words, she'll
have a difficult time finding a good man to marry her."

As she rolled up the embroidery she had been working
on, Miss Mason sighed. "Or any man at all, come to that,"
she said, as if to herself. Looking up and catching my eye,
she added, "I am sorry for her. I am. Truly."

I was surprised. I thought she loathed Louisa, but she
had sounded full of genuine regret. Would I ever understand Miss Mason?

Cameron Langley joined us for dinner that evening and
actually exerted himself to contribute to the conversation,
although I suspected it bored him to tears. My aunt re-
sponded by speaking more readily herself. It was just as
well. Louisa was preoccupied; once she had to be spoken
to twice before she replied. Miss Mason managed to ab-
stain from being provocative. It was quite the most pleasant dinner I had had since arriving at Moreston House.

Cameron left on his own pursuits immediately after his
port, and the two older ladies excused themselves not long
after. Louisa and I settled down in the drawing room before the fire. The pleasant day had turned to a cold rain. I
could hear it striking the window panes and gurgling in the
downspout at the corner of the house, and the crackling
fire was welcome.

For a while Louisa pretended to read a book. I say pretended because she rarely turned a page. I would look up
from my own book to see her gazing absently into the fire.
Sometimes I caught her frowning, her lips moving slightly
as if she were holding a conversation with someone only
she could see.

I did not mind. I was used to evenings like this at home

with my uncle. Rowley Parker was not given to idle chit-chat. After supper he would busy himself with the London papers even though they were several days old when we received them. Indeed, when I stooped to drop a kiss on the bald spot on the top of his head before going to bed, he was often startled.

I admit I was a little absent-minded myself that evening. Too often Hugh Carlyle's haughty face came between me and the page, or I would hear the Earl of Bryce's hearty laughter, see his face light up in that encompassing smile of his, and I would think once again what a nice man he was.

When the tea tray was brought in at ten, Louisa put her book down to pour out. She put away her abstraction as well.

"You had a pleasant afternoon, Connie?" she asked, forgetting she had said the same thing with a sneer before she closeted herself in this very room with Miss Hefferton earlier.

"Yes, I enjoyed the park, it was so sunny. It seemed everyone was there. It is too bad you did not come."

"I was there," she said as she handed me my cup. "Gloria's brother Robert took us out in his curricle. But it was so crowded it is no wonder we didn't see each other.

"You like Rosalind Beech, don't you?" she asked next.

"Yes, I do," I said honestly. "She is such fun. Besides, it's good I make other friends, Louisa. That way I will not have to be constantly in your pocket."

"Constant Constance?" she asked, smiling.

I smiled in return. When Louisa was like this it was hard to remember her tantrums or screams of displeasure, any of her harsh, hasty words.

She put down her cup and reached out to me. "I hope you do not feel that way, however. I enjoy going about with you. You are like the sister I never had. I'm sure you've noticed how few friends I do have. Your being here is delightful. Indeed, I've quite come to love you, dear coz."

Startled, I grasped her hand and squeezed it. Her gray eyes were dark with feeling. I must admit I was flattered.

"I do apologize for the way I acted today," she went on, her voice constricted now. "It was rude of me to twit you about Rosalind.

"No, no, don't say it wasn't," she added, although I hadn't had any intention of doing that. "I do have the most awful temper. And I was jealous, jealous you preferred her company to mine."

"I didn't think it mattered. You were with Miss Hefferton," I said, releasing her hand at last. This was a side of my cousin I had not seen before—humble, contrite. I did not know quite what to make of her.

"I've been trying to do better," she went on, smoothing her napkin over her knee, her eyes downcast. "I must be more comfortable or Bryce will never come up to scratch."

She looked up then and she must have seen some confusion on my face, for she nodded emphatically and added, "I am quite decided on it, you know. Here I am, all of twenty-one and unwed. It is more than time I changed that. Besides, haven't you noticed married women have so much more freedom than spinsters? And I've an urge to be a countess.

"You need not look so horrified, coz! I'll be a good wife to Paul, you'll see. I'll give him children if he insists on it, his heir anyway. Bryce has always loved me, you know. When we were children he was much nicer to me than Cameron ever was.

"I think he's been hesitant to ask me to marry because I have been having such a good time in the *ton*. I don't foresee any problems when I tell him it's time. But I must curb my temper—act more discreetly—pretend, at least, to be the demure lady I'm not."

She laughed at herself and I managed to smile. As she

chatted on about her wedding I tried to look encouraging. Deep in my heart, however, I was sure she had mistaken the earl's intentions. The two times I had seen them together he had shown her nothing but common courtesy. I shuddered a little at a mental picture of Louisa thwarted, spurned and disappointed, and I hoped I would not be anywhere in the vicinity when it happened.

Chapter Five

Another anonymous note arrived the next morning. It was as disreputable looking as the little boy Hibbert said had delivered it, all dirty and creased.

He had looked both superior and disapproving as he said so, and I couldn't blame him. The cheap paper, the crude outline of the daisy imprinted in the bright blue wax of the wafer were not at all the thing. I hoped Hibbert did not think I had some lower-class beau I was encouraging, and I sniffed as I took the note from his tray, quite as Miss Mason did when she was displeased, to show him that was not the case.

This time I did not read the note immediately. Instead, I tucked it in my pocket as if it were of no account and went in to breakfast. Louisa was there before me. She was full of gay conversation as I selected some eggs and fruit and a muffin from the array of silver dishes on the sideboard.

"What say you to a ride this morning, coz?" she asked as I sat down and poured myself a cup of coffee. "The rain has stopped; it promises to continue fair. Cameron has said he would join us, so we may dispense with a groom. Perhaps you would like to ride to Twickenham? It is a delightful village on the Thames—quite in the country, you know—and there is an inn there that serves delicious refreshments."

I told her that sounded grand, wondering at her enthusiasm. And the viscount was to join us as well. Would wonders never cease? Of course having to spend time in his taciturn company could hardly be considered a treat, but I told myself little conversation was necessary on horseback and no doubt we would not linger at this inn Louisa mentioned.

We were to set off at eleven, which gave me plenty of time to change to my habit. I had not brought a horse to London, but Moreston had provided a pretty mare for me. Louisa was fond of riding, although she tended to a neck-or-nothing style that was as dangerous as it was thrilling to watch. I trusted her brother could keep her in check.

Before I summoned my maid to change, I opened the note that had arrived. It was short again, with no salutation or signature, not that I had expected there to be. This time the writer was more blunt. She claimed my mother had taken lovers, many lovers, and there was no doubt at all I was not my father's daughter. I was a bastard, which was why I had been kept in North Yorkshire all these years. I was more than an embarrassment to my family, I was a disgrace. The writer ended by wondering what the *ton* would think if my illegitimacy were to become common knowledge.

Although I hated to do so, I reread the thing more carefully before I crumpled it in my hand. My heart was beating strangely and I could feel tears tickling my eyelids. I made myself take a deep steadying breath so I could think more rationally. I knew my parents had only been married a little over a year before my mother died giving birth to me. How could she, a new bride, have had "many lovers"? She and my father had spent that short time at Towers, the estate that had been her dowry which I had inherited.

I had seen portraits of both of my parents. My Uncle Rowley often said that although I had my mother's face, my hair and coloring were all my father's. I went and stared at my reflection in the glass on my dressing table. He was right. There had been no lovers. I was *not* a bastard.

Still, I thought as I tucked the note away in my jewel case with its fellow, it was hard to forget these nasty messages, no matter how easy it was to name them lies. The hatred in them, the sly, dirty sneering and satisfaction, leapt from the page and it was horrible—horrible. Who could hate me like this, I wondered again. Who could want so badly to make me miserable. And why? *Why?*

I forced myself to think of other things as I chatted with my maid while I dressed and she did my hair in the severe chignon I preferred when I was riding. And when I went downstairs pulling on my gloves, my crop under my arm, I was determined to forget the notes. I saw I was beforehand as usual. Indeed, I had heard Louisa scolding Emma Pratt for something as I passed her door. Of the viscount there was no sign.

I decided I would not stand about in the hall under Hibbert's disapproving eye. Instead, I went out on the steps to admire Hyde Park across the way. Our horses were already being walked up and down. The viscount's head groom touched his cap to me when he saw me, and idly I wondered what he would say if I suggested he ignore any order sent to the stables for at least fifteen minutes. That way there was a chance riders and mounts might arrive at the same time.

It was quite twenty minutes before Louisa came out, the skirt of her habit thrown over her arm. I admired the scarlet twill she wore with its braiding à la Hussar and its matching hat. The crisp white stock at her neck set off her dark hair.

My own habit was a dusky gold. The hat I wore swept up on one side and was adorned with a sweeping plume. I thought I looked very well and wondered what my Uncle Rowley would say if he could see me. For a moment I felt a wave of homesickness so intense it caused a pain to ripple through me. I wondered if it were a fair day in Yorkshire, or a cloudy, windy one with intermittent showers that left mist hanging over the distant hills and moors. I could see it all so clearly, the flocks of sheep grazing between the meandering stone walls, the lambs close to their mothers and the shepherd and his dog keeping watch over them. And I could see my uncle's spare, lined face, that disreputable old pipe clenched tight between his teeth, the twinkle in his eye as he looked me over. And I could almost hear him saying in his north country accent, "Think you're fine, don't you, my girl? Handsome is as handsome does, Constance." Then he would make me wait before he added, "You look blooming. The picture of your mother, you be."

I remembered the note I had just received then, and I frowned.

"Is there anything wrong, Connie?" Louisa asked. "You're not feeling ill, are you?"

I could hear the tension in her voice and I knew how disappointed she would be if we could not have our ride, so I was quick to reassure her. The groom helped me to the saddle and as I patted the mare's neck, Moreston came down the steps to join us.

Of course it was impossible for us to converse as we made our way out of town to the road leading to Twickenham and Hampton Court. It was not too crowded when we reached it. The farmers and tradesmen had come to London at dawn to sell their goods, and they would not leave until late afternoon. As I had suspected she would, Louisa set her horse to a gallop on the first straight. I prayed she would not meet a coach rumbling along on the crest of the road, but I had learned it would be useless to point out the danger of such a thing happening. Louisa scorned danger. She thought it wouldn't dare to touch her.

"A pleasant day for a ride, don't you agree, coz?" the viscount asked. "Hopefully it will not be marred by Weeza coming to grief in some way. Still, she does seem to live a charmed life. I don't think she's ever even broken her arm in a fall."

"I was frightened the first time I saw her ride," I admitted as we trotted along together. "I enjoy a good gallop myself, but not so near town on the high road."

"I'll wager anything you like she'll get it out of her system shortly and come back to chastise us for being so slow," Cameron said. I was surprised when he smiled and added, "I like that color on you, my dear. It flatters you."

Flustered, I could only nod. Then thinking to change the

subject, I told him how much I liked my mare and we discussed horses until Louisa did gallop back to us. For once her cheeks were full of color and her eyes sparkled. I thought she looked beautiful and wished she might lose her town pallor more often.

By the time we reached the large village of Twickenham we were all ready for some refreshment. While the viscount made the arrangements, Louisa and I walked along the banks of the Thames. The river was much narrower here than in London. A family of ducks paddled by in a line, the last duckling trying frantically to keep up.

"I wish we had some bread for them," I said, smiling.

"Are you happy, Connie, now you're in the country?" Louisa asked. "Are you taking deep breaths of the fresh air? Ignoring the smell of manure?"

"You're teasing," I said before I did take a deep breath. I could smell no manure.

As we started back to the inn in response to her brother's call, Louisa said, "Cameron has certainly been pleasant today, hasn't he? What did the two of you talk about when I left you?"

"This and that—you mostly," I said truthfully.

She grimaced. "I'm not that interesting, surely. Didn't he ask you about yourself, your interests, your concerns? I shall roast him for that. As most men do, he thinks himself irresistible, but he'll have to do better than that or you won't like him at all."

I swallowed a quick retort that no matter how ingratiating Cameron Langley became, I doubted I would ever like him any better. But he was my host for the Season. No matter how I felt about him, I had to be polite and agreeable. And then I wondered why the man had suddenly chosen to exert himself where I was concerned. After all, he had ignored me completely for an entire month.

I shook my head. Surely the anonymous notes I had received were making me ridiculous. I told myself Cameron Langley was a peer. He had important things to do besides taking care of his estate. He had to attend Parliament, raise important issues, guide the nation. Who was I to be critical? Many nobles were not particularly gallant. They had other things on their minds. But if that were so, why did the picture of Moreston guiding the nation make me want to giggle?

The food and drink that was spread before us in the private parlor the viscount had hired was delicious. Lemon cakes that melted in your mouth, glistening strawberry tartlets, a wonderful chocolate confection, and almost transparent almond cookies were only a few items on display. With them there was tea or chilled wine to drink.

We spent a pleasant hour at the inn and I was surprised at how gay we all became, the conversation flowing and the laughter frequent. Louisa especially was transformed, loving and happy and entertaining. I wished she might always be this way, wished her temper tantrums and moods could be banished for good. Moreston was a gracious host. I was almost sorry when we left the inn to ride back to London. Louisa did not go off by herself on the return trip, but spent the time reminiscing with her brother about their childhood. I noticed she did not mention either her father or her mother, not even once.

We were to go to the theater that evening. Louisa had bullied my aunt into getting up a party for a revival of one of Shakespeare's plays at the Drury Lane. A box had been hired and the Earl of Bryce invited, as well as two friends of Moreston's and Miss Gloria Hefferton. I suspected I was not going to have a good time. Inviting Bryce seemed so—so obvious.

I had seen so few plays I was no critic, but I thought this one well done. During the first interval Bryce came to sit beside me and ask me what I thought of the acting. In my ignorance I was hesitant to voice an opinion, but he was so easy to talk to I soon forgot my diffidence. He stayed beside me for the next act, leaving Louisa to the mercies of Clive Harkness, a dandy of Moreston's acquaintance. I could tell

she was not pleased by this turn of events, but there was
nothing I could do about it.

We were to go on to Grillon's Hotel after the theater for
supper and we found, once outside, we had to wait for the
carriages. There must have been some delay for there was
no sign of them. I was craning my neck, leaning out into the
street trying to spot them, when I saw a large coach approaching. It was then I felt a hand on my back.

It all happened so quickly I could not even cry out or try
to save myself. Instead, I fell into the street, just in front of
the team pulling the coach. How strange it was! I could hear
the cries of alarm, even feel the vibration of the street be-
neath me, as if all my senses were heightened, but I did not
think I could save myself even though I knew no one else
could reach me in time. It must have been instinct that made
me cover my head with my hands and roll back toward the
curb. I could still hear shouting, the frenzied neighing of the
alarmed horses as the coachman tried to swing them aside to
avoid me. Then I felt a quick hard blow and I lost consciousness.

When I woke up I discovered I was in my own bed at
Moreston House, although I could not remember getting
there. There was a bandage on my head, another on my left
arm and shoulder, and I ached—ached all over, if the truth
be known. It was even worse when I tried to move. I could
not help groaning and a moment later I sensed Louisa was
there. I could smell the perfume she always wore, a sweet
musky scent that reminded me of woods in the rain.

"Connie? Are you awake?" she asked, smoothing my hair
back from my bandaged forehead. "We've been so worried!
You've been unconscious for two days. Tell me, do. Are you
all right?"

I nodded, then groaned again. I had the most dreadful
headache and I was sure there wasn't a place on my body
that didn't hurt. Thankfully, I lost consciousness almost at
once.

I was to sleep a great deal over the following days. The

doctor who came every morning acquainted me with my injuries. A large lump on my head, a badly bruised shoulder where one of the horse's hooves had given me a glancing blow, and various scrapes and knocks elsewhere. I was told by everyone how lucky I was to have escaped worse injuries, even death, but the pain was such I found it hard to agree with them.

My room filled up with flowers and every day there were more notes delivered. To my disgust, I cried a great deal. I couldn't seem to help myself, I felt so weak and languid. Lady Rosalind's long letter full of her concern was touching, as was Bryce's short, encouraging note. John Geering's flowers and plea I recover quickly made me misty. And my Aunt Lavinia, Miss Mason, and Louisa sat with me often to keep me company. Even Moreston came once or twice. There was nothing however from Hugh Carlyle, no flowers, no letter. He did not even call and leave his card as some of the people in society I hardly knew did. I was disappointed although I realized how stupid that was.

Almost a week after the accident I woke early one morning to a gray dawn. The house was so quiet I knew the maids had not left their attic rooms to begin the daily routine. There was no one with me. I was finally well enough so I did not have to be constantly watched, and this was the first time I had been awake and alone since the accident.

But had it been an accident? I wondered as I pushed myself up gingerly on the pillows to a more comfortable position. I had been told I had lost my balance in the press of the crowd, or perhaps tripped over someone's foot, or an uneven place in the pavement. Nobody had suggested I might have been pushed. But I was sure I had felt a hand on my back just before I fell, sure someone had "helped" me to that accident.

I closed my eyes and tried to conjure up the scene. There had been a crowd of theater-goers of all walks of life. I remembered the gay chatter all around, the pungent smell of an orange someone was eating, the jostling that had gone on.

I remembered my aunt had been standing to my left. She had been turned slightly away for she too, as I, had been looking for our carriages. Moreston stood on my right. When I questioned how I could be so sure of that, I recalled how angry he had been at the delay, how he had muttered under his breath at the idiocy of the lackey who had called us from the theater before the carriages were at the door. I had no idea where the rest of our party had been. I concentrated even harder. Suddenly I seemed to hear some strange dowager announcing in a piercing voice that she thought Shakespeare vastly overrated and she did not intend to bother attending any more of his revivals. Nothing else came to me, and for a moment I despaired. Then clearly I heard a bitter little laugh—Louisa?—Bryce's deep questioning voice, and the aimless chatter of Gloria Hefferton. Surely I had also heard Mr. Harkness's affected tenor and Lord Faye's bored drawl, and that accounted for all our party.

But if it were true, it meant all of them had been almost directly behind me. Any one of them could have pushed me.

I shivered a little and pulled the satin coverlet higher with unsteady fingers. It couldn't be true, for it would have been too dangerous. Anyone might have noticed and later come forward with an accusation.

I remembered the notes I had received then. Perhaps whoever had written those notes had been at the theater that evening too. Perhaps this mysterious person had seen me there and managed in the crush to maneuver somewhere close to me. Perhaps, like me, that person had seen the coach and team racing toward us, and, intent on harming me, had pushed me directly into its path. But _who?_ And _why?_

I decided I would ask Louisa if she had noticed any strangers close by, even though it might be dangerous to do so. But deep inside I could not believe Louisa would want to cause my death. The problem was, I couldn't imagine why anyone else would want to either, unless they were insane. And if that were the case, surely that insanity must have come to someone's attention before this? Look at how crowded Bedlam was.

I rubbed my aching forehead. All this going over and over the accident was giving me a headache.

I never did have a chance to ask Louisa about that evening. Now I was out of danger she spent much less time in my room. And when she was there she was restless, pacing up and down or chatting gaily of her engagements, her new gown, some scurrilous gossip, so that all I wanted her to do finally was to go away.

My Aunt Lavinia was no better. She seemed to believe my misfortune was all her fault, that because of some negligence of hers I had come to grief. No matter how she was reassured, she began to cry whenever she saw me. Only yesterday she had confessed she had been unable to tell my uncle what had happened. I begged her not to write to him and at last I had her promise. I did not want my dear uncle upset, and I was sure any tear-stained, incoherent letter from Lady Moreston would have had him posting down to London within minutes of receiving it.

There was no one else I could ask. I guessed I would never know who had pushed me that fateful evening. I thought of something else then and I smiled grimly.

Ever since the accident I had received no further letters sealed with bright blue wax that featured a line drawing of a daisy for decoration. Surely that had to mean that whoever had pushed me had written those letters, and now, satisfied that I had been injured so badly, would write no more.

Chapter Six

By the day of the Duke and Duchess of Severn's ball, I was feeling much better. Bored with staying in bed, I had been getting up for longer periods every day, but I had no illusions my health was such that I would be able to dance until three in the morning. No, indeed. Furthermore, the bruise on my left arm and shoulder, although considerably less livid that it had been, was still colorful. In my pale yellow ballgown with its short puffed sleeves, I would have looked a sight. Resigned to my fate I went along to Louisa's room to watch her dress. She was to wear a new gown in the brilliant scarlet she so admired. When I saw the necklace she had on I could not help but gasp.

"Wherever did you get that?" I asked, coming closer to inspect it. A fine chain of small diamonds supported a pendant consisting of a single large diamond surrounded by a circle of rubies, it was splendid and not a bit suitable for an unmarried young woman.

"It was my mother's," Louisa said, defiantly tossing her head.

Emma Pratt, her elderly maid, mumbled under her breath as she tried to pin up an errant curl.

"I suppose you're going to tell me it isn't the thing for me to wear it. That I should clasp that insipid strand of pearls around my neck one more time instead," Louisa said quickly. Color had come into her face and I could tell by the bitterness in her voice it would be unnecessary for me to say a word since it was obvious others had already done so.

"I wouldn't dare," I said simply. "I'm not well enough yet to handle the explosion."

Her head came up and she stared at the reflection of my face in her mirror before she laughed. "Oh, Connie, I'm so sorry you won't be there, too," she said. "I'll be sure to remember everything so I can tell you about it tomorrow. Two years ago Severn had an enormous silk tent put up in his ballroom. It was all gold and white and the arrangements consisted only of white flowers in gold vases. Even the footmen wore gold and white. I wonder what conceit he will use this year?

"Ouch! Pratt, have a care. You stuck that hairpin right in my scalp."

The old maid mumbled again. Then looking sideways at me she gave me a look of such animosity it was chilling.

Louisa stood up and smoothed her gown over her hips, turning this way and that before the glass to capture the full effect. The diamond pendant sparkled in the candlelight. She reached up and touched it carefully with one gloved finger. "I know I should not wear this, but I don't care," she told me, her stubborn little chin set hard. "It was my mother's favorite jewel and she left it to me. It is not part of the estate. I've been waiting ages for a chance to wear it, and I'm not going to wait any longer no matter what anyone says."

Whirling, she picked up her evening wrap and fan. As she kissed me, I was enveloped in a cloud of her scent.

When she was gone I turned to face the elderly maid, who was setting the untidy room to rights. Taking a deep breath I said, "What have I ever done to make you dislike me, Miss Pratt? Please tell me."

She stared at me, her arms full of discarded clothes. "Why did you have to come here?" she whispered. "Why did you have to come and upset everything?"

"I don't understand," I said, bewildered. "My aunt invited me."

"Ah, *her*. Never was no good, that one. I took care of the

real Viscountess Moreston, and now I take care of her daughter."

She stepped closer, so close I could see the tiny mole at one corner of her left eye. "We don't need the likes of you, here," she said fiercely. "Go away! Go back where you came from!"

She brushed by me then and left the room mumbling to herself. I felt shaky and I was quick to return to my own room. I had no idea what the woman had meant, nor any idea still why she disliked me. Perhaps she was becoming senile? It would be hard for Louisa to pension her off, I knew. Why, she had known her all her life.

At eleven I sent my own maid to bed. The house was quiet. My Aunt Lavinia had gone to the ball with Louisa, not that she wished to. But although Louisa might be able to brazen out the diamond necklace, she could not go alone.

I read for a while, vaguely aware of the clock striking the half hour, then midnight. I was just about to blow out my candles when I heard a knock on the front door two flights down. I strained to listen, for who would call at this hour of the night?

I thought I caught the sound of a familiar voice and I got out of bed and went into the hall to peer over the bannister, just as if I were a small girl again. What I saw below made me gasp, and afraid someone might have heard me, I drew back quickly.

"Yes, yes, I understand you are shocked and you would like to refuse me admittance, but where's the sense of that, man?" Hugh Carlyle asked Hibbert. "I'm already inside."

The butler was standing before him, his hands clasped as if in prayer. Carlyle put him aside.

"Yes, bring in the harp. You there, with the flute, don't just stand about, help him. Ah yes, those baskets go by the stairs, the flowers as well. Jennings, see that all these things are taken to Miss Ames's room. Now then, which room is it?"

I saw Hibbert open his mouth and just as quickly close it. Carlyle glared at him.

"Try not to be so silly," he said, his voice frigid. "I can easily find out by invading all the rooms, but I dislike wasting time."

He leaned closer to the butler, then nodded. "Good. Two flights up, Jennings, second door on the right of the hall. It might be better to set the musicians up outside, but you will know what is best."

I didn't wait another minute. I raced back to my room, shutting the door softly before I jumped into bed. I could not believe it even though I had seen it with my own eyes. But true or not, Rogue Carlyle was coming up the stairs to *my* room. Wildly, I tried to think who I could summon to help me, now that Hibbert had capitulated so easily. There was no one but servants in the house. Moreston had been away from home for two days at a race meet, Louisa and Aunt Lavinia were at the Severn ball, and Miss Mason—the only one I thought would have any chance up putting Carlyle firmly in his place—was visiting an old friend for a few days.

I looked down at myself. I was wearing one of the nightrails I had brought with me from home. Made of white cotton, it was voluminous and long-sleeved, and it buttoned to the chin. Its only decoration was a little bit of lace at the collar. But what was I thinking of, worrying my attire might not be festive enough to receive Carlyle? He should not be here. I would be ruined if it ever came out.

Then there was my hair. My maid had brushed it out and tied it up with a ribbon. I must look like a milkmaid, I thought. Furthermore . . .

The door opened after a brief knock. A tall footman wearing black livery stood there holding two large wicker baskets. Bowing to me, he set them on the table before the window. Another footman similarly clad carried two vases of roses in. I saw him look around in confusion, for all the surfaces of the room held vases. As he set them on the floor before the empty fireplace, I heard more people moving about in the hall and whispering, even the twang of a quickly silenced harp string.

At last all was quiet. The two footmen took their places on either side of the door, their hands still at their sides as they stared at some fascinating spot on the ceiling behind my four-poster.

I felt as if I had been holding my breath for an age before Carlyle stepped into the room. He was resplendent this evening in well-tailored black except for his white linen and hose and an understated white brocade waistcoat. From his glossy dancing pumps to the top of his well-brushed dark hair, he was perfection. The lace at the cuffs of his coat made the small bit at my throat look pathetic. In a word, he was gorgeous, and suddenly I was furious.

Before I could speak, however, he strolled about inspecting the room. The vases of flowers on the floor drew a frown, and he ordered the footmen to remove my other bouquets, just as if I were not there at all. As they obeyed, he read the cards that had accompanied them while I sat there seething, the covers pulled up to my chin.

"John Geering, hmm? How touching. And Bryce. There's a conquest for you. Moreston, too? Ah, Lady Rosalind, of course. She has such exquisite taste."

When the room was cleared, he had the footmen place his flowers on either side of the mantel, then he stood, one hand on his hip and one at his chin while he considered the room.

"Of course! We will need more candelabra. See to it, Jennings. There should be some in the drawing room. Larson, be so good as to arrange the food and wine."

While the footmen bustled about, he went back to the hall. I could hear him speaking to the other people he had brought with him. Even concentrating on Carlyle as I was doing, I was aware of the footman spreading a white cloth on the table, then putting out crystal, china, and plate. A bevy of covered silver dishes followed and two bottles of wine. Two? Was the man planning a bacchanal? I resolved not to touch a drop.

At last, when everything was arranged to his satisfaction, Carlyle came back. Behind him the musicians began to play. I could hear the harp and flute, and there was a violin, a viola, and a violincello as well. I wondered how they had all fit into the hall, for it was not spacious.

As I stared at him, Carlyle made me an elegant leg. "Miss Ames," he said as he came toward the bed. "A very good evening to you."

"You must be mad," I told him, free to speak at last. He sat down on the bed and loosened one of my hands from the bedcovers to hold it in both of his. He looked me over very carefully and I hoped he could not feel how my hand was trembling.

"Yes, you have been having a time of it, haven't you?" he asked softly. "As for the question of my madness, hardly. I did ask you for a dance at the Severn ball, didn't I? I've come merely to claim that dance."

"But this is my bedchamber—I'm in bed," I stammered. "You shouldn't be here. You'll ruin me!"

"There, there," he said as if I were a small distraught child. "Rather, I'll make you. Besides, we are more than adequately chaperoned." He raised his voice a little and said, "Are you there, Mrs. Collins?"

"I am, sir," came the calm reply from just outside the door.

"And can you hear me clearly? And Miss Ames?"

"I can, sir."

"There, you see. We have a nonpareil on guard. Mrs. Collins is the widow of a former vicar. Her reputation is impeccable. She is even distantly related to the Duke of Cumberland. I assure you she will be on the alert to curb any untrammeled passion I might be tempted to visit on your lovely body if I am driven mad with lust by the location and your position."

I glanced at the two footmen. Unmoved by this insanity they continued to stand at attention on either side of the

door, their eyes resolutely fixed on the wallpaper above and
behind my head.

"You are mad, you must be," I whispered. "No one behaves this way, not even the wildest rake!"

"I am hardly 'no one,' " he said, his voice haughty now.
"Kindly remember that, Miss Ames. Jennings, some champagne.

"Shall we enjoy a glass before that dance, ma'am? And
some food? I did not neglect the best delicacies, including
lobster patties. I know how you ladies love them." As he
spoke, he spread an enormous damask napkin the footman
had brought him on the bedclothes before me; then he rose
to fill our plates.

In a dream I took the glass of champagne the footman presented and held it in both hands lest I spill it. To do so I had
to drop the covers, but I didn't even notice.

When I saw the plate Carlyle put on my lap, I stared down
at it in wonder. It all looked delicious and just as if we had
gone in to supper at the ball.

"Did you get all this from the Duke of Severn's?" I asked
for I wouldn't have been at all surprised to learn he had gone
there, baskets in hand, and calmly filled them while the
guests whispered behind him.

"No, of course not. My chef is superior to Severn's. I have
always said so," he told me, taking the chair beside the bed
while a footman positioned a small table for his use. "Do try
the duck breast in wine sauce. It is one of his signature
dishes. Claude used to be in Talleyrand's employ. He has no
equal in this country."

He held up his champagne. "A toast, Miss Ames? To the
evening and to your good health?"

"I shall drink to your ingenuity, Mr. Carlyle," I said, determined not to seem like a simple girl from a northern farm.
"And to your daring. I am sure this exploit of yours will
soon be common knowledge. Congratulations. You have
once again been outrageous. And dare I say, almost the equal
of your lady with the spray of ivy?"

He nodded as if to thank me. "I agree it is bound to come out. I fear Moreston's servants cannot be trusted to hold their tongues. But don't worry. I shall go to Severn's ball when we are finished here and tell everyone what I have done."

"You'll do what?" I demanded as I put down my fork, all my appetite gone.

"Tell them, of course. Not to do so would give rise to the belief we have something to hide. Most injurious to your reputation, Miss Ames. By treating it as quite the common thing—well, no, perhaps not *common,* I am sure I have never done anything common in my life—there can be no deadly gossip. Oh, there are those who will exclaim over it, naturally. I am often the subject of talk. It is nothing."

"Not to you, perhaps," I said bitterly.

"Nor to you," he replied swiftly. "I would never hurt you."

I had no answer to that. He had spoken in an ordinary voice, but the sentiment he expressed silenced me.

"Tell me, if you would be so good, about this accident you suffered. I assume it was an accident?"

I lowered my eyes and stared at my plate. Should I tell him my suspicions? Suddenly I wanted so badly to confide in him, to finally share my doubts and fears. But I did not dare. In spite of what was happening here, now, we were strangers. So I told him instead what had happened, saying I must have stumbled.

He calmly finished his duck and wiped his mouth before he said, "I find that hard to believe. You are an active, athletic woman. You would be the last to stumble."

"Wouldn't it be more flattering to say I was too graceful to do such a thing?" I asked, piqued. Athletic? My word!

"Please do not be offended. Of course I can praise your grace if you want the conventional platitudes. But it is your country upbringing that makes me believe you could not be so clumsy.

"Never mind. We'll discuss it at another time. I would tell

you how fortunate you were not to be more seriously injured, even killed, but I suspect everyone has been before me with that sentiment. You are recovering now? You will be well soon?"

"Yes, thank you," I said, determined to be as phlegmatic as I was sturdy. "I am almost healed. I am just not up to a long evening of dancing as yet."

He took my plate and signaled for another glass of champagne. Bemused, I saw I had drunk the first one without even being aware of it.

"But I hope you will be able to dance one or two." His smile when it came seemed less contrived and I nodded.

I admit it. I was fully taken up now with the spell he had cast over my more than prosaic bedchamber. The large candelabra gave off brilliant light and the scent of the roses he had brought was strong. Even the music issuing from the hall was enchanting. If I closed my eyes I could have sworn I was in the Duke of Severn's ballroom. Not that I did close my eyes, you understand, no, not even with the redoubtable Mrs. Collins on guard just outside.

Carlyle was lounging back in his chair now, looking at the wine in the stem he held as if fascinated by the bubbles that rose to the top of it.

"Let me see," he mused. "Is there anything I have missed? Please do not spare my feelings, Miss Ames. Tell me at once if I have forgotten to supply some necessary ingredient of the evening."

I tipped my head to one side as if deep in thought. "Well, I am afraid Mrs. Collins is not the equal of a row of stately dowagers watching the dancers with piercing eyes," I began. "Nor do we have the loud chatter and laughter that marks such a party . . ."

"No, nor the crowding, either," he added, getting into the spirit of things. "I have been most remiss. Should I jostle your arm a bit to make it more real? And surely I should have provided a young lady in her first season having hysterics because someone stepped on her gown? Two inebriated young viscounts? Three marchionesses, deaf but strident? And of course four retired military gentlemen reliving the battle of Waterloo even though none of them were there? And five . . ."

I giggled. I couldn't help it, I did. He smiled at me before he rose and took my glass—empty again, I noted with amazement—and bowed. As he snapped his fingers, the footmen came forward to take our glasses and put the food away.

"Shall we dance, Miss Ames? The waltz, perhaps?" he suggested. "I do not know if you are approved for the waltz, but knowing Louisa's reputation, I doubt you have been able to obtain vouchers from Almack's. It doesn't matter. We are quite private here."

He moved closer to the bed and I was suddenly reminded I was wearing nothing but my nightrail.

"I can't," I said with dignity, trying to hide the hint of panic I felt. "I am not dressed."

"Nonsense! From what I can see, you are more clothed than you would be at the ball. Unless, of course, you planned to wear long sleeves and a high neckline, that is."

He was right. My ballgowns showed considerably more of me than the nightrail I was wearing, and knowing he was quite capable of pulling down the covers to lift me out of bed, I capitulated. To my surprise Carlyle himself knelt to put on my slippers. I stared down at his dark head and wondered why I suddenly felt like crying.

As he rose and held out his hand I blinked my tears away. The musicians stopped what they were playing as if on signal and began a lilting waltz. I saw the footmen had rearranged the furniture and rolled the rug back so there was a clear area. As Hugh Carlyle took my left hand in his and raised it, I could not suppress a grimace for my shoulder was still tender. He let me go at once.

"You are in pain? Your arm?" he asked.

"No, my shoulder. That is where I think I must have been kicked by the horse," I explained.

To my dismay he began undoing the top buttons of my gown. I knew I should stop him but I did not want to call attention to his behavior, not with all those people in the hall.

He slid the gown down so he could inspect my shoulder, and as he did so his face darkened. The bruise looked worse than it was, all angry yellow and purple and green. Silently, Carlyle buttoned me up again.

"Take my hand, Miss Ames. Hold it where it is most comfortable for you," he said. I shivered, his voice was so cold and angry.

But I forgot that anger as we began to dance. How glad I was now that Louisa had insisted on a dancing master so I might learn all the latest steps. The lessons enabled me to follow my partner's lead easily, even, I hoped, appear more graceful than sturdy. As we turned together, I studied his face with wonder. Then Mrs. Collins coughed in the hall and he said, "I am sorry there is no harpsichord."

"It doesn't matter. The music is lovely. Do you know what song they are playing?"

We chatted lightly but our eyes remained locked, and they were saying things better not spoken aloud. But perhaps I was the only one who thought so, I reminded myself. Still, it seemed to me the arm that encircled my waist, the hand warm on my back to guide me, had drawn me closer than was customary.

When the music ended I made myself step back quickly to curtsey. Still staring at me, Carlyle raised his hand for a footman. "Pour Miss Ames another glass of champagne, then clear the room," he said. To me, he added, "It will help you sleep.

"Now you must not worry about a thing. You may be sure I'll take care of everything," he said as he helped me back to bed and put the champagne on my nightstand. Behind him the footmen were laying the rug again and repositioning the furniture. They worked quickly and efficiently. At last they left with the baskets and we were alone.

Carlyle arranged my covers before he reached out and

pulled the ribbon from my hair so it fell free down my back. Absently, he buried his hands in it till I felt him cupping my head and raising my face to his. As he bent closer Mrs. Collins coughed again. He sighed and let me go.

"Take care of yourself, Miss Ames," he said in a normal voice as he stood up. "I shall expect to see you in public very soon now."

He bowed to me when he reached the door. I could hear the scrape of chairs in the hall, the sounds of instruments being put back in their cases, but for me there was no one else in the world just then but Carlyle. I felt as bereft as Cinderella must have after the ball without the prince who had made her evening such a wonderful adventure.

Chapter Seven

I fell asleep easily, and just as easily woke up when my aunt and Louisa came home. I could hear voices raised in the front hall, and Louisa's hurried steps on the stairs, and I turned over and pretended to be deeply asleep. The light streamed into my room as she opened the door.

"Connie?" she whispered loudly. "Are you awake?

"Damn!" she said when she received no answer, but she did go away and I was grateful. I knew there would be a hundred questions on the morrow, but I needed this time alone to prepare my defenses as it were.

I slept late, but at last I rang for my maid. The girl's eyes were enormous when she came in with my chocolate, and when she saw the roses on the mantel, her face turned red.

"Shall I bring back the other flowers, miss?" she asked. "They're sitting just outside in the hall."

"No, leave them there, or better yet, take them to the drawing room," Louisa said as she pushed past the girl. "I'm sure Miss Ames only has eyes for red roses right now."

As she pulled a chair up to the bed, I dismissed the maid. No doubt she had already heard a version of last night's doings from the other servants. There was no need for her to hear any more.

Louisa barely waited for the door to close behind her before she said, "Tell. Everything!"

"What did you hear?" I countered, and sipped my chocolate with a fine air of unconcern.

"Carlyle come to the ball very late, and when taxed with

the hour by the duchess, explained he had been with you, wining and dining and dancing. And, if you please, here in your room. And all because it didn't seem fair you had to miss the festivities. Whew! The little bit of fuss about my necklace was forgotten immediately, although Mrs. Boothby-Locke did wonder if there were something in the air at Moreston House that made the young women there behave so wantonly. You may be sure Carlyle put her in her place with only one glance. I was glad. I hate Mrs. Boothby-Locke. I wish she were dead."

Shocking as that statement was, I let it go. "But it was all just as Carlyle said," I explained. "He came about midnight with a great number of people, even a small orchestra if you can believe it." I went on and told Louisa about the supper, the music—even Mrs. Collins—but I did not tell her everything. I did not tell her how Carlyle had looked at me while we were dancing, or how he had buried his hands in my hair, even how he had seemed about to kiss me until Mrs. Collins coughed.

"Well, I am sure I never expected *you* to catch Rogue Carlyle," Louisa said at last, sounding almost angry. I wondered at her tone, but she went on quickly, "Whoever would have thought *he* would fall victim to a raw country girl?"

I was hurt by her words but I managed to say, "I am sure you are making too much of the incident. You know his reputation for the outrageous. This is just another of his tricks to get attention, for he knows no one in London is talking about anything else right now."

Her face brightened. "Yes, that must be it. No doubt he hopes the print shops will issue another caricature of him. And he did protect himself by bringing Mrs. Collins. Mrs. Boothby-Locke was *so* disappointed to learn of her."

I drank my chocolate as Louisa chatted on. I wished I might spend the day in bed pretending I had had a relapse, but I knew I would only be delaying the inevitable. Today was my aunt's at-home day, too. The drawing room was sure to be humming.

Louisa picked up the champagne stem on my nighttable and twirled it in her fingers. It was so delicate I longed to beg her to be careful, but I held my tongue.

"Shall I have this returned, coz?" she asked archly.

I pretended indifference as I threw back the covers and got out of bed. "Not now. When the bouquets have died, I'll send it back with the vases. If I might have my robe, Louisa?"

She had to get up to reach it and as she did so I wondered why I had not insisted on wearing it last evening. It had been right there at the foot of my bed the entire time.

I managed to get through the morning unscathed, but when the knocker began to sound with great regularity that afternoon, I wished I might excuse myself. Only my aunt's anguished look kept me at her side.

I must have told the story a dozen times an hour that afternoon, trying to make light of it, pretending astonishment at Carlyle's behavior, yet assuring my avid audience it had been beyond reproach.

"Perhaps he still thinks of you as a young girl who should not be denied a treat," one of the more kindly ladies remarked. "It was very nice of him."

I did not think Carlyle had been motivated by such noble scruples, but I certainly did not say so. As one set of ladies left and another came in to take their place, I took the opportunity to go to the hall to tell the footmen more cakes would be required. Louisa found me there and took a letter from her pocket and handed it to me. I could see at a glance it was from my hated correspondent. Didn't I have enough trouble without this, I thought in despair. And here I thought I would never receive one again!

"Hibbert gave this to me this morning, but I forgot to give it to you," she said carelessly as she inspected it before handing it over. "What horrid taste your Yorkshire acquaintance has, Connie. This awful paper, and this common wafer! Now you are moving in such exalted circles, it might be well to end the relationship. It's hardly up to the Rogue's standards, now is it?"

I took the note she held out and stuffed it in my pocket. Fortunately an elderly couple and two other ladies arrived just then and I ushered them to the drawing room without having to answer her taunt.

It was late afternoon before the knocker was still and we were left in peace. I went immediately to my room and opened the note. I felt as if it had been burning a hole in my pocket ever since Louisa had given it to me.

The anger in it was so malevolent I cried out as I read it. "Whore!" it began. "Bastard whore!" And then it promised I would pay, pay dearly for my iniquity, that I would be exposed to the world in all my depravity, that I would die diseased and starving among the lowliest whores in London. That Carlyle wouldn't want me when he knew my true self.

My hands were shaking when I put it down. Finally the definite threat I had been fearing had been made. It was some time before I could think rationally. I worried about my uncle, how he would suffer when the accusations were made. I worried about my friends at home, and wondered which of them would stand by me, if any. I worked myself into a frenzy wondering how I was to face this, how live it down, or if that were not an option, live with it for the rest of my life.

At last my mind grew quiet. Nothing the letter writer had said was true. These filthy accusations were just that—accusations. There must be some way I could counter them.

I took the other two notes from my jewel case and spread all three out on the table next to each other. It was obvious they had been written by the same person, and I assumed in a disguised handwriting. I had never thought that tight, crabbed hand looked at all natural. I searched each note for some distinguishing mark—was the loop of the *y* and the *g* longer than usual? More slanted? That capital *w* with the curled serif, had it been used before? I began to see some patterns in the handwriting, patterns that were the same in all the notes. I wondered if the person who had written them had some of these same characteristics in their normal handwriting, and if I would be able to spot them if I got the chance.

At last I turned my attention to the words used. I decided at once whoever had written them was educated. The spelling was not perfect, but the choice of words was revealing. An unschooled person would not have written "iniquity," but "sin." And surely "depraved" was not a common, often-used term. But hadn't I always known my correspondent must be of society? It was true Hibbert and Emma Pratt were not champions of mine, but I couldn't see either of them mounting such a long, vicious campaign.

I tried to remember when the notes had arrived. The first had come two weeks ago in the morning, the next, three days later. Then there had been nothing until today. I did not know how today's note had come, but the first had been posted and the second hand-delivered.

This was all very interesting, but I couldn't see that it told me much, nor showed me any way to identify the culprit. As I put the notes away, I considered my acquaintance here in London, for it had to be one of them. Unfortunately, the first name that came to mind was Louisa's. I told myself it could not be she, for although she was often cruel in her comments and unfeeling, she had told me she loved me and I would swear she had been sincere. She did seem to like my company for she did not have many friends. Only Gloria Hefferton, I recalled.

How very nice and tidy it would be if it were Miss Hefferton, I thought. I didn't like her any more than she liked me. And she did seem the type of person who would take a great deal of satisfaction in writing poisonous letters, for there was no denying she was strange. She would know everything about me, too, from Louisa. I wondered if there was any way I could get a sample of Miss Hefferton's handwriting.

Another thought occurred to me then. I wouldn't need her handwriting if I discovered she kept tawdry writing paper, some garish blue wax and a seal with a daisy on it in her desk.

I had never been to Miss Hefferton's home, although I knew from things Louisa had said that she lived a short distance from fashionable Mayfair on Berwick Street in Soho. I gathered there were several Hefferton offspring and although the family was genteel, it was not wealthy.

But all the time I considered Gloria Hefferton and wondered how I could get myself invited to her home, in the back of my mind I could not forget Louisa—Louisa with her tantrums and moods, Louisa who could be so selfish and cruel.

I hated to think of doing it, but I knew I would have to find a way to look through Louisa's desk, and acquire a sample of her handwriting. As I rubbed the back of my neck, stiff from holding my head proudly all afternoon, I thought how strange it was I had never seen my stepcousin's handwriting.

Rosalind Beech sent a note early the following morning, begging me to visit her that day.

"I am sure you must be bored beyond anything, you have been kept so long in Moreston House," she wrote. "And since I know you are well enough for midnight rendezvous, surely you are well enough for a short visit. Do come and let me cosset you. And I will try not to ask too many questions, I promise."

I knew that besides enjoying the outing, it would permit me to avoid any further inquisitive callers. My aunt did not want me to leave her, but since Miss Mason was expected to return that afternoon, I did not hesitate to send an acceptance. To my surprise, and not entirely to my liking, Louisa announced she would join me.

"I always like seeing Rosalind," she said when she learned of my expedition. "And I've nothing else to do this afternoon. Are you well enough to ride, or should we take the carriage?"

I knew how useless it would be to point out she had not been invited, and remembering how I wanted to gain admittance to Miss Hefferton's house sometime soon, and might well have to use the same tactics, I said nothing except that I preferred the carriage.

If Rosalind was disappointed to see Louisa with me when she came out on the steps of her home to welcome us, she gave no hint of it. Instead, she led us to her own private sitting room and ordered tea.

"I've told my butler I'm not to be disturbed for any reason," she said with her warm smile. "I am dying, simply dying to know all about Carlyle's latest start. How did you feel, Miss Ames—oh, may we dispense with formality? Do call me Rosalind so I might call you Constance."

I smiled and proceeded to tell her what she wanted to know, in a carefully edited version. I could tell by her expression she knew what I was doing, but she did not press me. Louisa showed her boredom with the subject by leafing through the latest *Godey's Lady's Book* very ostentatiously. She even sighed once or twice.

"I know this is old news for you, Louisa, but you must allow it is not old news to me," Rosalind said, scolding her gently. "Just think how romantic! A midnight visitor dressed for a ball—and I can just imagine how he took your breath away for I saw him later—the dimly lit room, the way he swept you out of bed and danced with you—it was a waltz, wasn't it?—and you in your bare feet!"

"He ordered extra candles and he put my slippers on," I said in an effort to stem all this high-flown conjecture.

"Do stop being so prosaic," Rosalind commanded. "I quite envy you, you know. I imagine most women in London do, and wish they might meet such a man. But there is only one Carlyle, and he is such a conquest."

"He was only being kind," Louisa said flatly. "Connie told me so."

Our hostess looked thoughtful for a moment, but to my relief she did not contradict my stepcousin. Instead, she asked us if we would care to stroll in the garden. I was quick to say I would enjoy that very much.

As we left the terrace, I looked through the trees where I could catch glimpses of the roofs and chimneys of Carlyle's mansion. I had not heard from him since our midnight meeting and I wondered how he was and what he was doing.

Lord Beech and the Earl of Bryce found us in the garden a short time later. We were seated near the fountain to enjoy the play of the water as it sparkled in the sunlight. I saw Louisa brighten up immediately she spotted Bryce, and I was glad she had this opportunity to see him. He had not attended the Severn ball for he had gone out of town for a few days on estate business. For a while we all talked generally, but when Rosalind asked Louisa about some distant relatives of hers, Paul Hamilton moved closer to me, and turning his back on the company said in a quiet voice, "I am glad to have this opportunity to speak to you, Miss Ames. No doubt you will think me presumptuous, for I am not a relative. Promise me you will not be angry?"

I assured him I would not, although I suspected I knew what he was about to say. I was not wrong.

"I've heard all about Carlyle's midnight visit," he began. "Lord, who in London has not? It is unfortunate Moreston wasn't there to stop him. You are a nice girl, Miss Ames, I could tell that at first meeting, and I beg you to have a care. I fear you are over your head, in deep water here, and I would hate to see you ruined by such as he."

"Why don't you and Carlyle like each other?" I asked, amazed at my daring. But Paul Hamilton was such a comfortable man, much as I imagined a brother would be. I was sure he wouldn't mind.

"Not for any particular reason I can name," he said slowly. "I think we have always had this antipathy toward each other. We are different men, after all. He was wild as a youth, involved with older rakes and dilettantes. It's how he got the name Rogue."

Taking my hand and leaning closer, he said, "Think about what I have told you, Miss Ames. Be prudent, no matter how flattering Carlyle's attentions are. He is not a constant man."

He smiled then. "And surely Constance should have a constant man, don't you think?"

I smiled in return at the sally, but as I glanced over his shoulder, I saw Louisa staring at us. I was shocked to see her face wore a mask of hatred, and I was glad Rosalind was intent on something her husband was saying to her. Quickly, I removed my hand from Bryce's clasp. "I'll remember what you say, my lord," I told him. "Please, won't you talk to Louisa now?"

"No doubt she is unhappy because I've been speaking to you," he said coolly. "She should have been spanked more often as a child. However, I'll do as you ask, if only to spare you a session with her temper."

He turned away to ask Louisa what she had thought of the Severn ball, and if he might look for her at other parties soon to be given. Her face lightened, but I could tell she was still smoldering and I did not look forward to the ride home.

I had been right to dread it. She barely waited until the door of the carriage had been shut behind us and the groom taken his perch before she turned to me and began to rage. I am sure I have never seen or heard another human being in such a state. The accusations and hatred spewed out of her without pause, her words stumbling over each other in her haste to heap blame on me. How had I dared to try and take Bryce when she wanted him? What had made me imagine he would care for such as me, a nobody, a stupid little nobody? Didn't I think she could see me taking his hand and smiling at him, and all but falling into his arms? I was nothing but a slut, and she had always known it, right from the beginning. And this was how she was repaid for all her kindness to me, by this vicious ingratitude. But perhaps I couldn't help how I acted? She had heard there were women like that who couldn't get enough men. No doubt that was why Carlyle had come to my room as he had. She, for one, had never believed all that talk about a Mrs. Collins, or an orchestra, or footmen. No, she was sure that was only a subterfuge, done so I could get Carlyle in my bed . . .

I put my hands over my ears. I knew tears were streaming down my face and I was trembling, not only in revulsion but because I wasn't at all sure she might not attack me. Her face was distorted and her hands had formed claws as if she wanted to go for my eyes. And still she raged on at the top of her lungs. The coachman and groom must be getting quite an earful, but I was glad in a way because if I screamed, they might be able to help me.

Eventually, when I offered no resistance to her tirade, she stopped. I huddled on my side of the carriage, hardly daring to breathe or look at her except out of the corner of my eye. She was shaking, her hands still fists and her eyes flashing. When she turned her shoulder, so plainly excluding me from her sight, I could only be grateful.

Safely on Park Lane again, she ignored the groom's hand to sweep into the house without a word to anyone. I tarried, still feeling very weak from the ordeal, and I was glad to accept the groom's arm as he helped me down.

"Are you all right, miss?" he asked softly while the coachman ignored me and stared straight ahead.

I could not smile, but I nodded. "Thank you, Tom," I managed to say. "Thank you."

I went immediately to my room. There was nothing but a leaden silence in the house and I shut my door firmly, wishing there was some way I might lock it against any possible invasion by her. Then I sank down on my bed and tried to still my racing pulse.

Surely Louisa was not normal, I told myself. I had not been flirting with Bryce and if she had allowed me to speak I could have explained his interest in me in a few words. But this insane jealousy of hers, the things she had said to me—

surely she was not normal, she couldn't be. Again I wondered if she were the author of the notes. But no, I told myself, that didn't make sense. The first note had arrived before I even met Paul Hamilton.

I wrote a short note to my aunt excusing myself from joining the family for dinner, saying I was afraid my outing had been made too soon and asking not to be disturbed until the following morning. And then I undressed without calling my maid and crawled into bed to have a really good cry.

Chapter Eight

I not only did not go down to dinner, I had breakfast in my room as well. The thought of sitting across from even a quiet Louisa trying to eat coddled eggs and buttered toast made me feel ill. Now as I sat up in bed with a tray, my maid moving about the dressing room laying out my clothes for the day, I considered what I should do.

I could not hide in my room forever, that was certain. Sooner or later I must brave the dragon—and how easy it was to think of Louisa as a handsome dragon, all flashing eyes with fire and smoke issuing from its mouth every time it roared.

Perhaps the best thing to do would be to just go home. I had been in London for some six weeks, and it would be lovely in Yorkshire now. The entire landscape would be sporting the tender new green colors of spring. Down by my favorite brook there would be violets in profusion waiting to be picked, wild roses budding in the hedgerows, and the song of larks rising in the soft air.

I shook my head and stuck out my lower lip. To leave would be to admit defeat, give Louisa and that unknown correspondent the field. Admit I could be frightened away like any silly ninny of a girl who had more bosom than backbone. Besides, I didn't want to go. Not now.

I came to the conclusion it would be better not to follow that thought any further. Instead, I decided I would spend most of the time with my aunt when I was at Moreston House, and I would avoid Louisa, seeing her only at the dinner table in the company of the others, or at parties. And when we did meet, I would be polite but cool, and I would cultivate a considering expression when I looked at her as if I were trying to fathom what manner of creature she might be. I was practicing this put-down when I heard Emma Pratt in the dressing room, ordering my maid to leave.

I stiffened when Louisa came into my room after only the briefest of knocks, and wished I were not still lounging in bed, for I felt it put me at a distinct disadvantage. I did not know what I expected to see, but certainly not the humble creature standing just inside my door with tears running down her anguished face and her hands clasped to her breast as she sobbed.

"Oh, Connie, I am so very, very sorry," she gasped. "My wretched, wretched temper! I never meant a word I said, you know. It was just that I've been upset because Bryce went away before the Severn ball and didn't even tell me he wouldn't be there. And then he came back and didn't come and see me. And so I took my anger out on you, my dear, dear coz.

"Can you ever forgive me? I am so miserable—why, last night I could not sleep at all, so torn was I with remorse. To think I had said such things to one I love so dearly! Please, please say you forgive me or I will be in such despair I will go into a decline, I know I will!"

As she had been speaking she had been edging closer to the bed, and now she went down on her knees by the side of it to bury her face in the covers and sob uncontrollably.

I looked down at her perfectly coiffed dark hair and told myself, rather cynically I'm afraid, that I had just been treated to quite a performance. For I did not believe her, no, not for a minute. Yesterday, spewing filth at me, she had been sincere. This morning, her tears and pleading for forgiveness were much less convincing. Still, I mused as she continued to sob and twist the bedcovers in her hands, it would be easier all around if we could maintain some semblance of friendship.

"Louisa, stop that," I said as kindly as I could. "You will make yourself ill and there is no need for you to get in such a state."

She looked up, her expression begging for absolution. She was not lovely now. Her eyes and her nose were red, her face was blotchy, and she needed a handkerchief.

As if aware of that, she pulled one from her sleeve and blew her nose. Had it been put there in anticipation? I could not help but wonder.

"Please, Connie, say you forgive me, do! I have always had this bad temper and although I try to control it, it is impossible. It must run in the family for my mother was just the same."

"I think it would be better if we do not speak of this again," I managed to say.

She rose then and would have thrown her arms around me except I put out my hands to fend her off. "No, don't," I said. "I am still very upset by the things you said, the way you acted. I forgive you but I cannot forget. Not yet anyway."

Backing away, she kept her eyes downcast, her hands clasped in front of her again like a humble penitent. I wished she would not act her part quite so theatrically.

"I understand," she said in a stifled voice. "It is to be my penance. It is good of you to even speak to me, I know."

The tears began to flow once more and she sobbed. "I will wait patiently, dearest Connie," she said. "And I will pray we can be loving friends again. But you may be easy. I will not press you. I will not do anything you would not like."

She turned then and walked to the door, her shoulders stooped and her head hanging low. As the door closed slowly behind her, I wondered if I should applaud. Then I sighed to ease the tension I had been feeling, and told myself this cynicism I seemed to have acquired was not at all becoming.

I rang for my maid and dressed in a pretty new morning gown of white muslin, sprigged all over with tiny green leaves. I felt I needed the lift it gave me. I was about to join

my aunt in her sitting room when a footman came to tell me
the viscount wished to see me in the library.

I had not been aware he'd come home. As I went down
the stairs I wondered if he had heard of Carlyle's midnight
visit and wanted to discuss it with me.

I inspected his white face carefully as I curtsied. It was as
bland and expressionless as ever, but I thought I detected a
spark in his gray eye and hoped I was not in for more of the
famous Langley temper.

"Sit down, Constance," he said, indicating the chair set
before his desk. I did as I was told, trying not to feel like a
naughty schoolboy called to account in the headmaster's
study. "You are looking very lovely this morning," he added
which quite surprised me. Most of the time Cameron Langley didn't seem to notice I was alive.

"I have heard some disturbing news," he began. He sat
with his elbows on the desk, his hands clasped at his chin as
if in prayer.

"Yes?" I said calmly.

"It is all over London," he went on, and now a tinge of red
stained his cheekbones. "I am sure you know what I am re-
ferring to? Rogue Carlyle's unprecedented visit the other
evening. I must tell you I am appalled, Constance. Appalled!"

He looked at me as if there was something I should have
done to prevent such an invasion and I said, "I'm sorry for
it. I could not stop him. There was no one here to help me.
But you must not blame Hibbert. He did the best he could,
but Carlyle had brought such a crowd of his own people
there was . . ."

"I am aware. We must be thankful he had the good sense
to bring that Mrs. Collins as he did. She is the only thing that
prevents this debacle from being considered an orgy. And
from me having to call the man out and insisting he marry
you."

I swallowed the laughter I could feel tickling my throat at
the picture of myself standing beside Carlyle shortly on

some misty dawn, he with a dueling pistol in hand, I in gown and veil while over to one side waited a surgeon and a clergyman.

"But it was nothing of the sort," I managed to get out, although I must say Cameron looked at me suspiciously. Perhaps because of the wobble in my voice?

"The gentleman came with his footmen and chaperone, provided a delightful supper and an orchestra as well so we might dance. Then he went away. That is all that happened."

"He did not touch you?" the earl asked, looked suspicious.

"When we were dancing, he did," I said, determined not to mention how Carlyle had held me just before he left.

"It is all most unfortunate," Moreston said fretfully. "I never thought when you came here, coz, that I would find myself as concerned with your conduct as I am with my sister's. I thought you a modest, well-mannered miss."

"And so I hope I am," I said as I rose, quite tired of this discussion. "The *ton* will forget it as soon as something else takes their attention. I really don't think the man is apt to try and repeat it."

He rose reluctantly as well. "Oh, no," he said, his voice bitter. "The Rogue never repeats himself. He only comes up with more and more outrageous things to do, so I suggest, since you seem to have caught his fancy, you have a care. And I would appreciate it, coz, if you would remember that although you are not directly related, you are a close connection of the Langley family. And that your manners and behavior reflect on the revered name of Moreston."

I tried to hide my indignation as I curtsied again. How dare he take me to task, I asked myself as I went to the door. How dare he, when nothing I had done, or possibly could do, was a tenth as bad as Louisa's conduct every blessed day?

Once in the hall, I became aware of loud voices. Two men stood at the front door, arguing with a distraught Mr. Hibbert, who unfortunately was there alone.

"I know he's here and he'd better see me," one of them bellowed.

"Me, too," the other chimed in. "I'll not be put off no longer. I want what he owes me, I do!"

"My master is not at home to callers," Hibbert said valiantly, and I found it in myself to be sorry for him.

"You tell him Dan Henderson's here with the bill for repairing his curricle and that new saddle he bought four months ago—"

"And Larry Knoles, vintner," the other added. "Been over a year since I've seen a penny of payment for the cases I sent him for his cellar."

I walked to the front stairs. The two tradesmen saw me, of course, but they only stopped their harangue long enough to tip their caps to me.

As I went up the stairs I wondered if Moreston often found himself in dun territory. It was rather surprising. The family certainly lived as if they had endless amounts of money. Perhaps he had only mislaid the bills? Or forgotten them?

I met Henrietta Mason outside my aunt's door. She shook a finger at me. "Never fear, I don't care to hear your version," she said. "Got it all out of Lavinia last night. Warned you about Carlyle, didn't I?

"What's all that racket down below?" she added.

I explained about the tradesmen and she looked thoughtful. "Under the hatches again, is he? Money is the curse of the Morestons. *One* of the curses, I should say. Not a one of 'em has ever been able to keep his head above water. And this one's the worst of the lot."

I must have looked worried for she patted my arm and added, "Not to worry. Always land on their feet somehow. Besides, all the nobles do it. Don't know how tradesmen stay in business, indeed I don't."

When I would have knocked on my aunt's door, she said, "Tell me, what's the matter with everyone? I leave the house for two days and come back to trouble."

"What do you mean?" I parried.

"Why are the servants walking about on tiptoe and whispering in the halls if there's not trouble?" she said. "Louisa been up to her old tricks? Tell me, if you please. It's my place to shield Lavinia from as much unpleasantness as I can."

"Louisa and I had a disagreement coming back from Lady Beech's yesterday. I know the coachman and groom heard it."

"And now everyone in the house knows. And probably everyone in the houses on either side. Drat Louisa!" she said bitterly.

"She apologized this morning," I said, trying to be fair.

Miss Mason's shrew old eyes inspected me before she said, "Yes, she'd do that. But you've not forgiven her, have you, Miss Ames? Ah well, I was waiting for this. It's been too long."

She said nothing more, but I thought about her remarks often during the next few days. Louisa was quiet, too quiet, I thought. She seldom spoke and when she did, it was in an even, colorless voice. She never contradicted anyone, which was quite unlike the way she normally behaved, and when she went out, she always asked if there was some errand she might run for me. Her behavior should have been reassuring; instead it made me uneasy.

And then one morning as we both sat at breakfast and I read the Court News in the newspaper, hoping I might find out where Hugh Carlyle was keeping himself these days, Hibbert brought Louisa a note. I was not really attending so I was startled when I heard her exclaim.

Looking over the paper I saw she held a piece of paper that looked vaguely familiar. When I saw the garish blue blob on the back, my heart began to beat faster.

"But this can't be mine even if it is addressed to me," she said. "Surely this is the same paper and wafer as those your friend in Yorkshire uses. But why would she write to me?"

I could only sit there speechless as she slit the seal and unfolded the paper. "Oh no," she said moments later. "No, no, it cannot be!"

Her voice had risen and the footman busy adjusting the spirit lamps on the sideboard beat a hasty retreat to the hall.

"Who would do such a horrible thing?" she wailed, tears running freely down her pale face. "Who would say such things?"

"May I see it, coz?" I asked.

For a moment she held it out to me; then as I reached for it, she snatched it away. "No, I can't let anyone see it," she moaned. "It's too awful.

"But I don't understand," she went on, her brow puckered and the note clutched in her hand. "This looks exactly like the letters you've been receiving. But why is that?"

"Is your letter unsigned?" I asked.

"There's no signature," she told me as her tears continued to fall. When she mopped her face with her napkin I could see how her hand was shaking.

"There never was a friend in Yorkshire," I admitted. Surely only the truth would do now, for I did not have to see her letter to know it had been written by the same evil person who had been torturing me. "My letters were anonymous. I made the friend up because I didn't know how to explain them, and like you, I couldn't bear for anyone to see them."

"They were vile?" she asked. "Like this one?"

When I nodded, she said, "Perhaps we should compare them then. We might learn something about this person's identity. Two heads are better than one, you know, Connie. Ugh! If only I didn't feel so soiled. Soiled and violated somehow."

"As I have ever since the letters began coming," I agreed. I felt suddenly calmer. Was it because I was not alone anymore? Because I had someone to talk to about the anonymous letters? "Come to my room, Louisa," I said. "I've kept the three that came for me."

We did not speak again until we were in my room with the

door closed. When I opened the secret drawer in my jewel case, Louisa exclaimed over the cunning hiding place. But when I spread the three notes out on the table near the window, her face grew serious. "How awful," she whispered after she had scanned them. She took a deep breath before she held her note out in a trembling hand and turned away as if she could not bear to watch my face as I read it.

The note was the work of the same person who had written mine. There had been no effort to disguise the writing further. By the time I had finished reading it, my hand was shaking as well.

"Do you know, my lady, that your mother was mad?" it began. "Oh, yes, she was mad. This was kept from you, but she would have had to be confined in a barred room with an attendant on constant duty at Moreston Court if she had not died in that riding accident. Except it wasn't an accident. In her madness, she killed herself by riding her horse off the cliff over the sea.

"You are just like her. Every day that passes brings you closer and closer to the insanity that waits to claim you."

"Dear God," I whispered. Nothing I had received had been anywhere near as malignant as this. I saw Louisa was weeping quietly again.

"No, don't believe this, Louisa! It is not true," I said swiftly. "Here, see this note about my mother's lovers. She was a new *bride* and she was with child. How could she have had a lover, never mind more than one, with a new husband right there with her at Towers? All these things are lies."

"Do you think so, Connie?" she sobbed. "Really? You're not just saying it to make me feel better?"

She looked so pathetic, I forgot to keep my distance and put my arms around her to hug her tight. As I did so I wondered if she had been losing weight. She seemed almost fragile to me and at the same time, as taut as a steel wire.

"Yes, I do believe it," I told her. "Whoever is doing this

knows something about our families, true, but these accusations were invented to upset us."

I put her away from me to look at the notes again. "What I don't understand—and believe me, I've thought and thought—is *why*. Who could hate me so much? And now, hate you as well?

"Can you think of anyone who might know your family? Someone who bears you animosity because for the life of me, I can't."

She shook her head.

"Forgive me, Louisa, but you're not always kind. Perhaps there have been people you've offended or snubbed. Perhaps . . ."

"Of course there are! Their names are legion. But I don't think that's enough to make someone do *this!*"

As she spoke, she took her letter from me and put it beside the others on the table. "Are you sure it is a woman who did this?" she asked. "Surely men are vicious too."

I told her my reasons for suspecting one of our sex, pointed out the similarities in the handwriting, and she nodded and told me how clever I was.

"Still, I don't have any idea who wrote the things and you say you don't either," I said gloomily. "Perhaps we should tell your brother about them. After all, the slander involves him, too. He might have some ideas we haven't thought of, and he is the viscount, so—"

"Absolutely not!" Louisa snapped, that stubborn little chin very noticeable. Then in a softer voice she added, "I could not bear for him to know. No, surely the fewer people who are aware of this . . . this *filth*, the better. You must agree with me, Connie. Do you want this all to come out?"

"No, but surely your brother can be trusted to keep the secret, and—"

"The more people who know, the more precarious the secret," she said, shaking her head. "Besides, he might decide to make this public as a way to stop whoever is doing it, and I couldn't bear that, I couldn't!"

Forced to acquiesce at last, I put my notes back in the jewel case.

"Well, you may save yours—I don't know why you'd want to—but I intend to burn mine," Louisa told me.

Then she added, "What do you suppose will happen next? Do you think I'll get any more? And will the writer tell everyone these lies about my mother?"

Suddenly she wailed, "I cannot bear it! How will I ever persuade Bryce to marry me if he thinks my mother was insane!"

I hugged her again and made soothing sounds until she was calmer, but secretly I suspected neither one of us had seen the end of this horror. More surely lay ahead of us, although it was hard to imagine anything more vile that could be written. As for Bryce, I had never thought he would ask Louisa to marry him, no matter what the state of her mother's health had been.

After Louisa had left me, I sat down to do some thinking on my own. I had almost convinced myself that Louisa was the culprit before this morning—why, I had been prepared to search her desk! Now that she had become another victim, who else could it be? Gloria Hefferton? But she was Louisa's friend. She idolized her. Then who?

And a part of me that I deplored wondered exactly how the first Lady Moreston had died. I had not liked to ask if the version in the letter had been accurate, but still, I could not help wondering, and in my mind's eye I could see a slim, handsome woman who looked like Louisa whipping and spurring her mount until, in a frenzy, it took that last, deadly leap.

Chapter Nine

Now that I was fully recovered from my injuries and the bruises had faded away, I began to go about in company again. The first few occasions were most unpleasant, and I was glad to have Louisa beside me for support. Mrs. Boothby-Locke had subjected me to a probing interview during which she never lowered her quizzing glass. As well, several rakish young gentlemen had had to be put firmly in their place for making assumptions about my morals that I was quick to inform them were erroneous. In fact, by the time one of them had excused himself, red-faced and eager to escape, I had painted myself such a saint I was tempted to reach up to check whether my halo was on straight.

Still, at none of these evenings did I see Hugh Carlyle. Unable to ask anyone where he was lest I appear eager, I could only assume he had left town. It was depressing. Many were the nights I lay sleepless in bed listening to the hall clock strike one, then two, as I relived the evening he had brought a ball to me. Surely I had not been mistaken in his interest? Surely I had not just imagined he had wanted to kiss me at the end, had I? And hadn't he said he would look for me soon? Surely I was remembering that correctly.

But then I would punch my pillow into a more comfortable position as I told myself there weren't many men who wouldn't have taken advantage of a girl in that situation, and walked away afterwards not thinking a thing more about it.

You silly nitwit, I scolded myself. Of course Carlyle didn't take the moment as seriously as you did. He is not losing any sleep over it, nor weaving foolish romantic dreams. To him, it was only something he had to do to preserve his reputation as an original. You are naive if you think it meant anything more than that.

Such clear-headed thinking, however, could not make me forget the way he had looked, the intentness in his blue eyes, the firmness of his hand on my back—that hand I could almost feel still, so warm and intimate with only the cotton of my nightrail separating it from my skin. Nor could I forget how I had felt when he had buried his hands in my hair so I could not have escaped him if I tried. His mouth so close to mine, the warmth of his breath against my cheek, the clean masculine scent of him all tangled up with the starch in his cravat and some lotion he had used.

And that warning cough from the hall, I reminded myself lest I get completely carried away. Perhaps that Mrs. Collins had been brought not so much to preserve my reputation, as to keep him safe from any unwanted entanglements.

No more letters came for Louisa and me during those days. She confided she was quite relieved, but I could not be so easy. Instead, I literally held my breath every time the post was brought in.

One afternoon when Louisa and I were returning from a party where we had played silver loo, I asked her if she thought it would do any good to set one of the footmen or a groom to watching the house for that disreputable boy who had delivered one of my letters. She stared at me, perplexed.

"Surely that would be a waste of time," she said at last. "And how would they know who to look for?"

"Well, when a letter is brought—if one is, that is—they could follow the boy and see where he goes. Perhaps whoever is sending the notes does not pay until after the delivery is made."

"I see," Louisa said thoughtfully. "But the thing is, I don't know any servants here that can be trusted. They are all of them such gibble-gabblers! Our scheme would be common knowledge in a trice, and we don't want that, now do we?"

"What about your maid?" I asked, loathe to give up my plan. "Surely you can trust her."

"Pratt?" she asked before she began to laugh. "Forgive me, Connie, do," she said when she could control herself again, "it is just that Pratt is old and her eyesight is not what it was once. Besides, to even think of her trying to run after a young lad and keep him in sight is ludicrous."

She giggled again and I was forced to admit her maid was hardly an ideal accomplice.

One morning not long after, we met the Earl of Bryce while on a shopping expedition on Bond Street. As usual, Louisa glowed in his company, and all but forced him to invite us for a drive that afternoon in the park.

"We must hope Connie feels up to it," she added airily after the earl said he would call for us at five. I could tell I was expected to fall ill shortly before the time, and I resented it. Fortunately Bryce saw through her, too.

"Really, Louisa," he scolded. "Of course Miss Ames will feel up to it, won't you, ma'am? Because if she does not, there will be no drive."

For a moment Louise smoldered, her lower lip pouting in her frustration. Then she managed a laugh and I let out the breath I had been holding.

At five when the earl arrived in his landau, he insisted on taking the seat facing back.

"But you must sit beside me, Paul," Louisa said. "Connie always sits facing back. She likes it."

Paul Hamilton did not even look at me. "I have no intention of discussing Miss Ames's preferences in this case," he said. "I shall take that seat. It will give me the chance to admire two very lovely ladies.

"Drive on, Macon."

Both Louisa and I had parasols, and she wielded hers to great effect, practically hiding me from sight and putting me in danger of having an eye poked out. As we turned into the

Hyde Park gate, Bryce reached over and transferred the parasol to her left hand.

"Do try to be a little more subtle, Louisa," he said dryly as I smiled my thanks.

"Why?" she demanded, leaning forward and placing her hand on his knee. "Surely everyone knows how I feel about you, Paul. Why, ever since childhood I . . ."

"Be sure to drive slowly enough so the ladies may enjoy the park, Macon," the earl instructed his coachman as he removed her hand and put it firmly in her lap. I knew he was also instructing Louisa, not that she would heed it. Still, I was glad when she fell silent for a minute, and when she spoke again, it was only to call our attention to the quizz of a hat some lady was wearing.

The drive was very pleasant after that. Preoccupied with enjoying the colorful spectacle before us, I did not pay much attention until I heard the earl mention Carlyle's name.

"I hear he has just returned to town," he said. "Since he loathes the country so, I can't imagine why he left it. Do you remember when he announced he had not visited his ancestral acres for five long years? How he hired an agent to make sure all was running smoothly?"

"Yes, I heard that. He's a man after my own heart. How I have teased Connie about her woolies!"

Bryce gave me his warm smile and I sensed Louisa tense beside me. How impossible she was!

"There's Cameron," she said brightly, waving at her brother where he stood with another man by the side of the carriageway.

"Is that Lockwood beside him?" Bryce asked, frowning now.

"I believe so. Why do you look so disapproving? Lockwood's still good *ton,* I believe."

"He's a reckless gambler. Moreston should watch out or he'll find himself up the River Tick, keeping company like that."

"Pooh!" Louisa said. "My brother is not some green boy. Besides, they are friends."

"And Lockwood has no mercy on friend or foe when they are in debt to him."

I was glad when he changed the subject then for Louisa was looking rebellious. For myself, it was enough to sit back and admire the park. It was a beautiful June afternoon with an almost cloudless sky and a gentle breeze. The clear light intensified the green of the grass, the silvery blue of the Serpentine, and the brilliant colors of the costumes being worn. That pretty pink gown, the gold of a gentleman's coat, the bright flowers adorning a bonnet, all begged to be admired.

When Bryce set us down at Moreston House later, I thanked him for the treat. Louisa reached up and kissed his cheek before he could escape her, and she was laughing as we went into the house.

We were to attend a soiree that evening. It was such a crush when we arrived it was some time before I chanced to see Carlyle in a discussion with another gentleman. Quite near me, Mrs. Boothby-Locke remarked to her companion that she for one hoped Carlyle and that Ames chit would manage to behave themselves, although she wouldn't wager a groat on it.

When Carlyle came to my side as soon as he saw me, I resolved to be on my best behavior.

"Do me the honor of sitting out this set with me, Miss Ames," he said as he took me to a vacant sofa.

"You do not care to dance this evening, sir?" I asked, with only the smallest smile.

"No, nor take you for a stroll on the terrace as I see some couples are doing," came his quick reply. Sitting down beside me, he added, "I miscalculated and I admit it. I didn't think there would be such a fuss over our little adventure. I hope it has not been too unpleasant for you?"

I saw he was serious; his drawl noticeably absent. "Some of the older ladies have been almost scathing in their disapproval," I told him, not about to let him escape untouched after what I had been through. "And some of the younger, more free-spirited gentlemen seem to think me fair game now. No, no, do not concern yourself, sir. I soon put them straight."

"Who dared?" he asked. Even though his voice was still quiet, I felt a shiver run down my spine.

"I won't tell you. It's not important. That's all I'd need, you setting the *ton* to buzzing again by making an example of some green young man."

He leaned closer to peer at me. "You are not looking your best, Miss Ames," he said. "You look strained somehow. Is your shoulder still paining you?"

"My shoulder has healed and, as you can see, the bruises are gone."

"Then what else is the matter to make you so tense?"

"Nothing at all. To be sure I can't say I'm pleased to be told I'm not in my best looks. No doubt it is unreasonable of me. You do have the most awkward way of paying compliments, don't you?"

He waved an impatient hand. "I'm not paying you a compliment. Do have a little more sense and stop trying to divert me."

I took a deep breath. "Either we begin this conversation over or we part, sir," I said sternly, willing my voice not to tremble. "I understand you have been out of town. Did you have a pleasant return journey?"

"No. I wish you would tell me what is troubling you. However, I can see by the set of that enticing mouth—and that's the only compliment you'll have from me this evening, my girl—that you've no intention of revealing it. I wish you would trust me. I have not always done as I ought, perhaps, but I am not a bad man. Where you are concerned I have only the best of intentions."

"Thank you," I said, confused. He had sounded in dead earnest. I put his pretty compliment aside to consider later; now I mulled over this latest surprising offer. How I wished I might confide in him, pour everything out, those horrid let-

ters, my problems with Louisa, the feeling I had been deliberately pushed into the path of the carriage and team outside
the Drury Lane. I knew that was not possible, however. We
were not related, we were not even particularly good
friends. I knew very little of him but gossip. It would be
foolish of me to unburden myself. Still, I cannot tell you
how I yearned to, and in retrospect, how much better it
would have been if I had done so. How much pain and suffering would have been averted if I had only been open with
him. There are times it is wise to trust your instincts and
hang propriety. But I did not know that then, so I remained
silent, staring out at the dancers with what I hoped was a
pleasant, interested expression.

"It's no good," he told me. "Your face is too revealing and
you have not lived long or hard enough to have learned how
to school it to that perfect indifference you are striving now
to attain. I hope you never do master the look."

"Why not?" I asked, turning to him again. His blue eyes
were serious, intent.

"Because your freshness, your naïveté, is part of your
charm, Miss Ames.

"Whether you approve or not, I shall discreetly investigate the young cubs you mentioned. I have a fairly good
idea who they might be. I can assure you you will not be
troubled by them again."

"Please do not," I said swiftly. "It will call attention to the
situation and I was hoping people would forget it."

"If Lady Louisa keeps pursuing Bryce so fervently and so
obviously, you might have your wish." He nodded to where
Louisa was hanging on the earl's arm, standing so close to
him it was as if they were one person. As I watched, I saw
Bryce step away from her and, turning from the couple they
had been with, speak to her long and earnestly. I saw her
color rise, the way she clenched her fists, and I held my
breath. I was aware that we were not the only ones watching
them. Several other interested parties had turned in their direction, Mrs. Boothby-Locke among them. Bryce held

Louisa's eye until finally, after what seemed an age, she walked quickly away. I did not draw a deep breath until I saw her leave the room, however.

"Yes, she has always been difficult," Carlyle murmured in my ear. "I suspect she is well on the way to being impossible. There'll be an upset of truly heroic proportion one of these days. I hope you are nowhere about when it occurs."

"So do I," I said fervently before I thought.

"You intend to remain with the Langleys for a lengthy period of time?"

"No, just for the Season. I've been toying with the idea of going home in early July. Surely I will have trespassed on their hospitality for long enough by then."

"I think you would be wise to do so."

I waved my fan before my face to hide the distress I felt that he could say such a thing so casually. When I was gone north, would he miss me? Would he ever think of me and regret what might have been? Or would I leave his mind so thoroughly that perhaps next Season he would not even remember my name and I would become only that girl he had magically provided with a ball in her own bedchamber?

It was sad and sobering to think of, and I added it to all the other thoughts I had pushed to what was surely becoming a very crowded place at the back of my mind.

Looking around, trying to find something else to talk about, I noticed an older woman I did not know staring at us, her face showing her disgust.

"Do you know who that is over there, sir? That woman in the purple gown with the matching turban? She looks so very disapproving."

Carlyle raised his quizzing glass to such effect that the lady dropped not only her gaze but her handkerchief as well.

Lowering his glass, he said, "That is Mrs. Geering, your John Geering's mother. Although I fear he is not yours any longer. I do hope you were not cherishing any expectations there. Mama has obviously forbidden him to approach you again. My fault, of course. Should I beg your pardon?"

I thought for a moment. It was true I had not seen or heard from Mr. Geering for over a week, and although he was at the soiree this evening, he had not asked me to dance.

"It is unnecessary, sir," I remembered to say. "I never wanted Geering."

"I didn't think so. He is not worthy of such as you. No, you can do so much better than Geering."

"If I do find someone I want, should I tell you so you will have a care?" I dared to ask, even as I wondered I could be so reckless.

To my regret, he did not answer. The dance had ended and my partner for the next set was fast approaching. Carlyle rose. "Give you good evening, Miss Ames," he said as he bowed.

I did not watch him stroll away for I was determined not to be obvious. Instead, I worked very hard for the rest of the party trying to look not only entertained but vastly amused by my partners and the conversations we engaged in. I went in to supper with Moreston's friend, Lord Faye. We sat at a table that included Louisa. She was not in good spirits and she didn't even try to hide it. I felt sorry for her escort, a young gentleman new-come to London who had no doubt preened himself on the prize he had won and was now regretting it.

Much later, as I was returning to the ballroom, I chanced to hear Carlyle and another gentleman I did not know in conversation. They were standing on the other side of the doorway I was about to enter, their backs turned to me. I would not have eavesdropped, except the gentleman said, "I have heard the most engaging yet outrageous story about you, Rogue. You and a Miss Ames."

"Have you?"

"Indeed. Alone in her bedchamber at midnight, too. Was it really only champagne you plied her with? Rash, my dear fellow, very rash."

"Do you think so?"

"Everyone does. I'm surprised Moreston didn't insist that you marry the girl."

"How could he? You may be sure I arranged for us to be most adequately chaperoned."

"I still say it was risky. One of these days you'll find yourself in parson's mousetrap, just see if you don't."

"Not I. Deftness is all, sir. Deftness and audacity and perhaps a touch of insolence will always carry the day."

I did not wait to hear any more, but turned blindly away to seek the room I had just left, the one set aside for ladies who wished to withdraw. Fortunately there was no one there but the maid, and I ignored her.

What did you expect? I asked myself fiercely as I fought hot tears. He doesn't care for you. He is *the* Hugh Carlyle. He doesn't want a bride, especially not you. Do strive for some common sense, you silly twit!

I did not leave the room until Louisa came in search of me. Fortunately, she was so wrapped up in her own concerns she did not notice any distress of mine. She told me she had summoned the carriage. I was quick to agree the evening had turned flat. We spoke very little as we waited on the steps for that carriage, and even less when we were both inside it, alone with our thoughts.

Chapter Ten

After a thoroughly wretched night, somehow I was not surprised to see the morning post had brought Louisa and me more letters from our anonymous correspondent. Why not? I asked myself as I took it from the tray a disapproving Hibbert was presenting. It only needed this to make my day complete. I did hope, however, the butler would not feel it necessary to report the letters to Moreston, especially not today. I was feeling heavy and depressed and I didn't need anything else to upset me.

"I see you have also received a note from that impossible dressmaker, coz," Louisa said, staring down at her letter in disgust. "I have always said it was a mistake to teach the lower classes to read and write, and now I am convinced of it. As if we had any intention of giving the woman our trade!

"Oh, that will be all, Hibbert. I'll ring if I need you."

I wanted to applaud her quick thinking, but we only exchanged glances across the table before we broke those garish seals. As I did so, I resolved never, ever, to pick a daisy again.

"What does yours say?" Louisa demanded in a harsh whisper.

"How strange," I said slowly. "This one does not threaten me. It only says, "Do not fear I have forgotten you, Miss Ames." And yours, coz?" I asked. I thought Louisa looked badly this morning. Her face was not so much pale as a sickly gray, her eyes were blank, and her pretty mouth was drooping. You may be sure I had no intention of calling her looks to her attention, however.

She handed the note to me without a word.

"Have you asked the viscount if what I told you was true, Lady Louisa?" I read. "Don't bother. He knows it's so but he'll deny everything. I shall be writing again as soon as I decide how much money will be required to keep me from spreading this very delicious scandal throughout the *ton*."

"Louisa, you'll have to tell your brother," I said as I gave her back the letter. "For unless you have enough money of your own to pay this person, he's sure to find out. And won't he be angry that you kept it from him?"

"I can't tell him, I can't!" she said quickly. "Not that I have any money. My allowance is so pitiful I'm always in debt."

She paused before she added almost shyly, "If it should come to that, could you loan me the money, coz? No, no, I should say *give* it to me, for the chances of me ever having the large sum I'm sure this fiend will demand, are small."

"I can't," I told her. "I don't have much either."

She grimaced. "If you don't want to help me, just say so," she said. She was shredding the note she held with trembling fingers. I didn't think she even knew she was doing it. "But don't you dare to pretend poverty to me," she went on. "It's so hypocritical of you when all society knows your wealth."

"Then all society is wrong," I said firmly. "How did that story ever get started? I live on a farm. A large farm, to be sure, but still only a farm. And sheep don't produce gold."

She looked as if she didn't believe a word I'd said, but she was forced to give up the argument when her brother came in to take his seat at the head of the table.

"You're up late this morning, Cameron," she said as she pushed some eggs this way and that on her plate. "You look terrible, too. A bad evening at play?"

Moreston frowned. I agreed he did not look well. His face was as drawn as Louisa's, his eyes as shuttered.

"That, my very dear Weeza, is none of your concern," he

told her as he poured a cup of coffee. "Constance, if you would be so good as to pass me the jam? Thank you."

"Bryce said you should avoid Lockwood, that he's nothing but bad luck, confirmed gambler that he is. He says you'll find yourself in trouble if you get in debt to him," Louisa persisted. I wondered why she kept after her brother. Did she want to make him feel as miserable as she did this morning? Couldn't she rest until she had everyone in that state?

"Besides, if we find ourselves in the poorhouse, it *will* be my concern, now won't it?" she demanded. "I warn you, Cameron, I've no intention of marrying some wealthy nabob to save you, so don't count on that."

Moreston put down his knife and stared at her. The silence in the room stretched into long, long seconds and I wished I were anywhere but there, a part of it. A fleeting glance at Moreston showed me a face as black and dangerous as his sister's had ever been, and I admit I was alarmed. The anger and tension in the pleasant, sunny room was frightening enough without the viscount looking ready to do murder.

"That will be quite enough," he said at last, never taking his eyes from her face. "And I'll thank you not to discuss my affairs with Bryce, or anyone else for that matter. Langley business is just that—the Langleys'. As for your marrying a nabob, I'm afraid I'd have trouble finding one willing to take you on, you little shrew. You'd better not count on Bryce, either. *He* doesn't want you, no matter how you pursue him. He's too clever to willingly walk into a marriage that would only make him miserable."

Horrified, I watched Louisa jump up, her chair crashing to the floor behind her. Resting her fists on the table, she cried, "You're wrong! You don't know anything about it! I won't listen to you, I won't!"

As she spoke all in a rush, her voice rose to a scream, and I was glad when she dashed to the door, slamming it behind her.

"More coffee, Constance?" Moreston asked, picking up the pot and gesturing toward my cup. I shook my head, wondering he could be so nonchalant. Or had he witnessed so many scenes like this he had become hardened to them?

I excused myself a short time later. Louisa and I were pledged to join Gloria Hefferton that morning for a walk, but surely in the state she was in, Louisa would not remember that. As I went to my room I could not help recalling the uncontrolled display of temper—the angry spite—I had just been a witness to. It did not seem normal to me, but then I told myself that living alone with an indulgent uncle had hardly prepared me for ordinary family life. Perhaps all families had their arguments and disagreements. Perhaps in the seclusion of their own homes, they did raise their voices, even scream at each other. How could I know?

Miss Mason met me in the upstairs hall. "What set her off?" she asked bluntly when I would have passed her with only a little smile.

"You heard? Up here?" I asked.

"Hard not to," she replied. "We're all used to it, although it never ceases to throw Lavinia into a tizzy. What happened this time?"

"She had a disagreement with the viscount," I said, not liking to be specific.

Miss Mason inspected me shrewdly. "My dear Miss Ames, the Lady Louisa has disagreements with everyone she meets," she said tartly. "What was this about in particular? Lavinia will ask me, you know," she added, as if to provide an extra incentive for me to tell her.

"She was after him about his gambling," I confessed. "And he said some rather unpleasant things to her in return, about her chances with Bryce. And it just, well, it just went on from there."

"I can imagine." Miss Mason paused as if about to add something, but after a moment she went on her way to my aunt's rooms. I watched her, a little puzzled. I was still not sure about Henrietta Mason, nor her function here. I wonder if I should ask Louisa, I thought as I rang for my maid to help me dress for the street. But not today, I reminded myself, still hearing the way she had screamed, the cords of her neck standing out in ugly relief, the crazed look she had had.

No, I told myself quickly. Not crazed, of course. What had I been thinking? Louisa was only quick to anger with little self-control because she had been spoiled as a child. It was nothing more than that. Of course not.

She surprised me by knocking on my door half an hour later. She was ready for our walk and from her face and demeanor no one would have been able to guess she had ever had a temper tantrum, never mind the one of such heroic proportions she had indulged in this morning.

I was not quite ready for my maid was still arranging my hair. Louisa said she would wait for me downstairs since Miss Hefferton had already arrived. I was glad. I was getting tired of listening to her try to make her bad behavior plausible.

When we set off at last, I saw Miss Hefferton was wearing a long-sleeved dark brown gown this morning, made of some rough material that reminded me of burlap. Since it was a warm June morning, it looked very uncomfortable.

To my surprise, Miss Hefferton made much of me, admiring my walking dress and telling me I was in my best looks. It was soon apparent she did so because Louisa was annoyed with her. In fact, no matter what subject Miss Hefferton introduced for our consideration as we made our way to the Serpentine in Hyde Park, Louisa had little to say. I found myself in the unlikely position of Miss Hefferton's confidante and it was not long before I wished I had excused myself from the excursion. More than that, I was angry that Louisa should put her friend in the position of having to plead for attention. I also knew my witnessing her degradation would not endear me to her.

I was looking about for an acquaintance I might join when Louisa stopped walking and turned to her friend.

"I know how busy you are, Gloria. I believe Connie and I won't detain you longer. Come along, coz."

Miss Hefferton's thin face reddened, and her mouth opened and closed a few times before she said, "But Louisa, my love, I'm not busy. Oh please, Miss Ames, speak to her for me. It was just a misunderstanding on my part. I never meant—why, could anything be more unfortunate when I was just trying to help . . ."

Louisa, who had walked on a few paces, turned and ordered me to join her. Believe me, I would have refused, for to leave Miss Hefferton to make her own way home, unaccompanied, was not at all the thing, but I was given no choice in the matter.

"Go," Miss Hefferton said, giving me a little push in her direction. "She will be so angry if you do not, and I would not anger my dear Louisa for the world. But Miss Ames, please tell her I meant it only for the best."

Tears ran down her face as she spoke, and she was so in earnest that I nodded. When Louisa saw me coming she set off again and I had to hurry to catch her up.

"Now perhaps you will be so good as to tell me what that was all about, Louisa?" I demanded, so angry I forgot to consider the spell of temper I might provoke. "This goes beyond anything, to treat your friend in such a way! Why did you ever agree to a walk if you were angry with her? And slow down. Why are you hurrying? I do not understand you at all."

"No, you don't. You probably never will," she said, staring straight ahead and only moderating her pace slightly. "I am most distressed with Gloria. She has busied herself about something that does not concern her and I certainly never asked her to do it. Far from it."

"She probably did it because she cares for you," I said. "She asked me to tell you she only meant it for the best."

To my surprise, Louisa stopped, and, turning to face me, began to laugh. She had a deep, rolling laugh that seemed to come from the pit of her stomach, and it was so infectious I felt my lips twitch in response.

"What is it? Why do you laugh?" I asked when she was more controlled.

"I—I can't say, it's too silly," she said as she mopped her eyes.

"Oh, do look at that dear little boy rolling a hoop toward us. Isn't he adorable?"

She spent a few minutes admiring the child and talking to his nanny before we went on.

"But what *did* she do? For the best, that is? Miss Hefferton?" I persisted.

"Can't you forget her, Connie? I find the entire subject boring. And I've never thought you were even interested in Gloria."

"I'm not," I retorted. "But how can I help wondering what this is all about, since I was privy to such a scene?"

Louisa sighed. "It is a personal matter between Gloria and myself," she said in her coldest voice. "Of course I'm sorry you had to be involved, but I had to tell her immediately how displeased I was with her behavior. I am fond of her. We've been friends for a long time. But sometimes she takes advantage of that friendship, oversteps the bounds of what is seemly. Then it is necessary to put her firmly in her place."

I nodded and tried to look as if I agreed, although to be truthful I felt I had been spun a web of words that told me nothing at all. And for Louisa to mention "seemly" behavior in that disapproving voice was enough to send *me* off into whoops.

Before I could succumb, Louisa said, "Connie, I've been meaning to ask you something about those letters we've been receiving, and now we're alone and not likely to be interrupted would be a good time."

She looked around as if to make sure there was no one nearby before she added, "Have you ever thought our anonymous correspondent might well be Rogue Carlyle?"

I hoped my mouth had not fallen open as far as I suspected. "Carlyle?" I asked, stunned. "But why on earth would *he* do such a thing?"

"The very same—and no, don't say anything yet. Hear me out."

She paused, as if to put her thoughts in order. "I know you think the letters are more likely the work of a woman, and yes, I can see why you do. But Hugh Carlyle must not always be just leading fashion, he must forever be doing some outrageous thing to call attention to himself. Consider how he invaded your bedchamber and then hurried to tell everyone at the ball.

"Now, isn't it possible that after seeing you at Lady Beech's that first afternoon you met and strolled in the garden together, he determined to do this odd thing as a way of amusing himself? He is so dreadfully bored most of the time."

The tiny thread of doubt I had been feeling, vanished. "But I received the first letter the very morning of our visit, *before* we met," I told her.

"Did you? Well, perhaps that is the reason he singled you out at Rosalind's. He had seen you sometime in May—at a party, perhaps—and decided to find out if he could fluster you, perhaps force you to leave London and return to Yorkshire. He may even have had a wager with some friends that he could do just that. He likes his wagers, does Rogue."

"I'm sure you must be wrong, Louisa. What you say sounds so incongruous! And what if he became known as the guilty one? Would he take such a chance? He would lose everything. He would be scorned."

"Ah, but he is in no danger. He's using a woman's method for spite. And we're certainly not likely to talk about the letters, now are we?

"Tell me, hasn't he ever asked you if you were feeling quite the thing? Inquired if anything was bothering you?"

I had no answer for her. Clearly I remembered Carlyle saying he would never hurt me, but I also remembered just as clearly, how he had told me I looked strained and tense, and asked the reason for it.

No, I told myself. Even so, I don't believe it. I won't.

"I see you've thought of something," Louisa said as she patted my arm. "It is not his fault, you know. He must always be talked about, admired, marveled at. And surely you have known all along he was not pursuing you with any intent of marrying you."

"No, of course not," I said staunchly over the ache in my throat. Deftness is all you need to escape marriage, he had said to his friend that evening we had sat out together. Deftness and audacity and perhaps a touch of insolence. And, oh my, he certainly had insolence.

"Still, I find it hard to believe this of him," I said slowly. "I don't think he's the kind of man to do such a terrible thing, no matter how he pretends indifference. I—I just can't."

She patted my arm again. "I know. It's hard, isn't it? But we don't have many suspects, do we? Still, we might be able to make sure of his guilt or innocence if you're willing to try."

"How?"

"I've heard Carlyle is planning a party to be given soon. He does not do so every year, but when he does, everyone in the *ton* clamors for an invitation. They are so unusual, his parties! Two years ago he used a South American motif. There were exotic flowers, native drummers, even a wild jaguar wearing a diamond collar. The jaguar was in a cage, and the collar was for anyone brave enough to take it from him. No one dared, of course."

"But how would a party help us discover whether he is the one or not?" I asked to end her description of past delights.

"Well, while we're attending, one or both of us can search the desk in the library, even invade his private rooms. In such a crush as there is sure to be, it will be easy to do so unobserved. It only requires fortitude and determination.

"And if we find any evidence—the paper or the blue wax,

that awful seal—wouldn't that be proof he is the guilty party?"

I had to admit she was right, although I couldn't imagine the fastidious Mr. Hugh Carlyle ever using a wafer so garish a blue, not even when trying to conceal his identity.

"Of course chances are small we'll find anything," Louisa said glumly. "That would be too easy. No, I'm sure you were right in the first place. It has to be some woman who dislikes both of us so, she must take her revenge. If only we could think who she might be."

She began to name women who might harbor a grudge against her for some reason, but I barely listened. Was it Carlyle? I wondered. Could it be? Was he that fine an actor that I had never suspected his nefarious plan? And was he that despicable a man he could do such a thing to me only to amuse himself or perhaps win a wager?

A part of me wanted to leap to his defense, deny any wrongdoing hotly, tell myself Louisa was grasping at straws. But a part of me—the north country woman—had to admit there was no way I could be sure.

Hugh Carlyle was an enigma.

Chapter Eleven

Viscount Moreston left town early the next morning before anyone was awake. No one knew where he was going. No one knew when he would be back. His absence did not seem to affect the household very much—he was so often from home even when he *was* home, it was hard to tell when he had left London. When I went to bid my aunt good morning, I discovered she had no idea of his whereabouts either.

It was her day for making calls and I offered to go with her and keep her company.

"Why, how nice of you, Constance," she said, sounding almost surprised. "Henny doesn't care for visiting. It is so strange of her, don't you think? But never mind. I intend to visit an old acquaintance who lives near Richmond. The carriage is called for one."

The morning passed slowly. Louisa had gone out with Emma Pratt for a fitting on a new gown she had ordered, anticipating the invitation to Carlyle's party. Part of me hoped it wouldn't arrive. I couldn't see myself searching his desk or his rooms. Such an invasion would be especially painful for a man I suspected of being a very private person.

I tried very hard not to think of it, or the things Louisa had mentioned yesterday. Instead, I wrote a letter to my uncle and one to my former governess, who was now with a family in Dorset. As I did so, I wished she were here so I might pour out my problems and have the benefit of her advice and counsel. Then, of course, I found myself back where I had begun, wondering about Hugh Carlyle and the kind of man he might turn out to be.

It seemed fantastic to me, yet plausible, depending on how you considered the situation. Could Carlyle have written the letters? Of course. Was it probable he had done so? I had no idea. With what I knew of him, did I believe he might have begun this trick for a wager? Or because he was bored? Or merely to play God? Yes, unfortunately, I supposed I could when I was thinking coldly and rationally. Because when all was said and done, I did not know the gentleman that well, our midnight waltz notwithstanding. We had met and conversed exactly four times, hardly enough for me to be able to say firmly, no, of course he had not done it.

By one o'clock I was dressed and looking forward to the distraction the afternoon promised me. My aunt came down ten minutes later, trailed by her maid bearing her reticule, a parasol, and a light carriage robe to spread over her knees. I wondered she thought she needed it when the June weather continued warm and sunny. And then I remembered we were Going-Out-of-Town, a fearful and momentous undertaking, even if we were only traveling as far as Richmond.

We said very little until the carriage reached the outskirts of London. My aunt was always fearful of possible accidents when the roads were crowded, and she preferred to spend the time staring anxiously from the window beside her, clutching the strap tightly in anticipation of any disaster that might be in store. At the speed she insisted we travel, however, a disaster seemed most unlikely.

I was thinking as I so often did what a nervous, timid woman she was when she turned to me and said, "There, now we may have a comfortable coze. I've been wanting to talk to you privately, explain if I could . . ."

She paused for a moment as if to gather her thoughts.

"Perhaps it would be better if you began," she said finally. "I'm sure you must have wondered about us all."

"Yes, I have," I said, delighted to be able to ask about this strange family I was visiting, and determined to make the most of the opportunity. There were so many things that had confused me. "Do tell me about your husband, aunt," I began. She looked aghast; sorry now she had given me permission to question her, and I added quickly, "I'm sure yours must be a romantic story."

"Well, yes, I guess it was," she said, relaxing a little. "I met him here in London when I came to visit friends. I was twenty-seven at the time and for one reason or another had not married. Well, you know Yorkshire. So lonely. And it seems I spent my twenties in mourning for one relative after another. It's so unfair, mourning," she added darkly, and then fell silent.

It was the first time I had heard her make such a human remark, as if she were remembering how it had been when she was a young girl, forced to wear black for first an uncle or a grandparent, then no sooner freed of that restraint, having to learn another close relative had gone to his just reward. And all the time the years had gone marching on until she must have despaired that she was firmly on the shelf. I warmed to her then as I never had before, quite agreeing the length of time required to mourn was most unfair, especially to the young.

When I prompted her gently to continue, she came out of her reverie and said, "Oh, do forgive me! I was woolgathering.

"Now where was I? Yes, visiting London where I met Frederick Langley. I thought him wonderful, and when he admired me, told me he loved me, I was thrilled. His wife was still alive—Clara, her name was—so we could not marry. But even after I went home, Moreston wrote to me. When his wife died, he made arrangements for us to marry a year to the day later.

"It was quite the longest mourning I had ever done," she added, with a shy smile.

Something about her story bothered me beyond the viscount's infidelity to his wife, and I said, "But how did she die? Surely she could not have been very old?"

"No, she was only in her middle thirties. Her death was—unexpected."

It was obvious she did not want to say any more. She refused to look at me as she rummaged through her reticule for a handkerchief.

"Unexpected? How so?" I asked, determined to find out if the anonymous letter writer had known the truth about Louisa's mother. "It seems to me I heard she had had a riding accident."

It was several moments before my aunt nodded. "Yes," she said softly. "She was on horseback."

"But what happened?" I persisted.

"I—I'm not sure. I believe her horse bolted for some reason and so they came to grief. I know the horse had to be put down. It was badly injured."

I could tell by the way she folded her lips tightly together she wouldn't say any more, so I asked about the present viscount and Louisa. But if I thought the change of subject would make her easier, I was mistaken. She still clutched her handkerchief and looked at me with fearful eyes, huge in her thin, lined face. Not for the first time, I wondered about her age. If she had married the viscount in her late twenties, she couldn't be more than thirty-eight. How strange! She seemed almost elderly in appearance and behavior.

"The children?" she asked. "They are different, Louisa especially. She is so like her mother. Impulsive, quick to anger, unconventional. I am sure it is no wonder Moreston preferred *me*."

I wondered about that. For all Louisa's faults, she was alive in a way Lavinia Langley was not. Could the elder Moreston really have loved my aunt? I told myself I should not judge. She may well have been different when he was alive.

"It has never been easy for me, you know," she was saying, and I sat up and paid attention. "No, not easy at all. If you only knew what I have had to bear . . ."

She shook her head. She seemed tempted to brood about all her injustices, but she recollected herself and went on, "Cameron goes his own way. He has since he was a boy. I admit I don't understand him. Oh, you must not think he has been unkind to me," she added, reaching out to touch my hand as if to reassure me. "He has always given me the respect he owes his father's second wife."

I thought that a strange way to put it, and delivered in such a bitter little voice, too, but I did not say so. Instead, I asked about Louisa. Lavinia Langley sighed.

"You know her. You have seen how she is," she said. "I did try to teach her discipline when she was younger, but any reprimand of mine sent her off in hysterics. She can be so—so . . ."

"Frightening?" I supplied. My aunt turned to me so suddenly she startled me.

"Why do you say that?" she demanded. "No, no, she is not frightening, except perhaps when she is in a temper. But she doesn't mean the things she says and does then. It took awhile for me to learn that, accept it.

"You must remember she was twelve when I married Moreston. Too old for me to have any influence over her, or any way to change her. She had been terribly indulged, you know. I blame the viscount as well as her mother for that.

"But she has been much better since your arrival, Constance. You are so positive, so sure of yourself, so *forceful.* I cannot think it quite ladylike; still, I suppose I must thank you for keeping Louisa so well amused."

I longed to ask if I had been invited for just that purpose, but did not. How lowering if she said yes.

"She and the viscount do not seem especially close," I remarked instead.

"No, they aren't. It may be the five years between them, or the fact Cameron was away at school much of the time. I cannot say. He, of course, considered her an annoyance when they were younger, and now only a tiresome female. And she? Well, I've always suspected she envies him because he's a man and he inherited the title."

She fell silent and I thought about what she had said. Yes, it was possible Louisa envied her brother his position, his power, and the absence of the prohibitions that hedged her about, to say nothing of the freedom he had to come and go as he pleased. In a way that might explain why she had taunted him about his gambling.

"How came Miss Mason to join the household?" I asked next. "Is she a relative of yours?"

"Dear Henny? Oh no, she is a distant cousin of my husband's. She came to live with us shortly after we were married. When Moreston died, I discovered he had promised her she would always have a home with us. I am so grateful for that. She is more to me than a dear companion. I don't think I could have managed to survive it all without her."

I did not ask what "it all" was. Somehow I was sure it involved Louisa, perhaps Cameron as well.

"But enough of me. Tell me, are you enjoying your first Season? You have certainly taken, haven't you? All your beaux, Mr. Geering in particular—why, many a young miss would give anything to be so sought after. And then there is Mr. Carlyle and the attention he bestows. I am sure I am struck dumb by it. I would have thought the gentlemen would prefer a more retiring, modest sort of girl, but there! What do I know of modern matchmaking, old lady that I have become?"

She sighed and fell silent for a moment. Then she turned to me and said, "Tell me, niece, is there anything that bothers you? In spite of your success, there are times when I am sure I see a shadow in your eyes. Has anyone been unkind to you? Perhaps I could help. Do confide in me, Constance. I am your aunt and I would like to assist you."

"Why no, nothing is bothering me," I said as she peered at me, hands clasped before her. And then I wondered why I didn't tell her about the letters. Was it because I didn't feel there was anything she could do to help me? Or was it because she was not only ineffectual, she was so nervous I was afraid the knowledge someone had been writing poison to Louisa and me would upset her so dreadfully she would fall ill?

"I see we've arrived," she said as the carriage turned in between the gates of a handsome country house. I thought she sounded disappointed. But surely I had to be mistaken in that. She had been so reluctant to answer most of my questions.

As I took the groom's arm and followed her from the carriage, I considered the things she had told me, and, more importantly, the things she had not. Somehow I was sure a lot had been left unsaid. I wondered why my aunt had initiated the conversation at all. It seemed unlike her unless she had felt obligated to try and smooth over the rough edges of my stay at Moreston House.

There were several lady callers before us that afternoon, all of them considerably older than I. After a suitable interval our hostess, upon learning I was from the country, suggested I might enjoy inspecting the home farm. I was as delighted to excuse myself as I am sure the ladies were to see the back of me, for now they could air the more scurrilous gossip as well as be able to discuss candidly all their numerous female complaints.

I spent a pleasant hour admiring a herd of cows knee-deep in the lush grass of the pasture, a thriving henyard, even the pigsty with its odorous inhabitants, and if I muddied the hem of my gown and soiled my delicate kid slippers, I didn't care a jot. My aunt exclaimed over the color I had acquired, and on the return journey prattled on about the lotions and creams I might use to remove or at least fade it. I was brooding a bit and didn't heed her. It had been grand to be in the country again, free to roam where I would and talk to the farmhands and their wives. But somehow, even though I had enjoyed it, I had not been as happy as I used to be at home.

Carlyle, I admitted as I grasped the strap when the carriage wheels found a deeper rut than usual. It's because I've met Hugh Carlyle and learned to like him that nothing that once brought me pure pleasant can ever be the same. And suspecting him of infamy as I did troubled me deeply. It had to be that.

There was another letter waiting for me back at Moreston House. I was relieved to see Hibbert seemed resigned to all these unworthy missives that so often sullied his silver tray, for his face was an indifferent mask as he held it out to me.

"This came in the afternoon post, Hibbert?" I asked.

"It was delivered by hand, miss," came the measured reply. "By a dirty little urchin, just like before."

"The same one?" I could not help asking before I cursed my curiosity when he seemed surprised.

"No, miss, another one," he told me as I took the letter reluctantly. My aunt had already gone upstairs and now I followed her. I had no idea where Louisa was, but I was glad to have the time to read the note in the privacy of my room. It was longer than the last and all the time I was reading it I seemed to see Carlyle's hand moving over the cheap paper, the thin twist of his mouth and the coldness in his eyes as he sanded, then folded it. The disgust on his face as he heated the blue wafer, used the crude seal. It made me feel ill, but when I was finished, I shook my head. Carlyle had not written this letter. He hadn't penned these words, made the accusations enclosed in it. He couldn't have done it. It was too vile, and it was all lies.

For my father could not have been the monster the author described, a man who had had to be physically restrained from smothering me at birth because I was not the son he wanted; the man who had howled his threats and disappointment over my mother's bed until he had killed her as surely as if he had stabbed her to death.

Rereading the thing, I felt sick to my stomach. But before I sought relief in tears, I remembered the earlier letters. Then the author had claimed my mother had taken many lovers; that I was not my father's child. It seemed to me my correspondent wanted it both ways but that wouldn't work. Either I was my father's daughter and he had been angry I was not a son, or I was a bastard, in which case it seemed to me he would have been delighted and relieved he did not have to accept me as his heir to save face.

Could it be possible the writer had *forgotten* what he or she had alleged before? It seemed highly unlikely.

Once again I compared the letter with those I had already received. Except for the incongruity of this one, they were similar in every other way. As I put them in the hidden drawer in my jewelry case, I wondered the author had not thought to blackmail me rather than Louisa if what she had told me about London society thinking me wealthy was a fact. I had no brother to defend me as she did. I had only a weak, ineffectual aunt. I was as good as alone. Wouldn't it have been much easier to bleed me? But the author of the letters had not done so. Why, I wondered. What did he or she hope to gain if not wealth from all this venom?

I began to think about what would happen if I went home early to Yorkshire. Would the letters follow me there? A picture of Carlyle collecting his wager with that thin twist of the lips he called a smile came to mind, in spite of my fine sentiments exonerating him only moments before. I determined then and there he would never have that satisfaction, no matter what he wrote to me, and I would find a way to expose him if it was the last thing I ever did. If he was the guilty one, that is, I reminded myself, wondering if I were losing my mind.

One thing I did know was true, and that was I had to be the most confused person in London by a very wide margin. There could be no disputing that.

* * *

Louisa had invited a number of young people, including Lord and Lady Beech and Lord Bryce, to an evening of cards to end in supper. Somehow she had convinced my aunt to stay in her rooms with Miss Mason. It was unusual, but I told myself as long as Rosalind was there to play gooseberry, no one could truly find fault with it. Talk there might be, censure, no. How fine a line Louisa walked, I thought as I tried to decide which gown I would wear.

The evening began inauspiciously enough until Louisa suggested it might be more exciting instead of merely playing whist, to gamble on the outcome. If we all put up ten guineas, she said, then whoever had amassed the greatest number of points at midnight when supper was to be served would be declared the winner. I was horrified by the scheme and I could tell the others did not approve of it either. Rosalind seemed about to speak, but Lord Bryce was before her. "That will never do, Louisa! What are you thinking of, to turn your brother's drawing room into a gambling hell?"

"To say nothing of winning all, with her luck," Rosalind put in, before he say any more. "Oh no, Louisa, you'll not fill your purse as easily as that."

Louisa pouted, but when a glance at Bryce's handsome face showed her he was in earnest, she shrugged and went back to assigning seats at the tables. I was not surprised, nor, I was sure, was anyone else, to discover she was partnered with Bryce for the first game. I could only regret how obvious she was.

Still, it was a pleasant evening, due in part to Louisa's skill as a hostess. When she cared to, she could be charming, full of concern for her guests' comfort, and witty and amusing as well.

I am not especially adept at cards for I've had little practice, but I think I managed to acquit myself fairly well. At least none of my partners seemed distraught when they left me.

At Louisa's insistence, Rosalind took the seat at the end of the table at supper with her husband opposite. I was surprised to see her own place was some distance from Bryce's and wanted to applaud her tact until I saw she had seated him between the two homeliest girls at the party. As he assisted them, he chanced to look up and catch my eye and he winked broadly. I was hard put not to laugh until I wondered if Louisa had noticed. I wanted no scenes to mar the evening, not now, and not after the guests had left. Fortunately, the wink had gone unobserved.

After supper, Rosalind came up to my room with me. After using the close stool, she sat down to pull her gartered stockings tight while she asked me to join her on a shopping expedition the following morning. She told me in a demure voice it would be a favor, for Lord Beech was going out of town to look at another mare. I laughed.

"Would Louisa care to join us do you think?" she went on.

"She's agreed to see her friend Gloria Hefferton tomorrow morning," I said as I tucked a curl back in place. "She told me of the engagement when she came home this afternoon. They had a falling out yesterday—I still don't know what about—but hopefully Gloria can wheedle her way back into Louisa's good graces. She is such a faithful friend."

"I must admit I'm glad we can spend some time alone—is my gown hanging straight in back, dear?—I like Louisa, truly I do, but I'd like her better if I wasn't always waiting for the fireworks to begin. It's not a bit comfortable."

"I know exactly what you mean. Still, I'm sorry for her. She's not had an easy life, losing her parents as she did."

"I know. It was too bad," Rosalind replied. "But how you've managed to survive here this long is a miracle, dear Constance. She does have such a temper," she added as we went down to rejoin the others making their farewells in the hall.

"Ah, Louisa, what a delightful evening, even if you did cast me in the role of mother."

"I'll not deny it," Louisa admitted, and I admired her honesty. She had needed a chaperone and Rosalind had fit the bill admirably. That she did not try and pretend otherwise was a point in her favor, and from a glance at the Earl of Bryce's face, I could see he agreed with me.

If only I did not have that memory of her contorted face as she screamed at me and called me slut. If only I could erase that, and the picture of her fingers curling into claws as she confronted me. It's sad, isn't it, the terrible things you can never forget?

Chapter Twelve

The Beech town carriage came for me promptly at ten the next morning, and as I ran down the steps to it, I felt almost as if I were escaping. Rosalind did some shopping on Bond Street before we were driven the short distance to the newly erected Burlington Arcade with its luxurious shops and well-dressed clientele. I was amused to see how eagerly Rosalind inspected everything, how she exclaimed over a pretty fan or sighed at an emerald and pearl bracelet. But in spite of those years of exile in Jamaica, she bought very little beyond two pairs of dancing slippers and a few yards of lace. Later she collected a handsome snuff box she had commissioned as a gift for her husband.

"Dear Reggie. I suspect he'd rather blow a cloud," she said as we waited in the carriage outside Fribourg and Treyer for her groom to fetch it. Ladies were not welcome in that masculine establishment. "Still, he likes to carry a snuff box for evening. I suspect men are the same as women in that regard. We must have our fans, our hand-kerchiefs, after all."

Remembering how fond my Uncle Rowley was of his old pipe, I agreed, and resolved to buy him a handsome new one before I left London.

I was easily persuaded to go home with Rosalind to spend the afternoon after she promised to have her carriage take me back to Park Lane later.

We were strolling in the gardens of Beech House when

my friend said, "I'm sure you've heard of this gala Carlyle is giving?"

She waved her hand in the direction of the chimney tops we could just see beyond the trees in the distance. "It is to be the most wonderful evening! Not that he'll tell me a word about it, of course," she complained, wrinkling her nose in disgust.

I laughed. "Hugging his secret, is he?" Suddenly I was reminded of the secret I kept, of those vile letters, and I pushed them from my mind and added, "Surely you must know *something*. Tell me."

"I do know the invitations are to be delivered tomorrow. And he did let fall in a weak moment that all the ladies are to wear only gold, white, or black. Fortunately I have the most glorious white silk gown with delicate gold embroidery to hand."

"I wonder why he is so insistent on those colors?"

Rosalind smiled. "He is Rogue Carlyle, of course. He must always be mysterious. Men!" she added, and shook her head.

"What will you wear, Constance?"

"I have a gold gown I've not worn before," I said, wondering if I dared to do so now. Louisa had insisted I have it made up, but I had pushed it to the back of my armoire because I did not care for the low cut of the bodice. Louisa had said I was a hopeless prude, but I was not used to gowns that showed quite half my breasts. But perhaps if I had my maid raise the bodice an inch or so with some blond lace?

Suddenly we both stopped walking as we heard banging sounds coming from Carlyle's property. Staring at me, Rosalind said, "Do we dare?"

Without another word we picked up our skirts and set off at a run toward the noise.

A high brick wall separated the two mansions, but Rosalind led me to an arched gate in it. Unfortunately we could not see a thing when we reached it for the grounds beyond were hidden by greenery. We tried the gate but it was locked.

"Could he be building a pavilion, do you think?" Rosalind asked as she stepped up on the lowest bar of the gate to crane over it. "Or perhaps he's having an extensive arbor constructed. Or a pergola."

"Surely not. He'd need mature vines to cover it," I said absently as I continued to try and see through the bushes that blocked our view.

"He'd have vines dug from someone else's garden if he wanted them. I assure you, cost does not enter into Carlyle's calculations. Oh, this is useless as well as frustrating," she added as she climbed down. "Come along, I've a much better idea."

We went along beside the wall until we came to an old gnarled tree growing close to it. Some of its sturdy branches were well within reach. Rosalind hiked her skirt to her knees and climbed up until she reached the top of the wall itself. "Are you game to join me, Constance? The view's much better up here."

Amused at her agility, I climbed the tree myself and we were soon perched on top of the broad wall where we had a clear view of Mr. Carlyle's grounds. Below us, all was confusion. There was a lot of lumber about, and several workmen were busy working on something that resembled a trellis. Nearer the house I could see more men laying a wooden floor over a broad swath of lawn.

"For the dancing, no doubt," Rosalind said as I pointed it out.

"What if it rains?"

"On the evening Hugh Carlyle is giving a fete? It wouldn't dare!"

I saw a workman shading his eyes to look our way and I wasn't surprised when he hurried toward the house.

"We've been seen," I said reluctantly. "Best we climb down now."

"Nonsense," Rosalind protested. "I'm sure this is as

much my wall as Carlyle's and I may sit on it as often and for as long as I wish. Do look over at the rose garden, Constance. What do you suppose he's planned for there?"

I still felt uneasy, but when no one came from the house who looked remotely like Carlyle, I relaxed. Probably he was not even at home. We had nothing to worry about after all.

You may imagine my surprise when I heard his voice immediately below me. In fact, if I had not had a firm grasp on the wall, I would have tumbled down on top of him.

"Caught in the act, my lady, Miss Ames," he said as he stepped back so he could inspect us. He was in shirtsleeves and tight breeches and his dark hair was tousled, and not by his valet's expert hand, either. As I watched, he bent and put a roll of paper on the ground. The plans for the gardens? I wondered.

"How shall I punish you spies?" he asked, hands on hips as he looked up at us and scowled.

I suspected he wasn't a bit angry. Rosalind only laughed.

"If you will be so secretive, sir," she said as she shook her finger at him, "I'm sure 'tis no wonder Constance and I were curious. Do tell us what you are doing to the rose gardens. They are beautiful just as they are. I hope you're not planning to uproot them so you might divert the brook or some such thing."

"If you don't want me to, then of course I won't. And you Miss Ames? What would you like to see?"

"I don't know," I said airily. "A silken tent of cloth of gold? A fountain spurting champagne?"

"Here, let me help you down," he said, putting up his arms. "I'll show you around. It's the least I can do since you're so curious. You must promise me you won't tell another soul, however."

I wasn't a bit surprised when Rosalind jumped down into his arms, careless of the amount of silk-clad leg she revealed, but still I hesitated.

"Come on. I won't drop you," Carlyle commanded. His dark eyes held a dare it was impossible to refuse.

I moved to the edge of the wall and let my legs dangle over the edge before I let go. He caught me up neatly, quite as if I weighed little more than a feather. For a moment, he held me close to him before he set me on my feet. I tried to control my uneven breathing, tried to forget how the muscles in his arms had felt under my thighs, his hands spanning my waist, as he said, "I see you've been out in the sun again, Miss Ames. Shame on you. You're all golden."

We stared at each other and it wasn't until I heard the swish of Rosalind's skirts as she shook them out that I remembered we were not alone. And I remembered something else as well, then. That Mr. Hugh Carlyle might well be the author of the letters I had been receiving. That standing right there looking down at me with an enigmatic stare might be the man who had made all those vile, hateful accusations about my parents. Remembering that stiffened my resolve and I lowered my eyes and stepped away from him, resolved to treat him with no more than a cool dignity no matter how he teased or provoked me.

Carlyle offered us both an arm and we set off for the terrace that backed the house. As we stepped around the workmen, the lumber, and various barrows, our host let fall a few tidbits of information. I thought him very clever. For all his easy words, he told us little.

Seated at last on the terrace enjoying lemonade and fruit ices, Rosalind took him sternly to task for it.

"You might just as well keep your secrets, sir," she said, her voice scornful. "Yes, there will be a lot of flowers. Yes, you intend to have dancing and a lavish supper. Doesn't every soiree? Every ball? You haven't let slip a single thing that will distinguish your fete from the rest. Well, never mind. I'm sure Constance and I can contain ourselves till the evening in question."

"You're so sure you'll be invited?" he murmured as he poured more lemonade for us. "Both of you?"

Rosalind sniffed. "If we're not, we shall perch on the wall where you found us and make loud, rude comments about the proceedings and your guests."

"I'd be well within my rights to have you removed. That's my wall, not yours. But you need not fear, m'lady. Yours shall be the first invitation delivered."

"Only because I live next door," she retorted, not a bit appeased by this handsome concession. "Who is that dear little boy?"

Carlyle's glance followed her pointing finger to where a golden-haired toddler stood watching the workmen. "One of my gardener's children. He has been forbidden to bother the men, but we can't keep him away. He's very fond of hammers."

Rosalind excused herself, saying she simply must speak to the child. Bemused, I watched her make her way through the gardens.

"What is it? What's wrong?" Carlyle asked, his voice as quiet as if he were inquiring how I liked the weather.

I refused to look at him. "I can't imagine what you mean," I said, proud my voice was as even as his own. "Why do you think something's wrong?"

"You've said little this afternoon. Somehow I doubt it's because you feel guilty for trespassing. Have I done something to displease you?"

At that I was forced to look at him. He was leaning across the table, closer than I had thought he would be. Stifling an urge to press back in my chair, I said, "How could you? I've not seen you since we sat out at the last soiree . . ."

"Ah, and that displeases you? I do apologize for my neglect. I've been busy. The fete, you know."

"It's no such thing! Why do you presume that is the reason?"

"Perhaps because I wish it were?" he asked.

I had no reply for him. His voice had been without inflection or a hint of flirtation, and it confused me. Hugh Carlyle and I were acquaintances, no more. He had given me no sign he was interested in me, beyond that one moment in my room when I had thought he was about to kiss me before Mrs. Collins coughed. The things he was saying now might have been spoken by an anxious suitor. What could he mean by them?

I rose, taking care I did not upset my chair. Lazily, Carlyle followed suit. "I must be leaving," I said, pretending to adjust my bonnet and effectively hiding my face from his gaze. "It grows late and I have been from home since morning. My aunt will be worried."

"Will you promise to waltz with me again, Miss Ames? At my fete this time?" he asked as he escorted me down the terrace steps.

"If you would care for it, of course, sir," I said, keeping my eyes firmly on Rosalind's little figure and wishing it were closer.

"I care," he replied, and when I stumbled a little, he put his hand under my elbow for support. "Do watch your step, Miss Ames," he said, and now he sounded amused. "If you sprain an ankle I'll have to arrange another midnight visit to your room. And surely you've heard how I pride myself on never repeating an audacity?

"My lady, here is Miss Ames anxious to return home. Allow me to escort you to the gate you tried earlier. I have the key."

Rosalind bid the little boy good day. His quick bob was endearing, but I did not feel like smiling.

It seemed an age before we were safely on the other side of the gate in the wall, and I was able to turn my back on Hugh Carlyle. Of course then Rosalind began to question me.

At last I said, "Why are you so interested in what we talked about?"

"Because I'm quite determined you and Mr. Carlyle

shall make a match of it, my dear," she confided. "No, no, not a single word! I know you like him. I can see it in your eyes, hear it in your voice, watch the evidence of it rise in your cheeks whenever he is near you. And he is on the way to being smitten himself. Yes, it's true. I've never seen him so captivated."

"I'm sure you're wrong, Rosalind," I said weakly. "It cannot be so."

"Goose! Of course it is. It's why I went away to play with the little boy, to give you time to be alone together."

"I thought you liked children," I said in some confusion.

"I do. Not that one, however. He's pretty, but he speaks some language I'm not sure even his mother can understand. I had heavy going of it, I can tell you, and for that sacrifice I expect your hearty thanks."

She did not get it. Instead, I told her she was impossible, but I hugged her tight as I said good-bye a few minutes later.

All the way back to Park Lane I thought about what she had said. Was it true then? And were my feelings for Hugh Carlyle so obvious that anyone just looking at me would know? How mortifying.

But how was it possible I could fall in love with a man I suspected might be the person writing me vile letters? No, that just couldn't be. Rosalind had to be wrong.

I saw Louisa had just come in when I entered Moreston House, and we walked upstairs together. When I asked about her meeting with Gloria Hefferton, she shook her head, looking stern.

"She begged me so to forgive her, I had to," she said as she followed me into my room. "But then I was forced to spend the day with her at that little house the family has taken for the Season. It is so crowded there's no privacy at all. She had written this explanation of what she had done and why, to read at home."

She showed me some sheets of paper and I remembered I'd promised myself to acquire a sample of Miss Hefferton's script so I might compare it to the letters. Perhaps I could get a closer look at this example?

To my dismay, Louisa put it away in her reticule as she sat down on the edge of my bed and inquired about my day. I recalled I had not shown her the latest letter I had received and I got it out now, relieved I didn't have to mention my meeting with Hugh Carlyle. She looked as sick as I had felt when she finished it and my heart warmed to her, that she should care so obviously for my distress.

"I am more determined than ever that we must find out who this despicable creature is," she said, tossing my letter away. It landed on the floor and I picked it up to smooth it out.

"I'm so sorry, Connie," she went on, looking fierce. "How dreadful for you to have to read such filth."

"But what can we do even if we do discover the guilty one?" I asked. "If we expose them, we'll have to admit we received the letters, even show them. I don't think I could bear to do that."

"Nor I," Louisa said slowly. "But there must be some way we can make this fiend pay for what they've done. Don't you worry, I'll think of something."

I was sure she would. I could only hope it wouldn't be too outrageous.

"At one time I thought it might well be Gloria Hefferton," I said, watching her face carefully. "She's never liked me, you know. But when you began to receive the letters, too, I was forced to discard the notion. She might vilify me, but you? Never. Unless," I added as if I had just thought of it, "unless you think she might have done it just to put us off the scent."

Louisa looked incredulous. "Gloria?" she asked before she fell backwards on the bed, shaking with laughter. "Oh dear me, no, Connie. It couldn't be Gloria! She doesn't have the wit to compose the letters, nor the patience to conduct such a long campaign. As I've discovered, she's much too impulsive."

I nodded, but I wasn't entirely convinced. I still intended to study the woman's handwriting as soon as I got the chance.

It rained for the next three days and by the end of the week Louisa was as cross as a bear. Everyone in Moreston House was made aware of it too. I don't think a single person there, right down to the lowliest scullery maid, escaped her temper. I tried to reason with her. I even told her the weather had not been sent to plague her personally, which only made her stare. Even my cheerful remark that Carlyle's affair would surely have good weather after such a spell of bad could not make her smile. I must admit I found my stepcousin tiresome. Very tiresome.

The invitation had arrived, as promised, the day after my visit with Rosalind. It was delivered by the tallest footman I had ever seen. clad in severe black livery and sporting an elaborately curled wig. The invitation was written on heavy cream stock, bordered in gold. The writing had so many curliques it was difficult to decipher. I was relieved it in no way resembled the crabbed script of the hate letters until Louisa told me not to be an idiot, that of course Carlyle had employed a calligrapher.

She was intrigued by Carlyle's command that all the guests wear white, gold, or black and that everyone be masked. It took me most of the day to convince her that black would not be at all appropriate for her, no matter how stunning.

"But just consider, Connie," she enthused as she crushed the invitation between her hands. I wished she would not. I would have liked to tuck it away to smile over in the years ahead—my first London gala. "Just think how marvelous my diamond and ruby necklace would look with low-cut black silk and a damp petticoat."

Putting my daydreams aside, I set myself to the task of convincing her it just would not do.

At last she agreed, although she sulked for the rest of the

day, and when I looked up from the gold mask I was fash-
ioning, I could see her regarding me with a disdainful look.
I thought her most unfair. After all, I had not written society's rules for debutantes. It made no sense to blame me.
But I said nothing. It was impossible to reason with Louisa
when she was in one of her moods.

I noticed my aunt kept her distance and Miss Mason
treated her with heavy courtesy, and I was glad Moreston
was still out of town. It needed only his mite to stir the pot
to a boil.

The day of the gala dawned fine. As I lay in bed I admired the sunbeams that stretched across the floor of my
room. My spirits rose. I told myself it was only because I
was glad for Carlyle, that all his plans should not be
spoiled by rain, and that the bubble of excitement I felt was
not because I was happy to be able to see him again. After
all, he might well be the writer of those vile letters. I must
not forget that.

I thought I looked very fine that evening when we all
gathered in the hall. I had on the gold gown I had hesitated
to wear before but only because I had had my maid fill in
most of the bodice with rows of gold lace. Louisa had
mocked my modesty. She herself was dressed completely
in white. She had even powdered her hair. I thought her
eyes glittered strangely behind the white satin mask she
wore, a mask adorned with white plumes. She did not wear
her diamond and ruby necklace, but her pearls. Somehow
on Louisa, the ensemble did not look at all demure.

My aunt wore black silk, which only served to empha-
size her faded looks and her usual air of nervous exhaus-
tion.

Louisa and I had made plans to search Mr. Carlyle's
bedroom and his library, too, if we could manage it. I at-
tributed the breathless way I was feeling to qualms about
such a course, at war with a kind of dread anticipation. But
whether I was afraid of finding evidence of the man's guilt,
or afraid of what our meeting tonight might bring, I could

not tell you. I can only say I was both eager and reluctant at the same time.

Perhaps my Uncle Rowley was right after all. Perhaps women *are* very strange creatures.

Chapter Thirteen

It was necessary for our carriage to inch its way up Kensington Road for almost a mile before it reached Carlyle's front steps, and by the time it did I was quivering with impatience. When the carriage door was opened by a footman dressed in the black livery I had seen earlier I felt as if a curtain on a stage had been pulled aside, the lights dimmed—the play about to begin.

The doorway was lit by several flambeaux in tall holders that cast brilliant light over the scene. The steps had been covered with a gold, white, and black brocaded rug. As we gave our stoles to waiting maids in the front hall, I saw more footmen standing at attention along the walls. Idly I wondered where Carlyle had found so many men over six feet. I knew the nobility prized tall footmen. It appeared Carlyle employed most of them.

Our host stood at the door of the drawing room to welcome us. Unlike his guests, he was unmasked, and wearing formal evening dress of white knee breeches and hose, black pumps, and a fine black coat over dazzling linen. An emerald blazed in his cravat. I confess I thought him as handsome as his house.

When I curtsied, he smiled his crooked smile. As he drew me up, he said softly, "I hoped you would choose gold. It shows off your hair, and I know Titian never painted finer."

So much for any of us disguising ourselves behind a mask, for he called Louisa a minx to dampen her petticoat. My Aunt Lavinia had to content herself with a slight smile.

The drawing room we entered was lined in pleated gold silk and numerous chairs and sofas were set around for those who preferred a comfortable coze with friends to dancing or strolling about, seeing and being seen. At one end of the room a string quartet played softly and footmen offered glasses of champagne.

Fortunately, my aunt saw some particular friends of hers at once, and after I had her settled by them in a comfortable chair, I was free to investigate the gala. I could see the doors to the terrace were open wide and there were many more people out there and in the garden. I made my way toward them. Louisa, of course, had disappeared on her own pursuits.

I gasped when I stepped outside. Beyond the broad terrace where only recently I had sat with Rosalind and Hugh Carlyle enjoying lemonade and ices, there was a large tent made of gold silk. It enclosed the dance floor we had watched being built, and in its center was a fountain. Spouting champagne, I wondered?

There were many paths around the tent that led deeper into the grounds. They were lit by more flambeaux, and fairy lights gleamed in the trees and bushes. Here and there were large trellises covered with white roses. There was little natural light for the moon was new. How remiss of Carlyle, I thought, not to arrange for it to be full.

As I stood at the terrace edge, I heard a peculiar sound and turned toward it in time to see a large elephant appear. The beast had a basket strapped to its back, a basket containing several guests. As I watched, a keeper, dressed in black and gold and wearing a large turban, ordered the elephant to kneel in a language I did not understand. Obediently, the huge animal sank to its knees so the guests could alight. More guests crowded forward for the treat. When the basket was full again, the keeper made the elephant rise. As it did so, it raised its trunk and trumpeted. I thought it a wild sound for such a civilized setting, wild and lonely, and I shivered.

Lord and Lady Beech joined me then, and for some time we stood and chatted with various groups of people while we enjoyed some champagne. The orchestra in the tent was playing a country tune, and I watched the masked guests, all dressed in white, gold and black, whirl with the music and thought what a success Carlyle's gala was.

A short time later, Louisa materialized at my side. She was laughing at the elephant, who not only had its keeper to give it orders, but another less elaborately dressed Indian with a shovel to dispose of any dung. I was sure he was just as necessary.

"I wonder what other strange animals the Rogue has in store for us," she said. "Have you seen the snake charmer? He has a cobra in a basket and when he plays his flute, it rises and sways to the music."

"Where is it?" I asked, determined to avoid it. I don't like snakes, not even the ordinary garden variety.

She pointed to a small platform and tent near the wall. As I watched, I heard the thin reedy sound of a wooden flute, and I shuddered.

"It's almost eleven," Louisa said, moving closer to whisper. "I've had a chance to look around. I'm afraid the library is too well guarded—must the man have quite so many footmen? Luckily, there don't seem to be any servants on the upper floors. I did not want to linger there, however, so I've no idea which one is his room. We can discover that together."

"But how will we get up there if the hall is full of footmen?" I asked. "And don't forget the maids who took our wraps."

"There's a back stairway just beyond the room set aside for the ladies. Go there just before midnight. I'll be waiting for you at the top."

She must have seen the doubt in my face for she grasped my arm tightly and said, "No you don't! You're not backing down now, Connie! We'll never have a better opportunity to discover whether Carlyle is the letter writer and we're not going to throw that opportunity away, do you hear me?"

I nodded. She sounded quite fierce. Fortunately a pair of young gentlemen asked us to dance then, so there was no chance to discuss the plan further.

I wished I did not feel quite so hesitant, so full of a dread I did not understand. After all, there was little danger we would even be seen, the mansion was so crowded. And if we did happen to get caught on a floor where we had no business to be, it would be simplicity itself to talk our way out of trouble. No servant would dare question us, in any case. Still I could not quiet that little uneasy feeling, and I wished with all my heart I had never agreed to search Hugh Carlyle's home.

I was diverted slightly by a troup of dancers who swirled by. They were clad in beaded jackets and diaphanous silk trousers in brilliant colors. Several of them had gems set in a nostril or swinging at their ears. They were so lithe and acrobatic they made me wonder if they had the same bones the rest of us did.

All this time I had been constantly aware of Hugh Carlyle, where he was, and what he was doing. He appeared to be working his way through the ladies of the peerage according to rank, and now, finished dancing with the duchesses present, had moved on to marquesses and countesses. It would be some time before he arrived at an ordinary Miss Ames for the waltz he had requested—if he even remembered it, that is.

I saw it was almost midnight and I excused myself to make my way to the back stairs. I had to dawdle in the hall until two ladies coming from the withdrawing room passed me. I moved quickly then, but I did not draw a deep breath until I was around the landing and out of sight.

There were a few oil lamps lit up here, but it was not very bright. Louisa smiled when she saw me.

"I was beginning to fear you weren't coming," she whispered. "I've searched all the rooms nearest the stairs.

They're not in use." As she spoke, she lit two candles on a table nearby. Handing one to me, she went on, "You take this side, I'll do the other. There are only three more apiece. We'll find his room shortly."

None of the three rooms I looked into were Hugh Carlyle's bedroom. One was a guest room, the next a dressing room, and the third a small sitting room. Could it be he was up another flight? I did not think I could bear a longer search.

"Connie! Over here," came a harsh whisper. I hurried across the broad hall to join Louisa in a dressing room that was obviously in use. Towels hung over a marble tub and a gentleman's fittings were spread on a dressing table—a silver-backed sable brush, a comb, a toothbrush. Several cravats that had proved unsatisfactory were draped over a chairback.

"In here," Louisa beckoned from another doorway. Holding my candle higher, I followed her into a large room. A huge four-poster bed dominated the furnishings. It was draped in midnight blue hangings and the gold brocade coverlet was heaped with pillows. A tall chest of drawers with a mirror over it occupied one wall and chairs and a center table were placed by the hearth. I saw a pile of books on the table, an open one placed face down on one of the chairs, and wondered what Mr. Carlyle was reading. There was a faint, not unpleasant smell in the room, of sandalwood and bay rum which I remembered Carlyle liked to wear.

Louisa pointed to an escritoire placed before the windows that overlooked the drive. "There's his desk," she said, close to my ear. "Hurry now! I'll go out in the hall and stand guard. If anyone comes, I'll speak loud enough so you'll have time to hide."

Hide where? I wondered as she flitted away, extinguishing her candles as she opened the door and let herself out.

It was very lonesome, left by myself in that huge, masculine room—lonesome and scary. I drew a deep breath to steady myself. I did not begin with the desk. Somehow I was reluctant to touch it. Instead I went through the chest of drawers and found nothing but clothing. The drawers in the two tables that flanked the bed contained nothing either to indicate Carlyle was the writer we sought.

At last I approached the escritoire. It was lighter here near the windows, for the flambeaux illuminating the front door below cast some light upward. I riffled through the drawers of the desk quickly, afraid this was all taking too much time. There was paper there and note cards, but they were the heavy, expensive sort. There was also some sealing wax but it was gold, not garish blue. And there were several seals, one of them having Carlyle's initials, the others of various designs which I inspected carefully. There was no seal featuring a crude drawing of a daisy.

I remembered there had been some drawers in a small chest in the dressing room, and I went back there. It seemed so eerie to be here with only one flickering candle while below me the *ton* were dancing and drinking champagne and watching the performances Carlyle had arranged for their enjoyment. I could still hear the faint sounds of music. Was that a waltz?

I found the paper in the bottom drawer of the chest, placed carelessly under some pieces of cloth, a few stiff brushes, and some containers I did not bother to open. I could tell by the feel of it, it was the same cheap paper the letters had been written on, and at that moment I wanted nothing more than to cry. Cry because I had been wrong about Hugh Carlyle, and Louisa had been right. Cry because I had been building castles in the air and now, in one moment, they had all come crashing down around my feet.

Shaking slightly, I took a sheet of the paper for comparison and folded it before I tucked it in the evening bag that dangled from my wrist. The remainder I returned to the drawer.

"How glad I am to see you! The ladies room was so crowded I decided to look for another place," I heard Louisa say loudly in the hall. Looking around I saw a close stool and frantically I retreated to the bedroom, closing the connecting door behind me as quietly as I could. Hopefully the servant would show her the dressing room and leave her. I told myself there was no reason for anyone to search Carlyle's bedroom. I pressed both my fists tightly to my heart. It was beating so hard it seemed about to spring from my chest. I could still hear voices, but they grew fainter and fainter and at last all was quiet. I waited, exhausted, leaning against one of the massive posters of Carlyle's bed. I was just about to brave the hall to make good my escape when I heard another voice. I swear my heart stopped beating then for a moment.

"There is no one here, as you can see, Simkins. I'll look around the bedroom since you insist . . ."

Desperately I blew out my candle and dropped down beside the bed. There was no time to try to hide behind a drapery or in the large armoire, but I couldn't be seen there unless Carlyle ventured further into the room. If he did, I was undone.

Like a small child is apt to do when frightened, I closed my eyes tightly, as if that would make me invisible. I could not hear any footsteps, but I sensed the glare of a light against my eyelids. Still, I did not move.

"You may go, Simkins. There's no one here," Carlyle said. He sounded very close. I opened my eyes and saw him looming over me, his face dark. I did not move. It was as if I were frozen there. Numbly, I watched while he went to light more candles and the servant's measured tread faded away.

"I'm sure you have some perfectly good explanation for being here in my room, Miss Ames," Carlyle said as he returned to where I crouched and lifted me to my feet. "I can't tell you how interested I am in hearing that explanation," he added as he let me go.

"I don't have one," I managed to say although my mouth and throat felt parched.

He pretended surprise. "None at all? And here I always

thought you so quick-witted. Granted, your cousin used the need for a close stool as her excuse to be up here, but surely there are others just as good. You had made arrangements for a tryst with some gentleman and found yourself in this room by mistake? And then, hearing my voice, you became embarrassed and tried to hide? No?

"Well, how would pretending you had been told Lady Lavinia had been taken ill and you were up here searching for her, do? I could hardly dispute that, she always looks so wasted."

"Stop it," I said, unwilling to listen for a moment more to his cold, sarcastic voice.

"I will if you tell me why you are here," he said.

"I—I can't tell you that," I said, as conscious of the paper in my bag as if it weighed a stone. How could I admit what I had discovered? What might he not do to me, now I had found him out?

He stepped close and tipped my chin up with one hand. "Can it be you came here because this is my room, and you wanted to see where I slept?" he asked, sounding amused now. "Have you been indulging in fantasies, Miss Ames?"

I twisted away, sure my face was crimson. "No, no, of course I haven't!" I exclaimed.

He grasped my arm and reached out with his other hand to pull the mask from my face. To tell you the truth, until that moment I had forgotten I was wearing one.

"There's no need for this now," he said, tossing it casually on the bed. Then he looked down at the ruffles on the front of my bodice. "Or for these either," he added, nodding his head at them. "I am surprised such a bold piece as you have shown yourself to be felt in need of them. You should never have added them. They ruin the gown."

As he spoke, he reached out and yanked. The ruffles came away in his hand. I put up both hands, but it was far too late.

"That's better," he said, tossing the ruffles after the mask.

"Sir, you are mistaken in me," I said, trying to keep my voice from squeaking and ignoring the way he was staring at the vast expanse of skin the low-cut gown revealed. I was sure it must be crimson too. "I know it looks peculiar, but I had a good reason."

"A reason you refuse to divulge," he said almost pensively.

"I can't. But I assure you I wasn't here because I'm—I'm an immoral woman. Please, you must believe me and let me go!"

"I must? Why?" he asked. He touched one of the curls that dangled over my shoulder. "You have such beautiful hair. I've always admired it," he said. "I look forward to discovering if it is natural."

I was horrified. Did he mean what I thought he meant? But surely he wouldn't—not here, not during a party— surely his guests would expect—besides, if he tried anything I intended to scream, scream as loudly as I could.

Completely flustered, I began to back away from him, but he was having none of that. He pulled me into his arms and crushed me against him, my arms imprisoned at my sides. Staring down into my face, he said, "I think we'll forget the midnight waltz I was looking forward to earlier, Miss Ames. I can think of a much more enjoyable activity for us. I never thought to be so fortunate. You'll make my fete most memorable."

He bent his head then and captured my mouth. It was not a gentle kiss, nor a kind one. Instead, without regard for my feelings, it plundered and demanded. And his hands on my back didn't caress me, they insisted I yield to him. Still, I am ashamed to admit that I didn't want him to stop, the way I certainly should have. No, to my mortification I wished only that I might have had a different first kiss from him, one that began gently before it grew in intensity. One that told me I was cherished—desired. That I was someone special.

This rape of my lips, my mouth, did not do that and I couldn't stop the tears that escaped my closed eyelids and ran down my cheeks. Carlyle lifted his head the minute he felt them, his hands coming up to grasp my shoulders.

"Oh, spare me. Not tears," he said. I wondered he could sound so weary, so exasperated. I don't know what I might have said to him except I heard Louisa's voice just then.

"Connie? Are you in there?" she called, sounding as if she had bent to speak into the keyhole.

"It needed only this," Carlyle muttered, letting me go to walk to the door and fling it open. "Do come in, Miss Langley," he said. "Join the party."

She straightened up, looking stunned for a moment. Then she laughed. "Good heavens, Carlyle, I never expected to see you here," she said as she walked past him.

"I don't know why not. You are in my house. This is my room."

She laughed lightly again. "Is it? Then you must forgive me for choosing it earlier. But I only expected to see Connie.

"Whatever kept you, dear? Did you continue to feel ill after I left you here to lie down and rest?"

"It's no good, you know," Carlyle told her from his station by the door. "My valet told me he found you up here and the excuse you used. And I know how I found your cousin, crouched beside the bed in absolute terror."

"Because you frightened her, you brute," Louisa said. Her sweeping glance had revealed not only my mask on the bed, but the torn ruffles from my gown as well. "What have you been doing to her? Tell me at once!"

He stared at her for a moment before he began to laugh, long and hard. Louisa's face paled with anger. I doubted anyone had ever laughed at her in her life, and I wanted to beg Carlyle not to start now. Did he have any idea the havoc he might unleash with such provocation?

Fortunately, he stopped before she could work herself into a terrible tantrum. Shaking his head, he said, "As ill luck would have it, you interrupted us before I could do much of, er, anything. Should I admit what I had in mind? Or would you prefer Miss Ames herself tell you about it later, when you are alone?"

"I have no idea what you mean," Louisa said as she put her arm around me, her head held high. You would have thought her an elderly, affronted dowager duchess. At another time I would have been tempted to applaud.

"Come along, dear," she added, pausing only to pick up my mask before she led me to the door. "Here, put this on," she added softly for me alone to hear. "Your face gives everything away."

"I'm going to summon our carriage now, and send Connie home in it," she went on as we reached the door where Hugh Carlyle waited. "And may I say, sir, you may count yourself lucky I don't tell my brother what has happened here this evening. I do not refrain from doing so out of any consideration for you, no, indeed. I do so merely to save Connie from scandal, and from the horrible fate she would suffer if she were forced to marry *you*."

Carlyle's chuckle followed us down the hall.

"Damn him!" Louisa muttered. "Come now, Connie, get a hold of yourself. We've yet to pull this off, you know.

"Now, you stay here until I beckon. I don't want you to have to linger in the hall a moment longer than necessary."

As she left me in the shadows of the landing, I managed to straighten up and adjust my mask. I feel terrible and not because of any possible scandal either. Not even because of the way Carlyle had treated me. I supposed I had deserved that. No, it was because I had suddenly realized I was as good as in love with a man who wrote hate letters for amusement. Just thinking about it made my stomach crawl, and I had to swallow.

How I made it down to the hall, accepted the stole a concerned maid put around me, and allowed a footman to help me down the steps before he lifted me into the carriage, I don't remember. Louisa's pale face swam before my eyes, and vaguely I heard her ordering the coachman to return for her and the viscountess after he had driven me home to Park Lane.

I leaned back in the seat. Something made me look up at

Carlyle's mansion where it bulked against the sky, and above me I saw Carlyle himself standing at one of the windows of his room and holding back the drapery so he could see more clearly.

As the carriage lurched into motion, a part of me, a very reprehensible part I'm afraid, wished Louisa had not rescued me and I was still up there in that room held tight in his arms.

Chapter Fourteen

I told my maid I had been taken ill at the fete. I even remembered to tell her I myself had had to remove the ruffles from my gown when I found a loose thread. The girl had
looked indignant at the suggestion her sewing skills were
less than adequate, but she had known better than to contradict me.

I waited until I heard her trudging up the stairs to the attics before I got out of bed and opened the secret drawer of
my jewel case. My hands were shaking as I put the notes and
the paper I had found in Hugh Carlyle's dressing room side
by side.

They were all identical. They were the same color, the
same texture, they even had the same rough edges. There
could be no doubt Hugh Carlyle was the guilty one, and now
I did feel sick.

Still, it was a very long time before I fell asleep. Louisa
and my aunt had not even returned by the time the clock
struck four. As I lay there in bed, I tried to picture what Carlyle must have done after I left his house. No doubt he had
checked his appearance before he rejoined his guests. And
he must have smiled and chatted and laughed with them,
given his quiet orders to the servants, been attentive to the
most prominent people there. I wondered who he had
danced the waltzes with. Did he think of me at all? Did he
remember the kiss he had exacted as punishment because I
would not tell him what he wanted to know?

I turned over on my other side and pulled the coverlet up

to my chin. I knew I must stop thinking of that kiss, and Hugh Carlyle. I must not love him. He was not a good man. He was hateful and vicious and sly and I had to forget him. And somehow I had to let him know Louisa and I knew his secret, for only then would the letters stop. Somehow we would have to threaten him with exposure so he would never do such a thing again. I didn't have the slightest idea how we were to do that and I couldn't bear to think of it in any case.

I rose very late the following morning, but even so I was before Louisa and I had finished my breakfast when she came yawning into the morning room.

"You certainly missed a wonderful party, Connie," she said, covering her mouth. "Nothing but coffee, Hibbert.

"Carlyle had the most lavish breakfast served on the terrace at four. As we ate, we could watch the sun rise. It was beautiful.

"Of course from now on all parties will go on till dawn, or even later, for he has set fashion. How tiresome."

She paused to add sugar and cream to her coffee, waiting till we were alone.

"What happened last night?" she asked abruptly. "How did Carlyle come to find you in his room?"

"I think his valet went and got him after he took you downstairs. He must have suspected something was amiss."

Louisa bristled. "I don't see how he could," she said, indignant she might have failed in her role somehow. "I had a perfectly good explanation for my presence on that floor." She thought for a moment. "I have it," she said. "He had to have smelled the candle wax when he went into the dressing room."

"As Carlyle must have in his bedroom," I agreed. "I blew the candle out only a moment before I crouched down beside the bed. And he wouldn't have seen me if he hadn't come right into the room."

"But what happened between you?" Louisa insisted.

"And how did you lose your ruffles? I know there's a story there and I would hear it."

"He thought me loose because I wouldn't tell him why I was in his room. He pulled the ruffles off. He said they ruined the gown. But never mind that now," I added hastily when I saw more questions hovering on her lips. "I found the paper."

"What paper?"

"The paper the notes were written on."

"You *did*? Where?"

"In a lower drawer of that small chest in the dressing room. It was stuffed under some brushes and things. I'll show it to you later. I took a piece of it and when I came home last night I compared it to the notes I received. It is exactly the same."

Louisa's eyes were enormous. "Did you find the blue wax, too? The daisy seal?" she whispered.

"No, nothing more. They were probably there, hidden more cleverly, but I did not have time to look for them."

"My word," she said weakly. Then she sipped her coffee, made a face, and pushed it away. She had forgotten it as we talked, now it was cold.

"I never really thought it was he, you know," she said as if to herself. "Even now I find it hard to believe. Rogue Carlyle writing nasty letters to young women? Take my word for it, he's known for other things where women are concerned."

"I'm sure he is," I said in what I hoped was a wry tone to hide the pain I felt. "Still, there can't be any doubt he is the one. Louisa, what are we to do about it? Obviously we must confront him, even threaten him with exposure. But how?"

"No, no, we must not expose him!" she said, all in a rush. "Just think how it would make him feel."

"I fail to see why we have to consider his feelings," I said stiffly. "He's guilty. He should pay."

She thought for a moment. "Yes, but Connie, don't you see by now he must suspect we know? He has to have guessed we were onto him when he found you in his room and when I came up later. Surely he's wondering, even worrying about what we'll do. I daresay after the fete was over, he discovered you'd been rummaging in his drawers. You probably disarranged things. He'll be nervous—tense—and all he'll be able to do is wait. I agree we have to confront him eventually, but I suggest we punish him by letting him suffer for a time. It will serve him right."

I didn't want to agree. A part of me wanted to get this over and done with. But it was easy for Louisa to convince me, for another part of me really didn't want to confront Carlyle, accuse him. To do so would put paid to some very foolish dreams. I didn't want to say good-bye to those dreams. Not just yet.

"He said you'd tell me what he had in mind for you," Louisa said, looking at me closely. "Was he very angry?"

"Furious. If you hadn't come in, I'm afraid I would have lost more than my ruffles," I told her, for I knew she would pry and pry until she got it out of me.

"Never say so," she whispered. "How exciting! Oh, I wish Bryce would do something like that. Not that he will," she added morosely. "He's so conventional."

"Did you see him last night?" I asked, delighted for the chance to change the subject.

"Yes. He told me I looked very nice. Except for my petticoat. He let me know he didn't approve of a damp petticoat."

"Perhaps he didn't want other men seeing you exposed," I said, trying to cheer her up even though I suspected the earl would never dance to her tune.

We could be private no longer. Hibbert came to tell Louisa Miss Hefferton had called, and she asked him to bring her to the morning room.

"No doubt she wants to hear all about last night," she said as he went to do her bidding. "She made me promise to remember every little thing. Oh, not *that* little thing! That's our secret."

"If you don't mind, I'll be off. I don't think I can bear listening to a description of that cobra. Brrr!"

With Louisa's laughter echoing behind me, I passed Gloria Hefferton in the hall. I was reminded I had never seen an example of her handwriting. Now, of course, I would not need to. We greeted each other cordially, but I could tell she was delighted I was not to be a part of her tête à tête with her bosom bow.

A short time later I had a caller of my own, for Lady Beech came to have a word with me. I hated lying to Rosalind, but I certainly couldn't tell her the truth. And I thought she'd never leave. That bothered me the most of all.

"Constance, dear, I suggest you go back to bed," she said as she gathered her gloves and reticule. "You don't seem yourself even now. But what a shame you had to miss so much of the event of the Season. I know Carlyle was disappointed. He looked decidedly grim after you left, at least to me."

I forced myself to smile, although I had seldom felt less like doing so.

We had other callers that day, a surprising number of them. Louisa had to deal with them with only Miss Mason for assistance for I took the coward's part and went back to bed, and of course my aunt, completely prostrate after her raking, never left her bed at all. When I learned later from my maid that Moreston had returned, I excused myself from going down to dinner as well.

It didn't take the viscount long to hear about the gala, and my sudden indisposition. It appeared some ladies had seen me going up the back stairs after all, and others had seen Louisa coming down. None of them had been at all reticent about sharing this titbit all over town, as Cameron Langley was quick to tell me the following morning when he summoned me to the library again.

"I really don't know what I'm to do with you, Constance," he said, looking harassed. "And when I consider how I once thought you'd be a good influence on Weeza, well! What were you doing up there, anyway?"

Taking a leaf from Louisa's book, I said the ladies special room had been crowded and I had needed to find another place. Desperately, I added, looking down and hoping I was blushing. Of course Moreston could not question me further, but he said again how unfortunate the whole incident was. That was something I could agree with, although I would have used a stronger word than unfortunate. Perhaps disastrous? Shattering? Catastrophic?

Lord Bryce came to call that same day. I was beginning to think all London was determined to wander in and out of the drawing room. Bryce sat gravely as Louisa spun her tale and I contributed my bit. He did not look as if he believed a word we said. I wondered why. By now we had practiced it so, I'm sure it was beyond reproach.

The only person we did not hear from was Hugh Carlyle. Some said he had gone into seclusion, that people paying their respects had found the gates of his mansion on the Kensington Road closed and locked. I wondered where he was and what he was doing. Had he left town? Was he, as Louisa said she hoped, pacing his rooms, wondering when we would tell all and he would be ruined? Or was he even now preparing his defense, getting ready to claim we were only hysterical women making up a tale to call attention to ourselves? Women who hoped a connection with a leader of the *ton,* no matter how distasteful that connection might be, would shower them with reflected prestige? Still, every time I heard the knocker, I longed, if not for his abject, apologetic self, at least for a large bouquet with a card attached that said only "Forgive me" or "I'm sorry." No such bouquet arrived.

My aunt, recovered enough now to resume her place in the family, was stunned to hear the stories that were circulating about us. I steeled myself for her condemnation and I did not have long to wait. We were alone in her rooms. Even Henrietta Mason was excluded.

At first I was comforted by the way she commiserated with me, assured me she knew none of this could be my fault.

"Oh, yes, I know it is all Louisa's doing," she had said, handkerchief held to her trembling lips. "It is always Louisa! But truly, niece, you must have a care. If you don't, you'll find yourself old-cattish, and I can tell you from experience there is nothing good to be said about that state of affairs. For who will want to marry you if you are a care-for-nobody romp?

"I must say I am surprised, however. You have always gone your own way, acted as if you knew better than I, pretended a sophistication it is obvious now is completely missing. Perhaps from now on, you will allow yourself to be guided by me, lest you are forced to return to Yorkshire in disgrace."

I remembered I intended to leave London on the first of July. That was only a week away, but I decided to hold my tongue. Instead, I told my aunt I was truly sorry to have been so much trouble, and that I would try very hard not to get in any more.

"We must hope so," she said. "You are such a *forceful* girl. I have thought so ever since your arrival. So sure of yourself, so calm and practical. I did not expect a niece like you."

I am sure I looked perplexed for she hastened to add, "Not that I regret inviting you to Moreston House. Still, you must strive to be more modest and retiring. Remember Mr. Geering. Alas, he was such a wonderful catch. And now he's gone. For good."

I tried to look regretful, although to tell you the truth I hardly remembered what Geering looked like. And I stayed with my aunt, listening to her tales of the *ton* and how different everything had been in her day. By the time she went to take her customary afternoon nap, I felt thoroughly chastised.

Still, I didn't have to wonder why I hadn't told her my plans to leave town. I knew it wasn't only because I couldn't leave until the problem with Carlyle was solved. No, it was because I had to see him again. Do you understand? I *had* to. I had no choice in the matter.

I met Henrietta Mason in the hall. She had just returned from the lending library with an armload of books and I hurried to relieve her of some of her burden.

I had never seen her room before and I was surprised at how plain and bare it was. Yet somehow I thought it serene, even welcoming, with its soft color scheme and lack of clutter.

"Lavinia been ringing a peal over you, Miss Ames?" Miss Mason asked as she put her bonnet away in a band box. "I suspected as much when she sent me out to enjoy the fresh air."

"She did, yes, but in the gentlest way. I fear I've been a grave disappointment to her," I admitted.

"More than you know," the older woman said, and she chuckled. "Don't worry about it. All this clamor will die down eventually, and we'll return to our usual somnolence. Until the next time Louisa acts up," she added with a sniff.

I was reminded of how little I knew of Henrietta Mason, and since she seemed to be in a pleasant, open mood, I said, "Tell me, how did you come to live with my Aunt Lavinia? Were you friends before her marriage?"

She looked up from the pile of books she was arranging and the shrewd speculation in her eyes made me add hastily, "I only ask because you are so different! She is nervous, frail, and she worries so, whereas you . . ."

When I paused, she laughed. "Yes, I am everything she is not. Not only don't I have a nerve in my body, that body is as far from frail as it is possible to get. And I don't worry. What's the sense of it?

"As for how I came here, the late Viscount Moreston asked me to be her companion. He was concerned about her. She became so morose and timid after she lost the child. So easily agitated."

"I didn't know she had lost one. How sad," I said.

Was it my imagination, or did Miss Mason hesitate? "It is

not generally known," she said at last, intent on squaring up the books. "I think Moreston knew she could not be alone, and being so much older than Lavinia, he wanted to make provision for her while he still could."

I had not known my aunt's husband had been an older man. I realized I knew little of him at all, only that Louisa had adored him, he had fallen in love with my aunt while still married to his first wife—nothing but a few facts, none of which added up to a fully understood human being. Could that portrait over the fireplace in the library be he? I had thought it Louisa's and Cameron's grandfather with its thin white hair and heavy, lined face.

"How much older was he?" I asked.

Miss Mason stared at me. "Why are you so interested, Miss Ames?" she asked. "Surely this is ancient history. And ancient Langley history at that."

I nodded, to acknowledge the reprimand. It really was none of my concern.

When I reached my room I discovered Louisa there, pacing up and down in a regular temper.

"Where have you been?" she demanded. "I've been waiting for you this age!"

"Only with my aunt," I said, suddenly worried. "What is it? Is anything wrong?"

"The only place I never thought to look," she said, scolding herself. "Nothing's wrong, not the way you mean. But Cameron intends to take us walking in Hyde Park at five, and here it's gone four. I'll have to rush to be ready."

She was half out the door as she spoke, but she turned to say over her shoulder, "Bryce is coming too. As my escort."

I chuckled as I rang for my maid. The sea-green gown, I decided, with the chipped straw villager hat and its matching ribbons. There wasn't time to do much with my hair. I sat down to try and pin it back with a pair of amber combs.

Both Louisa and I looked slightly flustered when we came down to the hall shortly after five. Viscount Moreston was there gravely consulting his pocket watch. Fortunately, the Earl of Bryce arrived moments later.

Somehow the earl and Louisa preceded us. I thought what a handsome couple they made as I admired Louisa's pale lilac gown with its white lace spenser, the deeper purple of her reticule and sandals and lilac-trimmed bonnet, and Bryce's broad shoulders and straight legs, his regular, pleasant profile. But I still did not think they looked as if they belonged together. Louisa needed a tall slim man with an air of mystery and hair as black as her own, a commanding man who wouldn't stand for any of her foolishness. And Bryce? I assigned him a pretty blonde with roses in her cheeks and bright blue eyes and a merry laugh. An innocent girl and a steady one.

"He'll never have her, you know," Cameron Langley told me morosely, jerking his chin at the couple who walked before us. "Never thought he would, even without all her mad starts. Knows us too well, does Bryce."

And wants no part of you, I added silently. Small wonder. "She will be devastated," I told him. "She considers herself in love with him."

"Don't you think she is?" he asked, remembering to smile at the occupants of a passing phaeton who never took their eyes from us.

"I think she's imagined herself in love for so long, she believes it. But he's not the man for her.

"Oh, do forgive me, my lord! I shouldn't be saying such things, and to her brother, too."

Moreston captured my hand where it lay on his arm and patted it. "No need to pull your punches with me, Constance," he said in the warmest, liveliest voice I had ever heard from him. "If we're not the best of friends, I don't know who is."

I was delighted to be able to divert him by calling his attention to Mrs. Boothby-Locke going by in an old-fashioned barouche. We both smiled at this lady and bowed slightly. I fancied I could hear her sniff from here.

"Been meaning to talk to you," Moreston said after a moment. "The Season's almost over, and well, there's something we must get settled . . ."

"Oh, please do not remind me, sir," I said as quickly as I could. I had no idea where he was going with this conversation, but something warned me it would be better not to find out. Much better.

"I should be making plans to return home, I know. I've trespassed on your hospitality for far too long. But my aunt has begged me to remain awhile longer."

Before he could reply I chanced to look ahead to where Louisa and the Earl of Bryce had stopped walking and were now facing each other. "I'm afraid our companions are having an argument, my lord," I said, hoping I sounded concerned rather than relieved.

"You mean Weeza is attempting to argue and Bryce is quite rightly ignoring her," Moreston muttered as he hurried me after the two.

"We will not discuss it, Louisa," I heard Bryce say as we neared them. His color was as heightened as Louisa's was nonexistent.

"But I want to discuss it—*now*!" she retorted, snapping her parasol shut and clutching it in her hand. Furled it looked very much like a weapon. Both Bryce and her brother eyed it uneasily.

"If there is anything to discuss, you will wait until we reach home," Moreston ordered in a harsh whisper. "Smile! There go Lady Jersey and Princess Esterhazy!"

"I don't want to smile! And I don't want to wait until we reach home, and furthermore, why are you and Connie even here? I didn't ask you to join a private conversation and I would appreciate it if you would both go away! At once! Do you hear me?"

"You are impossible, Weeza," her fond brother said through gritted teeth and his own broad smile. "Come, we might as well return to Park Lane. There's no use trying to pretend everything's jolly, not when my dear, *dear* sister is sporting such an ugly frown."

Chapter Fifteen

I was prepared to excuse myself as soon as we reached Moreston House, but the Earl of Bryce was before me. I saw Louisa wanted to continue to argue this until she saw his eyes. They were angry and cold, and his face was rigid with distaste. I wondered what she had been saying to him, as pleasant a man as he was, to get him in such a state? I wondered as well how she could be so blind to his feelings? Or to anyone's, I amended as I went upstairs, leaving the Langleys to repair to the library where, I was sure, they would enjoy the usual family discussion at the top of their lungs.

My room was stuffy this hot late June afternoon, and I opened the window that faced the small swath of lawn and a tall elm tree, hoping for a breeze. As I did so, I heard my late companions clearly. There must have been an open window in the library directly below me. I would not have listened, except I heard Louisa say my name, and I lingered, my hands still on the sash.

"You say Bryce won't have me, Cam, but I tell you, you'll have no joy of Connie, either! She'll never wed the likes of you."

"You are wrong. She will agree to it as soon as I propose," came the measured, cold reply, and my mouth opened in astonishment. How could the man be so calm and certain and sure of himself? At the very least, one had to admire his gall.

"And I say she won't! You've been damned arrogant, Cam, going your own way, ignoring her, treating her to that stupid indifference whenever you are home—I tell you, Connie's in a fair way of falling in love with Carlyle."

"Even if she were so foolish, it wouldn't do her a bit of good. He wouldn't marry a nobody from Yorkshire. He's only been using her for his own advantage, and when I point that out to her, she'll see how good it is of me to ignore the reputation she's acquired and marry me. You'll see. She'll come around."

I heard Louisa's harsh laughter. "Fool! It would have been better for you to have stopped gambling, instead of planning on Connie's fortune to save you. How many additional debts have you managed to acquire on the strength of that fortune?"

"Hold your tongue, Weeza! My debts are my own business, no one else's. As soon as Constance and I are married they'll all be gone."

"She claims she's not wealthy. Perhaps your information to the contrary is wrong? What will happen to us if it is?"

Moreston snorted and I let go of the sash. I had been holding it so tightly, my fingers were cramped. As I rubbed them, I heard him say, "I'm not wrong. Her uncle has invested the profits of that sheep farm wisely in some very canny ventures. And there's the fortune her father left her as well. Naturally her uncle didn't tell a mere female ward anything about it. She wouldn't have understood if he had. But I'll enjoy the profits from now on, although I plan to let the old man continue to run the place. I've no taste for farming and no liking for the north.

"No more of this. Let me tell you I had a word with Bryce yesterday."

"You did? What about? What did he say?"

"Be still! How can I tell you when you go on and on? We discussed the possibility of a wedding between you. I brought it up because I knew you'd set your heart on it. But Bryce confessed he didn't feel for you that way and he never would. I told him I understood. And I do. *I* certainly wouldn't want to marry you, you impossible vixen!"

I waited, holding my breath for the explosion that to my great surprise didn't come. The viscount must have been waiting, too, for it was some time before he said, "I must say I'm relieved you are taking this so well, sister. If only you had managed to exercise this kind of control with Bryce, you might have had a chance with him."

Ah, no, I wanted to cry. Don't hurt her any more than she already is. Show some kindness!

"I don't believe you," Louisa said in her low, husky voice, and I had to bend closer to hear her. "You're making that up to distress me. Paul does care for me. I know he does."

"As an unruly little sister, perhaps. No more."

"No, he loves me! I know he loves me. And if he doesn't now, he will. I'll make him!"

"You are an idiot. A blind, silly idiot. Leave me. I'm tired of your conceit, your hysteria. By the way, tell our sensitive sad excuse for a stepmama I'll not be here for dinner. I'm promised to Fells for the evening."

I winced as the library door slammed, and moved away from the window. My governess had always maintained that eavesdroppers never hear any good of themselves, but in this case I rather thought the Langleys had had the worst of the bargain.

What had been said was not a surprise to me, with the exception of Moreston's plans for me because he considered me a great heiress. Me? An heiress? I found that very difficult to believe. And there had been something about Louisa's voice when she questioned the source of his information that made me uneasy. She had sounded almost frightened. I didn't understand, but I put it aside.

As for marrying Moreston, never. I didn't even care for him as a brother, which, I am happy to say, I'm delighted he was not. Thank heavens I had diverted him in the park from what I knew now was to have been a proposal. The arrogance of the man! The conceited, overbearing arrogance!

When he did ask me, I rather thought I would just say "no." Not "it desolates me to have to refuse you, sir," or "of course I am sensible of the great honor you bestow, but," or even "words fail me before the nobility of your sentiments, my lord." No, all I intended to do was look him in the eye and say "no." And I would say it coldly and so firmly there could be no mistake, no thought I might be pretending to be coy. But I had better have my trunks packed and a carriage hired when I did it, I reminded myself.

Carlyle. His name flew into my mind, and with it, impressions of his height, his style, his face, and his mannerisms. I seemed to almost be able to hear his voice. He had said he would never hurt me, but he had. Oh, yes, he had.

Gloria Hefferton came to call on Louisa late the next morning. I hadn't seen my stepcousin for she had not come down to breakfast. Busy with my own plans, I had been grateful. I hoped to make my escape before she forced me to listen to all her woes concerning Bryce. I intended to call on Rosalind, ask for her help, and I did not want to be delayed by a sullen, frustrated Louisa.

Miss Hefferton was resplendent this morning in a striped bright green pelisse worn over a yellow walking gown. To complete her outfit she had chosen to wear an elaborate bonnet featuring a large scarlet and gold cockade. I tried not to wince as I smiled at her, for it had occurred to me that a few minutes alone with Miss Hefferton might be of value. Certainly it looked bad for Hugh Carlyle and I might be grasping at straws, but a sample of Gloria Hefferton's handwriting might be useful. After all, it had not been proved conclusively that Carlyle was the guilty letter writer.

Accordingly, after ordering refreshments, I escorted the guest to the drawing room. We talked of the Season until the tray was brought in, and it was only after Miss Hefferton had enjoyed a cup of tea and a muffin that I broached the subject I had intended all along.

"I seem to remember you telling Louisa about a new shop you had discovered that sold unusual ribbons," I said. "Do you chance to recall its name?"

Miss Hefferton put her head to one side and thought for a moment. "Why, yes," she said. "It's called Farrington and Quent's. It's just off Jermyn Street in the little lane near the hat shop. You know the one."

When I confessed I would never remember for I had a terrible head for directions and names, she went willingly to the escritoire to write it down for me. I forced myself to linger for a few minutes longer after I had the paper she gave me tucked safely away in my reticule, not that I expected her to wonder if there had been anything underhanded in my request. Gloria Hefferton had to be oblivious to her appalling taste. No doubt she thought others admired her style. But just before I left her to enjoy another cup of tea, she said, "I'm sure I don't know why you need to search out unusual ribbons, Miss Ames. You're a lovely girl and a wealthy one, or so I've heard tell. Unlike myself, who must find ways to make people notice me."

I must have looked startled for she continued, "Oh, yes, I'm well aware my only chance of success is to become known as an eccentric. I'll never marry. I'm not pretty, my family background is ordinary, and I've no dowry. Who would want me?"

Fortunately I was not required to reply, for Hibbert announced the hackney I had requested was at the door and I was able to escape. But as I was driven out the Kensington Road to Rosalind's home, I thought of Gloria Hefferton and had the grace to be sorry for her. What an unfortunate life she led, dependent on Louisa for her place on the fringes of society. I had to admire her spirit, too. She had not asked for pity. She had spoken in a matter-of-fact way. Still, I was sure she must have wept many times that fate had been so unkind to her.

I found Rosalind in her charming morning room.

"What is the matter? I know something's wrong, I just know it," she said, searching my face as the butler closed the door behind him. "Sit down here and take off your bonnet. There, now tell me at once. What are you waiting for?"

It would have been funny if I had felt the least bit like laughing, for how was I get in a word until my hostess stopped speaking? Instead, I plunged right into my explanation. As I spoke, Rosalind's eyes grew rounder and rounder and her mouth dropped open in astonishment as I told her all the things that had happened, right from the first letter that had arrived, to Louisa's subsequent ones, to what had happened at Carlyle's gala. Of course I only hinted at what the letters had contained and I didn't mention Carlyle's kiss. I couldn't bring myself to tell her about that.

"You say he had the paper in his rooms?" Rosalind asked, sounding amazed. "But Constance, dear, I find that hard to believe. *Carlyle* write nasty letters to you? *Carlyle,* who sets fashion? Besides, under that weary air of superiority he affects, I suspect he is a nice man."

"I thought he was, too," I admitted, relieved now my tale was told. "The night he came to my room with the orchestra and champagne and chaperone—I'll never forget it, or our waltz."

"Yes, no doubt, but we can't waste time reminiscing now," Rosalind reminded me. "I wonder if what you have told me is the reason he has locked himself up next door and refused to see anyone? I would find that very encouraging if I were you, Constance."

"But he doesn't know why I was in his room, nor that I found the cache of paper. I'll be going home soon to Yorkshire. I can't go without seeing him. And I must tell him I suspect he is the letter writer, no matter how reluctant I am to do so. It wouldn't be right to just let him get away with it, you know!"

"Of course not. *If* he is guilty, that is. Yes, I agree you must see him, tell him your suspicions. Perhaps there is some simple explanation for that paper being there. After all, you didn't find the blue wafers or the daisy seal."

Before I could say I really hadn't had time to look for them, she went on, "But how are you to see him?"

"I thought if you would write a note to him, perhaps, he would come over here," I suggested.

I was disappointed when she shook her head. "No, that won't work," she said. "I've written to him twice since the gala and he's refused to see either me or Reggie."

"Then I shall have to go to him," I said, tilting my chin in a show of bravery I was far from feeling.

"But I doubt you can gain admittance," Rosalind protested. "He's probably given orders. You'll be turned away at the gates like all the others who've called."

"But what if I don't go in the conventional way? I could hardly do so anyway, without a maid to lend me consequence. What if I climb over the wall, go through the gardens, and find an unlocked door or window somewhere? I'm familiar with the house now; surely I'll be able to escape detection until I can discover his whereabouts."

Rosalind stared at me in what I hoped was admiration, "The very thing!" she said, clapping her hands. "But you won't have to climb over the wall. As it turns out, we have a key to the gate, too.

"Oh, this is perfect! How brave you are! And I'm sure Hugh will be able to explain the paper away. Somehow," she added. I thought she looked worried and I was suddenly reminded of the serious reason I was here. It wasn't only to see him again, be with him—be able to look into his eyes and talk to him. No, I had another purpose and it took first place. I must not forget that.

"Would you like a bite to eat before you go? Some tea?" Rosalind asked.

"I'm afraid if I delay I'll lose my nerve," I told her. "Will you come with me as far as the gate? Just to keep me from changing my mind?"

She laughed and went off to fetch the key. Much too short a time later, we reached the gate in the wall that separated the two estates. I listened hard, but there wasn't a sound coming from Carlyle's grounds.

"If I don't come back, will you save me?" I asked, only half in jest.

"You may rely on me, my dear. I'll storm the walls if necessary. But do send word as soon as you can. I'll be on pins and needles till I hear from you."

I hugged her and let myself into Carlyle's garden, carefully closing the gate behind me. As I went along the wall, keeping an eye out for gardeners, even the gatekeeper's golden-haired little boy, I remembered the cobra and prayed it had not escaped its keeper. But I told myself such a valuable reptile would surely have been watched closely. At least I hoped so.

Sheltering behind some thick rhododendrons, I inspected the extensive landscape before me. Carlyle's garden, or lair as I was beginning to think of it, lay quiet and empty under the warm sun. You would never have guessed that only a short time past most of London's masked elite had partied here, dancing in a silken tent with a champagne fountain, strolling through trellises covered with roses and fairy lights, laughing and talking and posturing. Now not even a bird sang in the afternoon heat, and the only sound I could hear besides the pounding of my heart was the drone of some bees busy in the rosebeds. I wondered if I listened long and hard enough, if I would be able to catch the echo of an elephant trumpeting, or if I searched diligently enough I might find a piece of ribbon caught on a thorn, or see a discarded mask lying forgotten under a marble bench. I realized I was wasting time deliberately to avoid the confrontation to come, and I scolded myself.

Cautiously I made my way up to the terrace, still without seeing a soul. That was eerie somehow, almost as if a wicked witch had cast a spell over the place and everyone there had fallen asleep.

When I cupped my eyes to peer into the drawing room, I saw it was empty as well. The French door I tried opened easily and I slipped inside, feeling less exposed now I was within doors.

Still, I held my breath and listened hard. Some dust motes floated in a ray of sunshine nearby. Nothing else moved. And it was quiet. Completely quiet.

I was shaking now and I was very careful as I made my way to the doors that led to the rest of the house. Any bit of noise might lead to my discovery and I dreaded the thought of servants finding me before I could find Carlyle.

Heart in my throat, I opened one of the drawing room doors a crack and listened. Again I could hear nothing. But surely the butler, some of those massive footmen I had seen the other evening, would be on duty in the foyer. I remembered the locked gates then. No one would be coming to call. There was no need for servants to be standing about when there was nothing for them to do.

Before I lost my nerve, I pushed the door open and inspected the hall. As I had expected, it was empty. I didn't hesitate now, but made my way boldly to the stairs. I would go to Carlyle's rooms first.

It was then I heard measured footsteps some distance behind me, coming from the back of the house. The footsteps were getting closer and closer and I let myself into the nearest room and shut the door of it behind me. For a moment I stayed where I was, one ear pressed to the paneling before I turned to search for a place to hide.

Can you imagine the shock it was for me to see Hugh Carlyle regarding me seriously from where he was seated at his desk some little distance away? Can you imagine how my heart stopped for a moment, then began to race as I faced him? I know I gasped and put my hands to my throat as he rose to lean on the desk and study me. When the expected knock came on the door, he only said, "Not now."

We both listened as the footsteps went away. Then, as if some spell had been broken, Carlyle came around the desk and approached me. He was stern and unsmiling, his mouth set in a hard line and his eyes—oh, his eyes were like pieces of blue gray flint.

How can I possibly explain what I did next? Even today I

have trouble accepting the way I behaved. It was most unlike me and completely insane when you stop and consider
the reason I was there. But I did not hesitate or stop to think.
No, on impulse I went to him and put my hands on either
side of his lean face. Still he did not speak to me or I to him,
nor did his expression change. Standing on tiptoe I pulled
his head down and I kissed him.

Can you believe it? Can you believe I kissed him when I
suspected him of such a terrible crime?

He did not put his arms around me. He made no effort to
kiss me back. It didn't matter. I didn't care. When I stepped
back at last, I said in an uneven voice, "I've been looking for
you."

"Have you now?" he said quietly. "Why?"

He did not look or sound angry anymore, and relieved, I
said, "I have to talk to you. There are things I must explain.
Things I must ask. It is important."

"Why did you kiss me just now?" he asked, searching my
face.

I couldn't look away. "I had to do that, too," I whispered.

He indicated a chair near the empty fireplace and waited
until I was seated before he took the one opposite. Not once
did he look away from me. A part of me wanted to reassure
him I wasn't a figment of his imagination, that I wouldn't
disappear, but I didn't speak. It was not a time for irrelevant
remarks, not now when I was in deadly earnest.

"Do begin, Miss Ames. I believe you are in charge here,"
he said as he leaned back and crossed his arms over his
chest. "At least for now," he added.

Chapter Sixteen

I took a deep breath to steady myself, thought for a moment, and said, "For some time now I've been receiving some very horrid anonymous letters. There have been five of them over a period of weeks. The first came the morning of the day I met you at Lady Beech's. These letters pretend to know something about my mother and father, something detrimental, and the writer threatens to tell the *ton*. I know what is written is false. Still, it is frightening.

"My stepcousin, Lady Louisa, had has some as well. All of these letters were written on the same kind of paper, fastened with the same wax, and sealed with a crude daisy device."

I was watching his face, but I couldn't see any sign he knew what I was talking about. Indeed, if there was anything to read there, it was carefully hidden bewilderment.

"Of course I'm very sorry you have been in such distress, but why do you tell me this?" he asked.

"Believe me, Louisa and I have thought and thought, but we couldn't come up with the names of any people who might have done such a thing. Then Louisa suggested you might have done it as a source of amusement."

I stopped, half afraid of how he might react to that. But he did not exclaim. Instead, he motioned me to continue. I swallowed and said, "We decided the night of your gala to search your rooms to see if we could find anything that might tell us whether or not you were the guilty party."

"And did you?"

"Yes, I did," I said, and at that he sat up and stared at me even harder than he had been doing.

"May I ask what you found, Miss Ames?" he said, still in that quiet, toneless voice that was all the more frightening for being so bland.

"I found the same paper that my letters were written on," I said. Reaching into my reticule I pulled out the sheet I had taken from his dressing room and handed it to him. I also gave him one of the letters for comparison.

It was very quiet as he studied them.

"Yes, the paper is the same," he said. "And I have never seen any like it in my life."

He rose then, the papers crushed in his hand. "What exactly do you think you are about here, Miss Ames?" he asked, his voice harsh now. "Do you think to blackmail me? Or will you be content to ruin me with these accusations of yours?"

"I don't want to ruin you. That's why I'm here," I said in a rush. Inside I was crying, crying and begging him not to look at me that way, not to hate me as I could see he was in a fair way of doing. Still I made myself add, "You claim you did not write the letters, but how can I be sure? There is no one else."

"There are hundreds of other people who might have done it," he said. "There is even the *innocent* Miss Louisa. Yes, yes, she received letters, too, but she could have sent them to herself to quiet any suspicions you might be having."

"If you could have read what had been written to her, you would not say that," I told him. "It was terrible. Vicious. Much worse than my letters."

"May I read your letters?" he asked.

As I handed them to him, I despaired. I've lost him, I told myself. Whatever chance I might have had with him once, it is gone now.

Carlyle read the letters more than once. I thought he would never finish inspecting them. At last he put them down on the table beside him. "The handwriting is obviously disguised," he said.

I remembered the sample Gloria Hefferton had given me so innocently that morning—had it only been this morning? It seemed an age ago!—and I took that from my reticule and looked at it before I handed it to him. "I managed to get this from Louisa's friend today," I told him. "She is jealous of me. I thought she might have been the guilty one until Louisa began to receive them, too."

"She has a distinctive hand, completely unlike your letters," he said after studying it before he handed it back. Then he rose and went to his desk. I wondered what he was doing as he went through some sheets of paper. Setting one aside, he pulled another sheet toward him and wrote a few words on it.

"Here is a sample of my handwriting, Miss Ames," he said as he came back and handed both sheets to me. "This one was done earlier, the other just now. I even tried to copy the writing on your letters."

I stared at him, troubled, and his mouth twisted in a sneer. "Go on. Look at them," he ordered. "Surely that is the real reason you crept into my house today and made straight for the library. How unfortunate you found me occupying it before you could begin your search."

I opened my mouth to protest and closed it just as quickly. He was furious. That fury blazed from his eyes, radiated from the tension in his body, his taut face. I looked away.

His handwriting was unique, black and slashing. Anyone would have known immediately it was a man's. No woman would form her letters so forcefully and so plainly with such abrupt endings. Neither sample was at all like the writing on the letters I had received.

"Of course there is the possibility I have a talent for forgery," he said as he towered over me. "Never mind that now."

He reached down and lifted me to my feet. Taking my

hand he went to the door, pulling me, a most reluctant captive after him.

"We're going up to my rooms," he told me as we reached the hall. When I began to struggle to get away, he grimaced. "You need not fear, Miss Ames. I've seldom felt less amorous. And I hardly think the location matters. Your reputation, or what passes for it, is in tatters now."

I stopped fighting him. It was useless and I would only hurt myself. Upstairs, he marched me down the corridor to his bedchamber. It looked very handsome in the daylight, rich and masculine. The huge four-poster seemed to loom over us. I made myself ignore it.

"Now just where did you find this paper, ma'am?" Carlyle asked, his voice rich with sarcasm.

"Not here. In the dressing room," I said, hating myself for the way my voice wobbled.

"Show me," he demanded.

I walked before him to the adjoining room and opened the lowest drawer of the small chest. To my surprise the supply of paper was still there under the rags and brushes, and neater than I had left it. Carlyle had sounded so confident, I had been sure he must have moved it.

I picked up a sheet and handed it to him. "I don't think there can be any question it is the same. Do you agree, sir?" I asked.

He didn't answer. Instead he went and rang the bell. We stood there carefully not looking at each other for what seemed an age before an older man, very neat and precise, came in. If he was surprised to see me, he did not show it by so much as the blink of an eye. You would have thought any number of women wandered in and out of Carlyle's dressing room on a regular basis. Perhaps they did, I thought drearily.

"You rang, sir?" the servant asked.

"Can you explain why this paper is in the lower drawer there, Simkins?" Carlyle asked, handing him the sheet.

The valet hardly bothered to look at it. "I keep it there, sir," he said. "I use it to make notes of any supplies I might bc needing. More blacking, or shaving soap, for example. That special lotion you use. There should be a pencil there, too. Yes, here it is.

"If I may be permitted, sir? I discovered someone had been in that drawer the day after the gala. And that someone had gone through your other drawers as well. I am sorry I did not mention it before. You seemed to have so much on your mind, I hesitated to bother you with it. And nothing had been taken."

"I see. That will be all. See that we are not disturbed."

I didn't notice the valet leaving. I only had eyes for Hugh Carlyle and all I could think, over and over, was, What have I done? What have I done?

Back in the bedchamber I found myself pushed down in a chair. "Don't take it so hard," Carlyle said in that same, distant voice. "Anyone might have made the same assumption. Except I did rather expect more of you, Miss Ames. You see, I've been thinking of you as not just 'anyone.' "

"I'm so sorry," I managed to say. "It was just I felt I had to find out who this terrible person was. That I had to stop it, if I could, expose him or her so what happened to me and Louisa wouldn't happen to anyone else."

"Yes, *her*," he said as he leaned against a bedpost. "I suspect when we do find the culprit it will turn out to be a woman."

"We?" I asked, pouncing on the one word I was astounded to hear.

"Oh yes. It is the only way I will be able to clear my name," he said carelessly, pushing his shoulders away from the bedpost and going to a table that held a decanter and glasses. As he poured out two tots of brandy, he said, "Now, Miss Ames, how did you get here? Who knows your whereabouts?"

"Only Rosalind. I should let her know I'm all right. I promised . . ."

"Quite. I've something to say to her, too, and I think when

she reads my note, any explanation from you will be unnecessary."

He went to his desk, sat down, and took a sheet of hot pressed paper from the drawer. I cringed. How could I ever have thought Hugh Carlyle would even soil his hands on the cheap paper that had been sent to me? How could I have been so stupid?

I watched him as he bent over the paper. His hand flew across it. Even as distraught as I was, I did not envy Rosalind the reading of it, his face was so dark and severe. He rang for his valet and sanded and sealed the note. With a gray wafer and one of the seals I had found in his desk. I noticed.

Simkins came quickly. I suspected he had remained nearby in case he was needed. He nodded and bowed when handed the note and left the room. I stared down into the snifter of brandy I held. It was still untouched. I did not think I would be able to swallow it, my throat was so tight with tears. As I did so, I willed myself not to cry. I remembered only too well how disgusted he had been with my tears the night of the gala.

Hugh Carlyle turned to face me. The sun was behind him. I could not see his face clearly, but I could hear the revulsion in his voice as he said, "And you thought I was the guilty one. You thought I could do such a despicable thing. That is what hurts the most. To be sure, I am not the most saintly of men, but to find someone I had come to care about considered me capable of such villainy completely destroys me.

"Of course it probably serves me right," he added. "There are those who say I've been riding for a fall ever since I appeared on the London scene. Too high in the instep, I've heard myself described. Too sure of myself and my worth. But never have I heard anyone say Hugh Carlyle was vindictive and depraved . . ."

"Oh, please, do not say such things! You're not, you're not!" I cried, bursting into speech as I reached out to him. "I didn't want to believe it. I tried hard not to. But Louisa said . . ."

"Louisa should be whipped," came the quick retort. "I still consider her the most likely suspect. Did you know, Miss Ames, she tried for me last year? Ah, I see I've startled you. She did not tell you that? Well, it hardly reflected well on her.

"There was no chance I could have been mistaken. She is never subtle, now is she? I was forced to be quite severe with her to discourage her advances. I see she's turned to Bryce this Season, poor fellow.

"But you do see she couldn't help noticing the attention I was paying to you. Perhaps she decided to take her revenge. On you, since she could not punish me . . .

"For she would take it personally, you know. And how dare you succeed where she had failed? She must have been furious."

Trying to ignore the wonderful things he was saying and concentrate on Louisa, I said, "Supposing she is the one. Why couldn't she retaliate? All she had to do was address her spite to you. What would have stopped her?"

"The knowledge that I would either ignore the letters or search out the author of them for punishment. And that her name would surely lead any list of suspects I might make.

"Drink your brandy. It will make you feel better. Then please explain why you said 'I had to,' when I asked why you kissed me. I'm afraid I don't understand."

I looked at him in wonder. Surely he must still be angry even though he did not sound it now. I took a deep breath. I felt that since I had lost him, it hardly mattered what I said. And I had no pride where he was concerned. Besides, I wanted to tell him the truth, confess.

"I kissed you because I love you," I admitted. "I've known that for some time. It made my suspicions of you twice the torture. And even though I knew my love wouldn't ever come to anything, it didn't matter. Love isn't something you can banish or forget.

"I hated that kiss you took when you found me hiding here in your room. You did it because you were angry. So I wanted, just once, to kiss you with love. To do it tenderly so I could erase the memory of that other kiss and have one I could recall whenever my life gets dark from now on.

"You need not be concerned," I added when I saw his face change, saw the way he half-rose from his chair as if to escape me. "I've no intention of embarrassing you, or even pursuing you as Louisa did. I'm going home to Yorkshire. I doubt I'll ever return to London."

"I hardly think it will come to that," he said lightly as he took my untouched glass of brandy. Wondering, I watched him put it down on the table beside me before he lifted me to my feet and pulled me close in his arms.

"In my experience, kissing is better when both parties participate," he said. "Shall we see if I am right?"

Do you know, he was wrong? The kiss we shared was not just "better." It wasn't even "much better." Instead, it surpassed everything I had ever imagined a man's kiss could be, and when it ended, it left me hungry for more.

Chapter Seventeen

A long, glorious time later, Hugh put me firmly away from him. He looked grim as he stepped back, his hands clenched at his side.

"What is it?" I asked, confused. "Why do you look that way?"

His one-sided smile was fleeting and strained as he indicated the four-poster behind us. I blushed when he said, "If we do not leave this room immediately, my love, I will not answer for my behavior."

"But I was just thinking how I adored your behavior, sir," I surprised myself by saying. "Besides, who cares?"

"I am astonished to find out I do," he retorted. "Believe me, that is not generally the case. But for Miss Constance Ames, everything must be done properly.

"Come, you wouldn't want to ruin this grand gesture of mine, would you?" he added. "Not when I am determined to behave so well?"

As he stooped to pick up my hat from the floor where it had landed somehow, he went on, "I suggest you use the dressing room to repair the damage I have done to your appearance. I'll wait for you at the foot of the stairs. We have a great deal to discuss, you and I, but unless we leave this room, we'll never get to it. Run along now, do."

I could hardly protest further even though I ached to be back in his arms. For some reason, Hugh had decided not to make love to me. Yet only a short time before, the evening of his fete to be exact, he had threatened to do just that. Was there anything so baffling as a man?

I had to blush when I saw myself in the glass in his dressing room. My hair had come unpinned and was streaming down my back, and my afternoon gown was open almost to the waist. I looked a complete wanton.

When I went downstairs several minutes later, Hugh greeted me with a warm smile, and when he kissed my hand, his lips lingered there.

As we went through the drawing room to the terrace arm in arm, I felt breathless, my heart beating strangely. I was glad there were no servants about.

"You look bemused, love," Hugh said, seating me at a small table laden with refreshments.

"I was just wondering if perhaps I am suffering from some sort of jactitation, sir," I told him, hoping my hand wasn't shaking as I took the glass of lemonade he had poured for me.

He put his head back and laughed and I was able to admire his strong throat and broad shoulders. For some reason, Hugh reminded me of an elegant racehorse. One bred for strength and endurance and speed, of course, and for just plain handsome good looks as well. Not that I intended to tell him that. I wasn't sure he'd consider it a compliment.

I forgot my musings when he said, "You are a delight in so many ways. But come, drink your lemonade and tell me what you thought of my fete—before you went upstairs to root about in my rooms, that is."

"I did not root about!" I said, indignant. "Indeed, I was astounded to hear your man say I had disarranged things. I was very careful not to do so."

"Ah, but Simkins is precise to a fault. Have some cake."

"I really should be thinking of going home," I said, noting the sun was already in the western sky.

"There is no need to hurry. In my note to Lady Rosalind, I asked her to send a message to your aunt, explaining she had persuaded you to remain overnight and promising to return you in her own carriage first thing tomorrow morning."

"Now why would you do that, I wonder?" I asked. I am sure I looked speculative, for his color heightened.

It seemed a long time before he said, his voice constricted, "I admit my intentions at the time were not good. Besides being upset and angry, I wanted you. Badly. I meant to keep you here all night."

"Why didn't you?" I dared to ask. "You must have known I wouldn't have protested."

He reached across the table to capture my hand. Squeezing it gently, he said, "I didn't because I came to see you were not just any desirable, available woman. That you were much more important to me than that. When you confessed you loved me, why, I cannot begin to tell you how elated I felt! I knew then I loved you too, and because I did, I couldn't do anything that would dishonor you. Do you understand, Constance? Do you understand how important it was to me?"

I nodded, unable to speak, caught in a glow of elation myself. A moment later Hugh asked me about my life in Yorkshire, and I followed his lead. For a long time we talked about our separate childhoods, our dreams and aspirations. Eventually we walked about the gardens, Hugh's arm firm around me as we discussed the unsigned letters and what we intended to do about them. I must admit I had a hard time keeping my mind on the problem. It seemed so distant and unimportant compared to everything else that had happened to me this afternoon.

It was sunset before Hugh took me to the gate in the wall and kissed me once more before he held my face in his hands and stared down into my eyes. "Don't forget what you are to do," he said. "I'll come to you as soon as the business I must see to allows."

I smiled as he added seriously, "Be careful. Very careful."

"I shall. Don't worry so," I told him. "Nothing can hurt me now."

I waved good-bye from Rosalind's terrace. Only then did he turn away. As I let myself into the house, I wondered at my happiness. Yes, I missed Hugh already, but inside I felt strong, invincible even, because he loved me.

The minute I stepped into Moreston House the next morning, I knew something was wrong. It was very quiet, but that was not it. It was often quiet when Louisa was out. No, there was something else, something I could not put a finger on but was still conscious of, something that raised the hair on my arms and set an insistent clamor to beware going in my head.

"Where is my aunt, Hibbert?" I asked as I began to work my gloves from my hands.

"She has not left her rooms this morning, miss. Miss Mason is with her."

"Viscount Moreston? Is he at home?"

"M'lord left for his club not half an hour ago, miss."

"And Miss Langley?" I persisted.

"In her room, miss."

I shrugged. Whatever was wrong, I would not discover it from the butler, that was sure. Perhaps Louisa would tell me more.

As I put my hand on the bannister, Hibbert said from behind me, "Miss Hefferton is in the drawing room, miss. She has been there for some time."

I hesitated but I did not turn. Stranger and stranger, I thought as I climbed the stairs. Why would Louisa leave Gloria to twiddle her thumbs while she remained secluded? I knew of no recent estrangement. They were friends again.

When there was no answer to my knock on Louisa's door, I opened it a crack and peeked inside. Still dressed in her nightrail, Louisa was seated by the window staring blankly at the curtained panes. I had rarely if ever seen her so still.

"Coz?" I asked as I let myself in. "What is going on? Is everything all right? Something has happened, I'm sure of it."

She turned then and I was startled by the look on her pretty face. She had been crying, but she was also deeply angry. I admit I wished I had gone immediately to my own room even as I braced myself for the unpleasantness I was sure was coming.

"So, you have come home at last, have you?" Louisa asked as she rose from her chair and grasped the back of it. "How very good of you to finally remember us."

"What are you saying? I've only been gone overnight," I said, trying for a rallying tone. "Rosalind sends her love," I added. "She asked me to tell you . . ."

Louisa took a quick step toward me, her fists raised. "I don't care to hear what *Rosalind* said, or what *Rosalind* does, or what *Rosalind* feels," she said. "Isn't it bad enough that you deserted me for *her*? Must I also have to hear all about it in my own room?"

Her voice had risen and she was panting. I could see she was in a fair way of working herself into a fit of hysterics. But where before I would have cringed and tried as best I could to placate her, now I only said coldly, "I'll leave you. I've no intention of remaining here and listening to you scold me for visiting a friend . . ."

"Oh, yes, a *friend*. Your dear, *dear* friend! It's plain to see she's more to you than I am . . ."

"Why, you're jealous!" I exclaimed. "How very silly you are, Louisa. Of course she is my friend. Yours, as well. No, don't say another word. I'll talk to you when you are more yourself."

As I shut her door behind me, I wondered at my last remark. It seemed to me that what I had just seen had been the real Louisa, that the patina of courtesy and cousinly affection she had shown me almost all the time I had been here had been nothing but a facade put on to disguise the real Louisa Langley.

I did not go immediately to see my aunt. I felt I had had enough of family, for the moment at least. Instead, I asked my maid to bring me a cup of tea. Alone, I removed my fashionable hat. Rosalind's own maid had done my hair, and I was as neat as a nun. On the outside, that is. Inside I was a tangle of emotions I did not even try to fathom. Still, I hugged the warm glow I felt whenever I thought of Hugh Carlyle, and wondered what he was doing. He had been very mysterious about this "business" he had to take care of before we could meet again. I wondered what it was all about and how soon it would be over.

My aunt did not look at all glad to see me when I finally went to her rooms. She was still in bed, as white as the pillows heaped up behind her.

"Are you ill, Aunt Lavinia? I do hope not," I said as I bent to kiss her faded cheek.

"I have had to have the doctor," she said in a faint voice. I eyed the damp handkerchief clutched in her thin hand with misgiving. "I had an awful spell, didn't I, Henny?" she went on, turning toward her companion.

Miss Mason looked up from the fringe she was knotting. "You were certainly not feeling well, Lavinia. I told you not to get yourself into a state, but you did not listen.

"Louisa treated us to one of her most memorable scenes last evening," she told me. "There was no one to stop her; the viscount had gone out. At the height of her performance, she even threw a platter of veal in a hunter sauce to the floor. I had to slap her to get her to control herself."

I thought Miss Mason looked grimly pleased as she recalled that slap, and I did not blame her.

"It was just dreadful, dreadful!" my aunt moaned. "And it was all your fault, niece."

"Because I stayed at Rosalind's," I observed. "Louisa's already rung a peal over me, unreasonable girl. And poor Miss Hefferton sits all forlorn in the drawing room because Louisa will not see her. Was anything more absurd?

"Well, I'll not take the blame, although I'm sorry you were distressed, ma'am," I continued, ignoring my aunt's gasp, Miss Mason's stern glance. "Louisa is not a normal person. I can't do anything to change that.

"I think it would be better if I left Moreston House. I have trespassed on your hospitality for far too long, dear ma'am. Perhaps when I am gone, Louisa will forget me and things will return to normal. I hope so, for your sakes."

"Leave here? Go home to Yorkshire?" Lady Lavinia said faintly. "Oh, no, you can't do that! Lord Moreston has said—that is, I mean . . ."

"Nothing definite has been decided, Lavinia," Miss Mason said, folding her work and stuffing it in the capricious workbag she was seldom without.

"Have you forgotten the Throckmorton ball this evening, Constance?" she asked pleasantly. "What gown are you going to wear?"

I had no desire to attend any balls unless Hugh Carlyle would be there with me, but I could hardly say so. Instead, I excused myself to speak to my maid. I doubted my aunt would feel strong enough to accompany us; perhaps we might still cancel the invitation?

I spent most of the day alone, writing to my uncle and making lists of things I still wished to purchase before I returned to Yorkshire. I hoped there would be no trouble about my leaving. My aunt had mentioned Cameron Langley. Did she know of his plans to marry me? Why? How? But it had been the way Henrietta Mason had spoken, almost as if she were sure the viscount would stop me, that gave me pause. Not that there was a chance he could, I told myself stoutly. Even if Hugh had not been coming for me, I would have been happy to leave this place and these people.

I remembered then that although he had said he loved me over and over, Hugh had not mentioned marriage, not even once, and I had not liked to do so either. I was sure that was what he intended, but still I couldn't keep a small quiver of doubt from invading my thoughts every so often.

I told myself I wouldn't worry about it. Instead, I spent a great deal of time dreaming of the day just past, the wonder of it—the joy.

To my surprise, my aunt came to the dinner table dressed

for the Throckmorton ball in one of the lavender silk gowns she favored. Louisa was there as well. She wore white this evening, but her stormy expression wasn't at all demure. To my relief, she had little to say for herself and she ignored me completely. I didn't care. I conversed with my aunt, Miss Mason, and the viscount. Cameron Langley had come home late in the afternoon. Now he announced he would escort us to the ball. He looked determined as he did so, and during dinner I was often aware of his brooding gaze. I found it disconcerting.

Society had been leaving town in ever greater numbers now the Regent's departure for Brighton had been announced. Still, there was a crowd at the Throckmorton's town house in Cavendish Square. Viscount Moreston hovered at my elbow and I was glad when other gentlemen came and filled my dance card.

The Earl of Bryce was at the ball. I wished he had not come. It could only upset Louisa further to see him there, and not dancing attendance on her as she had hoped. I saw her staring at him, but to my relief she made no move to accost him or linger in his vicinity.

It was a long evening and a boring one. I seemed to have had the same conversations a dozen times before, laughed at the same witticisms, complained of the same few subjects—the weather, how tiresome this particular Season had become, the lack of anything interesting and new left in the world to do. I began counting the minutes until we should be able to leave, but once we reached home, I found myself regretting the safety the ball had provided.

Louisa went immediately upstairs without saying good night to anyone. Lady Lavinia scurried up as well. When I would have assisted her, Moreston took a firm grip on my arm and said, "A moment of your time, Constance. It seems we never have a chance to talk, you and I."

I held my tongue as he led me to the library. I was resigned now to the confrontation I suspected was coming, and it would do no good to point out our lack of communication was entirely his fault. That would be to start on an argumentative note that could hardly bode well for a friendly conclusion.

"Some brandy?" he asked, already pouring us both a tot. I took the glass from him, careful not to touch his hand.

"I am sure you have a very good idea why I wished to see you alone, haven't you, you clever little puss?" he asked. His attempt at a playful manner was ludicrous. I'm sure my expression betrayed me, for he coughed and added, "Lady Moreston tells me you are thinking of going home. We—I especially—would be very sorry if that were so. I must tell you I have come to not only approve your excellent qualities and sportive sense of fun, but your handsome good looks as well; indeed, I may say I have seldom admired a woman more."

And do you admire my handsome bank account as well? I thought cynically when he paused, to my great relief, to take a breath.

He came closer then and pulled me to my feet and into his arms before I could protest. Sorry that I had put the brandy down, I began to fight him as hard as I could. The very thought of him kissing me after Hugh had done so was repugnant. I didn't think he looked too keen on it either. His pale face was white and there was a sheen of perspiration on his brow.

"No, stop this, Cameron," I exclaimed, trying to loosen one of his hands while I moved my head rapidly this way and that to avoid his kiss.

"I can't," he panted. His kiss fell on my ear and I kicked him. Unfortunately, I was wearing satin sandals and no damage was done, but I did manage to push him away. Quickly I darted behind the chair I had recently vacated. "If you don't stop this, I'll scream," I threatened.

He stared for a moment before he chuckled and said, "Can it be you do not fully comprehend my intent, dear Connie? You are so innocent!"

You've got that all wrong, I told him silently.

"I want to marry you, puss," he went on. As he moved one way, I feinted by moving the other. I'm sure we must have looked as if we were engaged in some strange dance. "I've decided to make you my viscountess. Now what do you think of that?"

You don't want to know, was my silent reply as I moved smartly right.

"You'll like being a viscountess," he assured me. "And running Moreston House. Admit it, now."

"No, I won't. I don't want to marry you . . ."

"Of course you do," he interrupted. "Try not to be so silly.

"I did not bother to ask your uncle for your hand, you know. Can't quite see what he has to say to the matter anyway. He's only your mother's older brother, isn't he? No, we'll be married in London as soon as the banns have been called. *Stand still!*"

Stunned by his loud order, I stopped moving and he pounced. Dragging me around the chair he pushed me down into it and handed me the brandy again. At least he seemed to have discarded his amorous approach, for which I was extremely grateful.

"Now then, that's all settled," he said as he took his own seat, wiped his brow, and raised his glass. "Shall we drink to our future together, my dear?"

He took a healthy gulp and I waited until he swallowed before I said, "It is not all settled, sir. I will not marry you. And I am leaving Moreston House in a short while."

His face took on an ugly cast. Reminded of Louisa's angry fits, I added hastily, "There is no sense in discussing it. My mind is made up. Besides, I must tell you, there is someone else . . ."

He waved a careless hand, looking a little easier. "I assume you mean Carlyle. I do assure you there is no sense of your hoping in that direction. Rogue Carlyle will not have the likes of you. When he marries—if he ever does—it will be to one of the nobility. Little Constance Ames from Yorkshire, of all places, won't be given a moment's consideration. No, indeed. I am sorry you have been misled by his attentions. It is often his way, you know, to single out one young lady a Season, flirt with her madly, pay her all kinds of attention, and then drop her without a moment's regret. He is not a nice man, not at all."

I was angry now, but I resolved to keep a civil tongue in my head if it killed me. I rose and curtsied. "You will excuse me now, my lord. I am tired."

As he was forced to rise, I added, "Of course I thank you for your proposal, but I do decline to accept. And I think it would be best if we left my reasons for doing so unspoken."

I had almost reached the door, trying not to scurry there, when he spoke up from behind me. "I simply do not understand your arrogance, cousin. To turn me down without so much as a by-your-leave—well! I see your manners are nowhere near good enough to grace the Moreston title. Surely I have had a fortunate escape."

I counted to ten before I turned to face him, made brave by the doorknob I held tight in my hand and the distance between us. I looked straight at him and, remembering the conversation he had had about marrying me with his sister in this very room, I said steadily, "Not nearly as fortunate as the escape I have had, sir."

Chapter Eighteen

I went to bed wrapped in the armor of righteous indignation. I knew the way I had spoken to Cameron Langley had been rude, but I didn't care. How dare he say Hugh was only toying with me? How dare he imply Hugh was the kind of man who would steal a woman's virtue and then discard her? I knew better, but oh, how I wished Hugh would come back! It was going to be so hard, living these days alone.

We had discussed ways I might find out the mysterious writer's name, and I was reminded of that the following morning when another familiar note arrived while I was enjoying my breakfast in solitary state. I did not open it immediately. Instead, I calmly finished my strawberries and clotted cream, shirred eggs and ham, and a scone covered with marmalade. I even poured myself another cup of coffee before I slit the ugly seal.

This note puzzled me. Although it had been written by the same hand, it was unlike the others I had received. It rambled so, going on and on about my pride and my pertness, and my bad manners, which the writer claimed were the result of a suspect upbringing and peasant ancestry. For the first time as well, the writer ridiculed my looks. I did not mind "Your horrid red hair, so common; those cat-colored eyes," but I did take exception to the comment that my breasts made me look like a new mother. I was sensitive about the size of my breasts.

I had almost forgotten being pushed the night we had left the theater. I now believed it had been unintentional, what with the crowd and the way everyone had been pressing forward to try and find their carriage. When I had mentioned this to Hugh he had looked severe but he had told me not to worry about it since he himself intended to find the culprit. His face and voice when he said this had made me shiver.

He had suggested then I try and obtain a sample of all the Moreston House women's handwriting. He had stressed I was not to put myself at any risk. Now I decided that in spite of my reasoning, I would add Cameron Langley to my list of suspects and I would begin my search at once.

I knew the viscount had left the house early for his place at the breakfast table had been cleared away. The maids would have finished sweeping and dusting the library long ago. There would be no one to wonder at me.

Alas, I forgot the butler. I met him at the door to the library and he went so far as to inquire what I might require in his lordship's private room. I glared at him, my head high. "I really do not see it is any of your concern, Hibbert," I said in my frostiest voice. "Since you are curious, however, I shall tell you I am looking for a particular book to read. You are excused."

Hibbert could do nothing but bow and open the door for me. It was several moments however before my heart resumed its normal tempo.

The first thing I did in the library, once the door was safely closed behind me, was to select a book. Having obtained my alibi, I went to Moreston's desk. There were some papers on it covered with his handwriting but I did not dare take one. It might be missed too readily. Instead I began to go through the drawers. One of them was crammed with bills—unpaid bills, I noticed. There seemed to be hundreds of them. No wonder Moreston had been so intent on marrying a woman he considered an heiress. In another drawer I found the draft of a letter to Mr. Lockwood, begging for more time to repay a debt of honor. There were several attempts and I folded one of them small and put it in the pocket of my morning gown. I felt soiled somehow, searching the viscount's desk, but still I went through all the drawers that weren't locked, looking for blue wafers and a daisy seal. I did not find them, but then I had not expected to.

Safely upstairs in my room I wondered how I was to get the other samples. My aunt was almost always in her rooms. I would have to wait for her to go out of the house. As for Miss Mason, I might be able to search her room while she was with my aunt, but it would be risky. Better to wait until she too was absent from the house. And then I must avoid being caught by the maids. I could see this was a more dangerous endeavor than I had imagined, held close in Hugh's arms. Then it had seemed a simple matter, easily accomplished.

I forced myself to forget that time and think of Louisa. Hugh had considered her the most likely candidate, but since we were at odds now I could think of no good reason to visit her room. And there was her maid, Emma Pratt, who hated me so much. If the maid could write—if she had sent the letters—I would never know, for just thinking of braving the women servants' quarters in the attics made my blood run cold.

I was startled when Louisa came to see me only minutes later. She did not apologize for her behavior, and her voice was cold when she said she had received another letter and needed my advice. After she had handed it to me, she went to the window. I read it while her back was turned and I was horrified. The note demanded the princely sum of five hundred guineas, and if the money was not forthcoming, the writer threatened to tell the *ton* Louisa's mother had killed herself during one of her mad spells. It ended by saying directions to pay the money would arrive soon.

"You must tell your brother of this, Louisa," I said to her stiff back. "You must see this threat involves him as well as yourself."

"You will not let me have the money?" she asked over her shoulder. "After all we have done to launch you in the *ton* this Season, you will not help me?"

"How can I?" I replied swiftly. "I do not have that amount, indeed, not even a tenth of it, at my disposal. And I am sure my uncle does not either. We are only farmers, Louisa, *farmers,* in spite of what you think."

"I see," she said, still in that toneless voice. "May I have the letter back? Thank you."

She started for the door and I held out my hand to her. "Please, Louisa, can't we be friends again? I am sorry you were upset by my staying at Beech House, indeed I am. And I will be going home soon. I do not like to leave like this."

She stared at me for a moment before she let herself out and closed the door sharply behind her. I sank down on my bed. She had not spoken again, but then there had been no need for her to do so. The look she had given me had said it all. I would not be forgiven for anything. She was prepared to hate me from this moment on.

Later that same day, after I had returned from doing some errands on Bond Street with my maid, I met my aunt in the hall. She was accompanied by her companion, and both ladies were dressed for afternoon calling. I declined to accompany them, intent on using this opportunity to search both their rooms.

The upstairs maid had long since finished her day's work and I knew my aunt's abigail was probably having a cup of tea in the kitchen. Still, I waited for some time and even carried a book with me when I went so I could say I was returning it to my aunt if anyone inquired.

The house was very quiet in the midafternoon heat. I met no one in the upper hall and no one in my aunt's rooms. Her desk was set against a wall and I went to it at once. Again I found a half-finished letter on top, but I dared not take that. I saw Lavinia Langley's handwriting was spidery, with a great many elaborate curliques. It was not at all like the writing on the letters I had received. Still, when I found an earlier attempt in the basket beside the desk, I took it with me. It had been discarded because my aunt's pen had spattered and left a large blot. I did not bother looking through the desk drawers.

Feeling more confident, I went along to Miss Mason's room. I felt almost invisible now, and I investigated her desk thoroughly. There was no cheap paper, no blue wafers, and no daisy seal. Neither was there any sample of her writing. Miss Mason was a neat woman. Too neat.

Disappointed, I went back to my own room. I did not think Henrietta Mason had written the letters. There was no reason for her to do so unless she took some sort of perverse satisfaction in causing others pain, and I did not think she was that kind of woman. Still, I reminded myself, *someone* had written them.

I did not dare invade Louisa's room even though I knew she had gone out with Gloria Hefferton. I was afraid Emma Pratt might find me there. It was entirely too dangerous.

Four more days passed uneventfully. I attended an afternoon party of silver loo with my aunt, purchased the handsome pipe I had decided to give my uncle, and some excellent tobacco, and tried not to wonder where Hugh Carlyle was more than once every half hour.

Rosalind came to call, fortunately at a time when Louisa was absent from the house. I told her what had happened with my stepcousin and she exclaimed, but she was more intent on her own news. Lord Beech had found a property he liked in Kent and had been persuaded to purchase it. I was glad Rosalind would not be leaving England and happy for her when she confided she thought she was with child. Lord Beech joined us then and from the way he hovered over the mother of his heir, I did not envy my friend the next several months.

Seeing them together made me sad and I lingered in the drawing room after they took their leave, standing at the window and staring at the traffic on Park Lane. Where was Hugh, I wondered. Why hadn't he come back to me? The hateful words the viscount had said echoed in my mind and

I tried to push them aside. It was getting harder to do so. Could Hugh have said he loved me, yet left me as Moreston had implied he was wont to do? Was I deceiving myself thinking the love I felt for him was returned?

I had seen little of Cameron Langley. He was out most days and he was seldom home for dinner. I was glad of that. I knew he was wondering when I would leave. It had been almost a week since I had refused his hand. My remaining here was beginning to look odd.

A footman brought me a note that had just arrived, and I took it listlessly until I saw the handwriting. Then I barely waited for the footman to leave before I ripped it open.

"My business now concluded, Miss Ames," it said, "I shall do myself the honor of calling for you tomorrow at ten in the morning. Wear a pretty gown and your best bonnet. Till then—Carlyle."

It was formal and it was short, but he had written. And he was coming for me! The hours to be spent between now and ten tomorrow seemed endless. I resolved to be patient, well aware there was nothing else I could be.

You may be sure I was ready long before the hour appointed. Indeed, I had been awake at dawn. What my maid thought of my request for a morning bath, I neither knew nor cared. I had her wash my hair as well, and I brushed it dry myself to help pass the time. I chose to wear a gown of fine willow-green cambric in the empire style with bishop sleeves. With it, I wore an Angoulême bonnet that tied on the side with matching ribbons. I did not take the writing samples I had obtained with me. They were too bulky for my reticule. I would have to arrange to get them to him some other way.

I almost laughed at the formality of our meeting in the foyer under Hibbert's eye. Hugh bowed, his face carefully indifferent. I curtsied, and willed myself not to blush. It wasn't until we were going down the steps that he leaned close to whisper he loved me.

The tiger watching the team was left on the paving and we were alone at last.

"Where are we going?" I asked as he turned the rig smartly around a corner, heading away from Hyde Park.

"To church, of course," he replied, a smile teasing the corner of his mouth. "We are to be married this morning."

I am sure my mouth dropped open. "Are we indeed?" I asked.

He spared me a sideway glance and my heart began to pound. "I am so glad I made that grand gesture the other day. Now when I take you to bed, you will be Mrs. Hugh Carlyle. I assume you have no objection to such a program, ma'am?"

"Of course I don't," I told him. "I wonder if saying I am ecstatic will enlarge your already burgeoning conceit? Oh Hugh, I have missed you so!"

"And I, you. But our separation was necessary for I had to find the Archbishop of Canterbury without delay."

"Why?" I asked, confused. Hugh Carlyle had not struck me as a particularly religious man.

"When one does not care to wait three weeks for banns to be called, a Special License is necessary, my love. And only that archbishop or one of his appointed minions can part the waters, as it were."

He patted his breast pocket. "Now we're all right, my soon-to-be Mrs. Carlyle. I've arranged for a private ceremony at St. George's in Hanover Square. It's an attractive church. The naval hero Nelson married his Emma there, which is the kind of nonsensical bit of romance women seem to find irresistible."

I wisely ignored this provocation. I was determined there would be no arguments to mar my wedding day.

One of Carlyle's grooms was waiting for us in Hanover Square, to walk the team while we were in church. The man did think of everything. We went inside arm in arm and found the cleric who was to marry us waiting. Witnesses were provided, an elderly verger for Hugh, a shabby young seamstress for me. I suspected Miss Mary Hatfield had been in church praying for a new position and I was glad when Hugh rewarded her so liberally for helping us.

It is strange, looking back, how little of the ceremony I remember. I can't even recall what Hugh wore that day, only that he was fashionable and impossibly handsome. The single thing that remains clear in my mind was the moment Hugh slipped my mother's thin gold wedding band on my hand. He had borrowed it for the occasion and I wondered about that. It seemed so out of character for him not to provide a ring when he had seen to everything else so efficiently. But he explained as soon as we drove away from the church with only Miss Hatfield to wave and wish us well.

"You may be sure I have a ring for you, darling," he said, even though I had not asked. "But when I put it on your finger, it will stay there. And you cannot wear it until we have discovered the identity of your mysterious letter writer."

I admit I was disappointed. "You mean we are not going to announce our marriage today?" I said. I had been looking forward to telling the Langleys, ordering my trunks to be packed, removing to my new husband's house.

"If we do and you leave Moreston House, we may never find out who has been bedeviling you. Or discover the identity of the creature who tried to push you under those carriage wheels."

He sounded grim and I knew this was important to him, more than it was to me. To be truthful, I didn't care about the writer anymore. Whoever it was could not hurt me now or ever again. But of course I would agree to whatever Hugh wanted to do.

We entered Hyde Park through the Stanhope Gates and Hugh slowed the team to a sedate walk. As we went along, he asked what had been happening in his absence. I told him of the writing samples I had obtained and mentioned the latest letter I had received, Louisa's as well. He seemed especially interested in that and asked a number of questions. I also mentioned Viscount Moreston's proposal and was surprised when he grinned.

"He was after your fortune, of course," he said with a chuckle.

"How can you be sure?" I asked, a little affronted. "You wanted to marry me. Why shouldn't he?"

"Because, my pet, Cameron Langley has no interest in women. There now, don't frown. Not today.

"He is very discreet. I've heard nothing of any scandal which would be fatal in any case."

I thought hard. Yes, it was true the viscount had rarely sought a partner at any ball or soiree, and he had seemed almost reluctant to kiss me the night he proposed.

"I do wish everyone wouldn't assume I have a fortune," I said crossly. Learning I was only entrancing because of my dowry hardly raised my spirits, I can tell you.

"But you do have a fortune. However, you may be sure I don't care about it for I've a tidy one of my own. You may use yours to dower our girls, ma'am."

That statement made me forget everything we had been discussing and we had been twice around the park before I recalled the mystery.

"What exactly are we to do and when, my dear?" I asked. "It is so uncomfortable for me at Moreston House now. I'm sure everyone is wondering why I don't go home. I said I was going a week ago."

"You will. Shortly. I am flesh and blood, you know. I expect we will be able to convene everyone at Moreston House tomorrow. There are one or two little details I wish to look into first. If only you had managed to get a sample of Louisa's writing . . ."

"You are so sure it is someone who lives there?" I asked. Oddly I did not want it to be one of the Langleys now, nor Miss Mason either. Secretly I had hoped it might be Gloria Hefferton, and I did not understand why in the slightest. I had not had a comfortable time of it on Park Lane; Louisa especially had made my life miserable on more than one occasion. But to think someone that evil had been living in the same house with me, eating their meals beside me, sleeping in a room close to mine, was not a pleasant thought.

"It has to be one of them," Hugh said curtly. "And I want you out of there as soon as possible, and I am not speaking just as an eager bridegroom now. So, here is what you will do. I'll set you down shortly and you will say nothing of this morning's activity. Put the ring back on your other hand before anyone notices. There's a reception at Lord Marshall's this evening. I'll contrive to meet you there.

"Now, why are you looking so pensive, love?"

"Because I'm so sorry we must be apart tonight," I said honestly.

"As I am," he replied, turning slightly to stare down at me. The light in his eyes made me catch my breath. It was so powerful I felt as if he had put his hand on me. "We will not be parted again," he promised. "Trust me to see to that."

"I do trust you, Hugh. In everything," I said, my voice only a little shaky. "After all, I married you, didn't I?"

We left the park a short time later. I wondered Hugh had not kissed me except for the light pressure of his lips in church. When I asked him about it shyly, he grimaced.

"If I kiss you, I won't be able to stop. I think you have bewitched me, Constance. I don't trust myself around you. In fact, I feel as uncertain of myself as any boy. Whoever would have thought a little Titian-haired beauty from the north would have been able to turn me into a quivering blanc-mange? I'm not at all sure I like it."

"Ah, but I do," I told him, caressing his arm. When I felt the muscles there tighten, I smiled.

Chapter Nineteen

We arrived at Moreston House just as Cameron Langley was getting out of a hackney. He was about to run up the steps, but he paused and stared as Hugh stopped the phaeton expertly in front of the house and the tiger who had been lounging against the palings ran to the horses' heads.

I thought the viscount looked distraught somehow and I knew something was wrong when he said, without even greeting Hugh, "Thank heavens you are home, Constance. Come inside at once!"

I would have obeyed him instantly except Hugh's hand on my arm kept me next to him.

"There is something amiss, Moreston?" he asked, his drawl noticeably different from my stepcousin's hurried speech.

"No, there is nothing—that is, thank you, but—Connie, get down! I need you!"

"But I insist, sir," Hugh said as he came around the carriage to lift me down. Such was my concern I did not even notice his hands at my waist.

"Shall we go inside?" he asked. "I'm sure whatever has happened is better not bandied about in the street."

Defeated, Moreston led the way. As we entered the house, Hugh said, "It is Lady Louisa, of course. What has she been up to now?"

The viscount did not answer. Instead, he went to the drawing room and we followed closely in his wake. I was surprised to see my aunt was there, half lying on one of the sofas while Henrietta Mason waved a fan before her face and kept her vinaigrette ready to hand. Lady Lavinia moaned when she saw me and closed her eyes tightly when she spotted Hugh Carlyle behind me.

"Now, my lady, if you would be so good as to explain that rather garbled note you sent to my club, summoning me home?" Moreston began. I saw his face was white with strain and although I was repulsed by what I had learned of him, I did feel sorry for him then.

"It is Louisa, Cameron," came the weak reply. "She is gone!"

"Gone where?" he demanded.

"I have no idea. Her bed was not even slept in, which is how we discovered she had disappeared."

"But she went up to bed last night. I remember seeing her do so. Never mind. Our conjectures are useless and they waste time. Where is Pratt? She'll know what this is all about."

"Pratt is Lady Louisa's abigail?" Hugh asked softly in my ear. We were still standing behind the viscount, but now Hugh led me to a chair and took up his position behind it. His hand pressed my shoulder for a moment; it comforted me.

The elderly maid was sent for and Lady Lavinia began a dreary monologue. She had always dreaded the day Louisa would do something truly outrageous and shame the family—why had God punished her by giving her such a disastrous stepdaughter?—she was sure she would never be able to show her face in society again, her life was over and she wished she were dead . . .

No one cared to interrupt this dirge, but I noticed that not once did my aunt express any concern for Louisa's safety. No, all her attention was centered exclusively on herself. I had not realized just how selfish a woman Lavinia Langley was, and I was sorry Hugh had to find out so vividly what kind of family he had married into.

I thought of something then and I rose and said, "You

must excuse me for a moment, Aunt, my lord. I will return
as quickly as I can."

I did not wait for them to reply, and I ignored Hugh's
questioning look. As I ran up the stairs I congratulated myself for remembering what a perfect time this was to search
Louisa's room. Not only was she gone, her maid was on her
way to the drawing room.

Louisa's room seemed very empty. The bed was neatly
made, there were no clothes flung about, no gloves dangling
over a chairback or bonnets perched on the tops of her four-
poster. I shivered a little as I went to her desk. She had left
some lists there, and I grabbed one and left as quickly as I
had come. I did not go downstairs immediately, however. Instead, I went to my own room, opened my jewelry case, and
removed all the samples I had collected. Stuffing everything
into my reticule, I ran back down to the drawing room. I did
not want to miss a word of Emma Pratt's account, if I could
help it.

I had been very quick. The maid had not even made an appearance when I took my seat again after giving Hugh a
smile and patting my reticule. He nodded.

Emma Pratt barely curtsied after she had shuffled into the
room. She was twisting her hands in her apron, and I saw the
worry on her lined, old face. Moreston questioned her ex-
tensively, but she had no knowledge of Louisa's whereabouts.

"She said I wasn't to wait up for her last night, that she'd
put herself to bed," the maid confessed. "She knew I had a
tooth that was bothering me."

She darted a malevolent look in my direction and added,
"My girl's not been happy these past months, no, that she
hasn't. And now my girl's run off. To get away from the
likes of *her,* no doubt. Why was *she* allowed to upset my
dear mistress? Why doesn't she go away?"

"That will be quite enough," Moreston interrupted.

I sat frozen with horror. I knew the woman didn't like me,
but to be accused like that, to be told I was the reason for

Louisa's moods was not at all fair. I reminded myself both my aunt and Miss Mason had claimed my coming had been a godsend, that Louisa had been much calmer and easier to live with since my arrival. Emma Pratt was clearly riddled with jealousy. Once again I wondered if she could write. She had not spoken as a common, uneducated servant.

No one spoke until Pratt had left the room.

"I do apologize, Constance," Moreston said then, two red spots high on his cheekbones. "Pratt has been with us forever and I suppose we have allowed her too much freedom. She was my mother's maid, and after her death, she took over Louisa's care. Obviously, she should be pensioned off."

"Most unfortunate," Lady Lavinia breathed. "So unpleasant."

"Shall we return to the problem at hand?" Hugh asked briskly. "And may I point out that wherever Miss Langley went, she planned the move. She was not kidnapped or spirited away. I am sure we will find her safe and sound."

Moreston nodded glumly. "She does have the most uncanny ability to land on her feet like a cat," he admitted.

"Bryce," Hugh said.

That one word brought everyone to attention. The viscount straightened up, his eyes growing distant, my aunt abandoned her sodden handkerchief, and Miss Mason stopped fanning her.

"I imagine she's gone to Bryce, don't you? If she hasn't prevailed on that eccentric friend of hers to take her in, that is," Hugh said.

"She'd never go to Gloria Hefferton," I told him. "The family is large and they are crowded into a tiny house. Besides, Miss Hefferton could not help Louisa. She's as poor as a churchmouse."

"You think my sister needed money?" the viscount asked stiffly. "May I ask why you say that, coz?"

I didn't want to reveal any more than I had to, and I did not need the pressure of Hugh's hand on my shoulder to remind me of it. "She has on occasion mentioned she was in debt," I said reluctantly. "I thought she had told you about it. I told her she should."

He shook his head, looking grimmer than ever.

"Perhaps we had better send to the stables to find out if she took a horse," Hugh interrupted. "Bryce is not in London any longer. He has gone to his estate in Kent. It is no great distance from town, but still I hardly think Miss Langley would care to trudge all that way."

Moreston did not bother to answer. Instead, he went to the door and gave the order to Hibbert. I am sure the butler had had his ear to the door, but I stopped thinking of him when Hugh whispered, "Quickly! The samples!"

I glanced around. My aunt and Miss Mason had their heads together, whispering. They were not paying any attention to us. I reached into my reticule and pulled out the papers. They disappeared under Hugh's coat.

"The one on top is Louisa's writing," I told him as the viscount started back toward us. "I got it just now."

"Good girl," he breathed. "That will help immeasurably."

I thought Moreston looked as if he wished Hugh Carlyle was miles away, a fact my new husband blandly ignored. Aunt Lavinia seemed to have accepted him as one of the family. What Miss Mason was thinking I had no idea. But then, I had never been able to understand the woman. She was as much a stranger to me now as she had been the night I had first arrived.

The head groom duly reported that Louisa had ordered her mare late the previous afternoon to be ready at ten that night. She had said she was going on a moonlight ride with a party of friends, said party to stay overnight in the country. He had thought it was a rum deal, but not worthy of calling milord's attention to, Miss Louisa being known for her mad starts.

"Yes, yes, that will be all," Moreston said, running his band through his already disarranged hair. As the door shut behind the groom, he muttered, "When I get my hands on Weeza, she will be sorry. Very sorry!"

"One can only commend such sentiments, sir," Hugh agreed. "However, you must *get* your hands on her before you can begin a program of reeducation. Still, I really don't think there is any need for either of us to scurry about. I'm sure Bryce will return her as quickly as possible. I assume he's no wish to be saddled with her? At least I've seen no sign of it, this Season."

"No, no, he doesn't," Moreston admitted. He seemed to recall he was host here, no matter how reluctant a one, and he added, "Some port, sir? Or sherry and some biscuits, perhaps? I am sure my aunt could use a restorative, Miss Mason as well. Coz?"

I nodded, and he went to give the orders. Hugh took this opportunity to step over to the window. With his back turned I saw him remove the papers from his coat and look them over carefully. He seemed to spend a lot of time on Louisa's, but it was hard for me to tell at a distance. Strange that I had never seen her handwriting, and I had not taken the time to look at the paper when I had snatched it from her desk. Was there something there that gave her away? Was she the guilty one? I cannot tell you how I wished Hugh and I were away from Park Lane, pounding down the Kensington Road behind his matched pair of blacks and exchanging smiles. How much I wanted to be quit of this family, this house, this whole unsavory situation!

Hibbert was majestic as he served the port and sherry and passed the biscuits. At last he bowed and left the room.

There was little conversation. Hugh and Moreston talked about a horse race they had both attended and the unplacing of the favorite at the last minute, which had almost caused a riot. From the turf they went on to a rural prizefight that was to take place the following week. The viscount grew quite animated as he explained why he intended to place his blunt on Wee Geordie, a huge Scot who had rarely been beaten due to his ability to last twenty or thirty rounds until his opponent could not come up. I managed to catch Hugh's eye and convey my dislike of possibly being abandoned for Wee

Geordie. His quick grin assured me I would have no such rival.

Over on her sofa, my aunt fell into a kind of reverie, her eyes closed and her hands clasped in her lap. Miss Mason abandoned her fanning and settled down in a straight chair a little to one side. She was soon hard at work on the latest project she dug from her workbag.

I was left with nothing to do and no one to talk to. When I had finished my sherry, I went to the windows that faced Park Lane and so it was that I saw the coach that pulled up, Louisa's mare ridden by a strange groom coming along behind. Bryce stepped down first and extended his hand. He looked not only stern but exasperated. I did not wonder at it. It seemed an age before Louisa stepped out, disdaining his assistance. She held her head high as she looked past her rescuer. Behind her, a large, imposing maid followed and I grinned. Trust Bryce! He would not be compromised, not he!

"Louisa is here," I said as the party made its way to the front steps. "Bryce has brought her home."

Hibbert announced the newcomers with such an air of studied indifference I almost applauded. I could see Louisa's face was white and her hands clenched into fists, and I hoped we were not about to be treated to a scene of majestic proportions. I need not have worried.

Bryce grasped her by the arm and took her to a chair where he seated her with what could only be called a push. When she glared at him, he said, "We'll have none of your dramatics, miss! You will sit there quietly or I'll have Tilda remove you to your room."

I assumed Tilda was the large maid standing at ease against the far wall. What a shame one like her had not been available during Louisa's formative years.

"Louisa came out to Brycedale late last evening," the earl began, taking the glass of port Cameron Langley handed him with a nod of thanks. After a healthy swallow, he continued, "She said she could no longer abide living at home, that she was throwing herself on my mercy—well, we need not get into that. There was also a rather convoluted story of some horrendous debt that she wanted me to lend her money to cover. She said she could not ask you, Moreston, for this would be the fourth quarter in a row she had outrun her allowance."

"How much was this debt?" the viscount asked. He sounded as if he were strangling from either rage or embarrassment.

"Five hundred guineas," Bryce said.

My aunt gasped and moaned and Miss Mason put her work away. I had not thought it possible for Cameron to get any paler, but he did. For myself, I looked closely at Louisa. She was staring at me defiantly as if to say, If you had only helped me, Connie, it would never have come to this. It is all your fault.

I wondered how she had done the thing. I could easily picture her galloping down the moonlit roads grinning to herself in the excitement of her adventure. Then dismounting from her spent horse and demanding Bryce. Or had she crept around the house and tapped on the window of his library perhaps? Yes, that sounded more like Louisa with her love of drama. And then no doubt she had told a tale of persecution, undying love, passion. I could almost see her throwing herself in Bryce's startled arms. And when that hadn't worked, she had settled for begging for money. Suddenly I was reminded that the blackmail demanded in her last letter had been five hundred guineas, the exact amount she had asked Bryce for. How odd her debt should be the same. Or was it?

"I assure you, Moreston, Louisa was adequately chaperoned at all times," Bryce was saying, and I made myself concentrate. "My mother is visiting Brycedale with two of my sisters."

Lady Lavinia groaned. Miss Mason uncapped her vinaigrette.

"I was unable to make Louisa see that what she had done

was wrong, coming to a bachelor's home alone and worrying her family. It was too late to bring her back last night, and some time before we could leave this morning. She feels little remorse. She seems to consider me one of the family and I am sure I am glad to serve as such."

I knew Bryce was giving the Langleys a way out of this unsavory situation and I wanted to hug him for his thoughtfulness. He was a very nice man. I hoped some day he would find that pretty agreeable blonde I had mentally chosen for him a while ago.

"I must thank you, my lord," the viscount said stiffly. "You have been more than kind and accommodating and I am sorry you have been troubled. I apologize for my sister. She has had her own way for far too long and I have been most remiss in not seeing to her discipline at an earlier age. I shall attempt to do so now, however, and . . ."

"Oh, do stop, Cameron," Louisa said. She sounded disgusted. "So abject, so cringing, so very, very remorseful. There's no need to *writhe*. I'm not ashamed of what I did. I did it to help you. I thought if I could get the money, you wouldn't have to learn about my debts. After all, you've a great many of your own, haven't you?"

"Hold your tongue!" Moreston roared, and she shrank back in her chair. Perhaps her brother's anger had never been so fierce before. She was obviously frightened.

"Well, that's all," Bryce said, putting down his glass and rising. "I'll be on my way. Er, no need to worry that any of this will get about, Moreston. I'll see there's no talk about it at my end."

"Good of you. I appreciate it," the viscount said.

"I hope I can convince you to remain, my lord," Hugh said, coming from his place against the wall to the center of the room. "You see, there is something to be discussed by all of us. I had intended to convene this meeting tomorrow, but I find I would like to get it over. I have something rather ravishing planned, not only for this evening, but for tomorrow as well."

His glance swept over me without pausing and I hid a gasp at his audacity. Then I forgot it quickly for it was obvious he was going to bring up the poisoned letters. I wondered why he wanted Bryce to stay. Surely he didn't consider him a suspect, did he?

"If you would dismiss your maid, sir?" he said, nodding to Tilda. "And Moreston, if you would be so kind as to give orders we are not to be disturbed? Not for any reason? Thank you."

The two men looked confused, but they did as they were bade. I was so proud of my new husband. These gentlemen held respected titles, yet such was the power of his personality, they obeyed Hugh Carlyle without question.

"I don't understand," my aunt complained. "What is it all about, Henny? Why is Carlyle giving orders in Moreston's drawing room?"

Hugh gave her his crooked smile. It was so potent, she smiled back. "It will all be explained in a short time, ma'am. Just be patient, if you please."

He looked at everyone in turn then, slowly, considering them one at a time. "I suppose it would have been better if we had had Gloria Hefferton here as well, but I think we can dispense with her," he said.

"Now then, Constance has shown me some very ugly anonymous letters she has been receiving. They have been coming for several weeks now, some by the post, others by messenger.

"These letters were written in a disguised hand. They cast aspersions on her mother's virtue, raised the possibility her father was, among other things, a murderer, and questioned her right to use the name Ames."

"What's this you say?" Moreston demanded. "Letters like that came here? Why, you never said anything of this to me, coz."

"I saw you so rarely. I did not like to bother you," I said. As I spoke I glanced around. Not a single person looked anything but perplexed and my spirits plummeted. Was it possible we had been wrong, and the culprit was not here?

"Miss Langley has also received some letters. As I understand it, hers began coming some time after the ones to Constance.

"I think we might be able to clear up this mystery today. Now. Here in this room."

"Let me understand you, sir. Is it possible you are accusing one of us of being the author of these letters?" Bryce demanded, his jaw set. I was reminded he and Hugh Carlyle had never been friendly.

"Why, yes, that is exactly what I'm doing," Hugh said pleasantly.

Chapter Twenty

The silence that had reigned in the drawing room erupted in a torrent of sound. My aunt screamed and collapsed on the sofa. Miss Mason called for brandy. The Earl of Bryce blustered his indignation, while Louisa assured him she knew he had had nothing to do with it. Moreston threatened Hugh with the law and shook his fist at him. Only Hugh and I were silent. It seemed a very long time before everyone settled down again.

"Now then, having gained your attention, may we go on?" Hugh asked as he went to the center table and pushed the half-empty plate of biscuits aside. He spread out the letters I had received, and beside them, the samples I had found of everyone's handwriting. They crowded around, even my Aunt Lavinia, who tottered over supported by her faithful companion.

"There would be other examples, but I understand Miss Langley burned her letters," Hugh said. "Is that correct, Miss?"

Louisa nodded, biting her lower lip.

"A shame, that," Hugh said, moving one of the letters a trifle. "I would have liked to compare them to Constance's."

"What do you mean?" Louisa asked, her voice cold.

"What do you think I mean?" he countered.

Before she could answer, Cameron Langley held up a sheet of paper and said, "Did you take this from my desk in the library, coz? I am appalled to think you would rummage through my drawers. Appalled!"

"Why, here is the letter I was writing to Ann Mannering. The one I had to discard and begin again," my aunt interrupted. "See here, Henny, the blot I made. Well, niece, I do not know what to say of you, indeed I don't. Surely it is very bad manners to creep about in others' rooms, taking their personal letters!"

"I see you have a list I was making too, Connie," Louisa said, staring down at the latest paper I had acquired. "You think I was the one who wrote to you? How misplaced my love for you has been! You are a sneak. A thieving, filthy little sneak. I suspect you wrote those letters to yourself to get attention, yes, and mine as well, to hurt me. Well, you succeeded. I hate you now. Do you hear? I hate you!"

"That will be quite enough," Hugh said. Such was the authority, the power, in his quiet words, Louisa subsided and hurried to her seat again. I swallowed the large lump in my throat. It was ghastly to be called names—accused. I felt miserable.

"I told Constance to take the papers after she confided in me and asked my advice," Hugh said. "She did not want to do it, but I insisted."

Bryce had been very quiet. Now he looked up from one of the letters he had been comparing to the handwriting samples and said, "Yes, but I can't see that it did any good. None of these look at all like the letters she received."

"Perhaps not at first glance. However, after careful study I have found some similarities in one of them," Hugh told him.

My aunt swayed and Miss Mason persuaded her to go back to the sofa. No one spoke until she was seated, clutching her handkerchief in her hands. Then Hugh continued, "There is also the evidence of the paper the letters were written on, that ugly daisy device and the hideous blue sealing wax. We do not have to rely on the writing samples alone."

He paused and I wondered if he were waiting for someone to break down and confess. When nothing happened, he continued, "The paper is cheap and ordinary. It can be pur-

chased at any stationer's. My own man has a supply he uses
to make lists of things he requires.

"The seal and wax are not unusual either."

He reached into his coat as he spoke and brought out a
small parcel tied up in string. Holding it up so everyone
could see it, he said, "But there is no need to question tradesmen. Someone here used the seal and the wax. I have the
proof in my hand."

Louisa whipped around and glared at me. She did not
speak, but I could see she was accusing me of finding the
items Hugh held in his hand in her room. I felt sick. So, it
had been Louisa all along.

"Yes, I purchased the seal, the wafers, too," she said almost defiantly. "I did so after I discovered the letters that
had been written to Connie. But I didn't write those letters.
I only wrote to myself, and that's no crime, is it?"

Everyone looked at her, appalled, and her chin went up
another inch. Proud, contemptuous, fighting with her back
to the wall—however dreadful you might consider Louisa
Langley, there was something still to admire about her.

"Why would you do such a thing, Weeza?" her brother
demanded. "What possible reason could you have?"

For the first time, Louisa looked uncertain. "I had at-
tacked Connie, accused her of trying for Bryce, and we were
at odds. I thought if I got a letter too, she would feel sorry
for me and we could be friends again. I know I have a
wretched temper. But even though she did forgive me, it was
not the same. The letters were my only hope of reconcilia-
tion."

She turned to me then. "I found the secret drawer in your
jewel case long before you showed it to me, Connie, and the
letters, too. When I needed it, I took one to copy. It was
easy."

"And later you thought to pretend someone was black-
mailing you?" Hugh asked. "Because you hoped to get Constance to give you the five hundred guineas you needed to
pay your debts?"

Louisa clasped her hands in her lap again. "Yes, I confess I did," she said. "I was desperate."

"Well!" my aunt spoke up, surprising us all considerably. "To think you would scheme this way, Louisa! I am sure you are also the person who wrote to Constance. There is no one else it could be. You, and you alone, are guilty."

She wriggled forward until she was sitting on the edge of the sofa. I saw Miss Mason was looking at her with an arrested expression, and I wondered why.

"Wretched girl!" my aunt said, pointing a bony finger at her stepdaughter. "I have known all along you were not normal. No, you are just like your mother, and mark my words, you will come to the same end she did. She killed herself, you know. Rode that horse right over the cliff because she had gone mad and Moreston threatened to lock her in the attic. Oh, yes, he told me all about it . . ."

Cameron Langley started toward her and she shrank back on the sofa. She looked like a frightened rabbit. I did not dare look at Louisa and I hoped no one else was looking at her either.

"How dare you say such things about my mother?" Moreston demanded, leaning over her. "She was not mad! She was a wonderful, spirited woman, and my father mourned her sincerely."

"Then why did he marry me a year to the day later?" Lavinia Langley managed to say in defiance.

"Perhaps because you told him he had got you with child?" Miss Mason asked. Her voice was cold and full of disgust, and I shivered. My aunt only stared at her out of dark-ringed eyes.

Relentlessly, Miss Mason went on, "Because you made sure there was one indiscretion, probably soon after the funeral when he was distraught and seeking comfort, didn't you? Then later, after you returned home from Moreston Court, you wrote saying you had had a miscarriage. I've always wondered about that miscarriage.

"Of course, since he was an honorable man, Frederick felt

he had to marry you anyway, to make it up to you. Then you had what you wanted, didn't you, Lavinia? You had a husband at last and you were a viscountess as well. How splendid for you.

"But the feeling didn't last, did it? You became nervous and easily upset and you had trouble sleeping. And you found marriage, even to an older man, more than you bargained for. Did that riding accident the late Lady Moreston died in begin to prey on your mind? Because it wasn't entirely an accident? Because you goaded her to it? I've wondered about that, too."

"I will not listen to this, any of it," my aunt said. "It is all lies. I have no idea what caused the accident. I wasn't with her. You all know I don't ride. I am afraid you will have to leave Moreston House, Henny. I do not care to have you here any longer."

"You have no power to dismiss me, Lavinia. Your husband saw to that and it was put down clearly in his will. I think he foresaw the time I would be necessary to you, as you grew more and more unbalanced. I promised him I would stay for the family's sake, and so I shall."

The viscountess opened and closed her mouth a few times before she sank back on the sofa, silenced.

I did not know what the others were thinking. I was horrified. I could suddenly see so easily how all the things Miss Mason had told us could be true. I looked at Hugh helplessly and he sent me a silent message to be strong, for this would soon be over.

"Yes, that is certainly interesting, but it takes us rather far afield from our original discussion," Hugh said. "And that is, who was it who wrote to Constance if Miss Louisa did not. I don't believe it was Miss Hefferton either."

Louisa shook her head. "No, it wasn't Gloria. It's true she was jealous of Connie and wished her gone, but all she's guilty of is pushing her the night we were at the theater. Not that that's not bad enough, of course."

I gasped and she went on, "She saw Connie talking to

Bryce, saw how he remained beside her for the second act, and she wanted to help me. It was all done on impulse and she was horrified when the carriage appeared and Connie was struck by the team. I was very cross with her when she confessed to me."

I remembered the day in the park when Louisa had dismissed her friend so coldly. And I remembered how heartily she had laughed when I served as Miss Hefferton's agent, begging for her forgiveness. I suppose it was ludicrous, me taking the part of the woman who had almost caused my death, but I did not feel like laughing. I wondered if I would ever feel like it again, after today.

"I will remember Miss Hefferton," Hugh said coldly. "But if she is not the guilty letter writer, we're left with few suspects. There is only my lords Moreston and Bryce, Lady Moreston and Miss Mason. Of course anonymous letters are rarely a man's weapon, and to be truthful I can see no reason for Bryce at least to be involved."

"I suppose I must thank you for that," the earl said, his usually pleasant voice sarcastic.

Hugh bowed. "You are just not the type, sir. You are too open, too straight, too—is there such a word as undevious?"

"I don't think you did it either, Moreston. From what I have gathered, you had other plans for Constance. You wouldn't want to frighten her away.

"So that leaves only Miss Mason or Lady Moreston," he concluded. We all turned as one and stared at the two ladies, side by side on the delicate striped satin sofa.

"Of course it is Henny," my aunt said quickly. "She is so secretive! And you all heard what she just said to me! She will say anything to avoid being accused, even to name me, a poor, sick woman, to save herself. It is dastardly, but I will try very hard to forgive her. It is my duty as a Christian."

Miss Mason did not respond, but I saw her hands tighten on the neck of her workbag.

Hugh held up the parcel once more. "Have you forgotten

the wafers and the seal, ma'am?" he asked. "They tell us plain who the culprit is."

My aunt looked even more agitated. "No, no," she said. "If you found those things in my room, it is because Henny put them there. I wondered what she was doing last week with an old bandbox of mine. It is always kept on the back of the top shelf of my armoir. What would she want with it, if not to hide the wafers and seal inside?"

"That is a lie," Miss Mason said steadily.

"I know it is," Hugh told her kindly. "You need not worry, ma'am. I know who the guilty party is now."

I felt as if my head was whirling. My aunt had written those horrid letters? My *aunt?* But why would she do such a thing? What possible reason could she have when she herself had invited me to stay at Moreston House for the Season?

When she saw the way we were all staring at her, the viscountess began to scream and pull her hair, her words tumbling over each other as she tried to deny her guilt. I felt sick when she tore her gown and scratched her face, leaving bloody trails on her cheeks. Bryce hurried to help Miss Mason restrain her and Moreston went to send a footman running for the nearest doctor. When my aunt fainted, Bryce picked her up and carried her out of the room, Miss Mason right behind him.

I never faint, but I came close to doing it then. When I was myself again I became aware of Hugh kneeling before me, holding my hands tightly and willing me with all his strength to hang on. I saw Cameron Langley had his sister in his arms. Louisa was weeping softly. I did not think she even knew the tears were coursing down her face. I will never forget the stricken look she wore as the enormity of the situation came to her.

I didn't suppose we would ever learn what happened all those years ago, even if my aunt had had a hand in the first Lady Moreston's death, nor how she had contrived it. If she did, I reminded myself. I decided I would really rather not know. What good would it do? And if that makes me a coward, so be it.

It was several minutes before the renewed keening from upstairs died away and Bryce and Miss Mason returned. Cameron poured us all another drink. It was more than welcome.

"She is sleeping," Henrietta Mason said, gratefully taking the glass he handed her. "I gave her a heavy dose of her medicine to make sure of that. And the earl has left his maid to watch over her."

As she sat down in a chair as far as she could get from the sofa she had used before, Bryce said, "But why would Lady Moreston do such a thing? Miss Ames is her niece. I assume she is here at her invitation. What possible reason could she have had to torture the poor girl in that despicable way?"

No one spoke as we all pondered his question. At last Miss Mason sighed and said, "From some things she has said, I think she did not expect Constance to be the young woman she is. She wanted a timid, retiring girl she could gently bully. One who would ask her advice about everything. One she could feel superior to, guide and caution. She had never had that kind of relationship with her stepchildren. Cameron was seventeen when she married his father, and beyond her control, and Louisa never heeded her and let her know she despised her as well. So she wrote to her niece, all prepared to play Lady Bountiful. But then Constance arrived, blooming and beautiful, and so sure of herself. Here was no shrinking violet afraid of society. Here was a young woman running toward life, to grab it with both hands."

As Hugh pressed my hand, she turned to me and said, "Do you remember the first evening you arrived in London, Constance? We were all out, and Hibbert tried to send your traveling companion on her way. He knew she was unimportant, only someone's retired governess. But you wouldn't stand for that. You ordered him to have a room prepared for her, quite as if you were mistress here. I know this because I heard him complaining of it to Lavinia the next day. And there were other things, things that after a while she began to find unbearable. Why, you wouldn't even let her choose your gowns! So she thought to pay you back. I think she hoped you would come to her with the letters; beg her to help you. When you didn't, she wrote more, and again, more."

We all sat quietly, thinking of what she had said. Hugh still held my hand in his.

"There is another thing I don't understand," Bryce said, and now his voice was stiff. "What business is all this of yours, Carlyle? Why have you taken it upon yourself to settle it? You're not one of the family, you are only an acquaintance."

"In a manner of speaking, I am one of the family, although a very recent one," Hugh said, looking around at everyone before he added, a touch of pride in his voice, "Constance and I were married this morning at St. George's, Hanover Square."

Bryce exclaimed and came to kiss me and offer his congratulations. I was glad he was there. He made the situation seem almost normal. Louisa just stared at me, Cameron would not meet my eye, and Miss Mason seemed a million miles away, lost in her thoughts.

"It was a very good thing you found that seal and those wafers in Lady Moreston's room, Miss—I mean, Mrs. Carlyle," Bryce said, bowing as he used my new name.

"But I didn't," I protested. "I have no idea what is in the package Hugh is holding."

He held it up again and smiled. "It is not evidence. I only pretended it was, hoping to flush out the culprit. It was dangerous, I know, but it worked.

"The package contains a box from Rundell and Bridge. In it is Constance's wedding ring and a set of diamonds for her bride gift.

"Which reminds me, it is time for us to be on our way. Constance, please give one last order to that butler. Tell him you want your maid to pack up all your things and bring them along with her to your new home. Tomorrow should be time enough."

I prayed the blush I could feel rising in my body would not reach my face. Louisa had still not spoken to me. I wondered if she ever would again. Cameron, however, did come and take my hand to wish me happy, although his voice was strained and he did not meet my eye. Miss Mason, too, had a word for me. I hugged her, not envying her her future at all. At last, just as I reached the door, Hugh's arm tight around my waist, Louisa rose and said, "I am sorry, Connie. I begin to see what a terrible person I have been. I hope someday you will forgive me for my part in your troubles here."

She did not sound as if she were playacting, but still, I could not answer. I only nodded.

My last order given to Hibbert, Hugh swept me from the house. He tossed a coin to his tiger, telling him to find his own way home, and then we were rolling down Park Lane, headed toward the Bath road.

"I wonder what will happen to them all," I mused, looking over my shoulder for the last time.

Hugh appeared to give it some thought before he said, "I imagine the viscount will take his sister in hand. One can only hope so. He will probably send her down to Moreston Court until she learns to be more conformable. If she ever does. I wonder if he might be able to get Bryce to release that maid to him.

"Your Aunt Lavinia is mad, you know, as mad she pretended her predecessor to be. It will probably be put about that she suffers from delusions. Unfortunately, she may get worse as the years pass but I do not think she will ever be a danger to anyone. Still, Miss Mason looks equal to anything she might get up to. And in the end, she may well be the saving of the family. Your aunt, not Miss Mason, I mean."

"I don't understand. How could that be after all the evil she has done?"

"Moreston's deep in debt and now he has his sister's

obligations to satisfy as well. What has not occurred to him yet, but will shortly, I'm sure, is that his stepmother is a wealthy woman in her own right. It's common knowledge his father left her considerable dowry to her discretion, and settled a large amount on her as well, or so my uncle claims. I expect when she learns how bad things are—that they might have to sell Moreston House and the Court—she'll fork over the ready. She likes being a respected member of society too much not to do so."

"What a terrible woman she is!" I shuddered.

"I'm so glad you think so. It will give us the perfect excuse not to invite her to visit us, come for Christmas, or attend any christenings we might be having."

Hugh had spoken blandly. He had his hands full of the reins; we had reached the road out of town and the team was cantering. Still, I saw the love in his eyes when he glanced at me, and it was almost as if he had touched me.

Sighing, I settled back in the seat, grasping my bonnet lest I lose it. "You seem in a hurry, sir," I remarked. "Now why is that, I wonder?"

He only smiled his crooked smile and I went on, "Can it have something to do with those plans you mentioned you had for this evening? And tomorrow as well? Because if it does, there is a slight problem."

"Yes?" he asked, his tone encouraging. "And what could that possibly be, Mrs. Carlyle?"

"Well, doesn't the word 'ravish' imply the other party involved is unwilling, Mr. Carlyle? And if that is the case, you have it all wrong. You see, I have every intention of not only being a willing but an *enthusiastic* partner in your plans. . . .

"Oh, my. Do you really think it wise to urge the team to a gallop, sir?"

Coming in August 1999

A Man of Affairs by Anne Barbour

Well beyond the normal age of courtship and marriage, a young woman resigned herself to a quiet life on her parents' estate. Then the adopted son of the Duke of Derwent arrived. His kind manner and passionate glances brought new, unfamiliar joy to the lady's heart. But the dashing gentleman had too many duties to his father to properly court her. It would take a scandalous heartbreak to bring them both together in a love that would go against their families and society....

The Bartered Heart by Nancy Butler

Abandoned by his mother and raised by a tyrannical father, a young rogue vowed long ago to harden his heart against emotion. So when his fortune is lost, he sets his sights on a marriage of convenience and riches. But as he makes his way to the estate of a very eligible young mistress, he finds his route riddled with treacherous bogs, bungling thieves, and a beautiful waif in petticoats who may mean much more to him than any amount of money.

Miss Treadwell's Talent by Barbara Metzger

Still unwed at twenty-one, an unconventional high-spirited woman finds her affections sought by a handsome, devilishly charming earl. Though at first she fights his advances, slowly she forms a heated alliance with him. But sparring with words soon turns into a succumbing passion....